The Lives and Times of Jerry Cornelius

Stories of the Comic Apocalypse

by
Michael Moorcock

Four Walls Eight Windows
New York · London

"The Peking Junction" originally appeared in *The New SF*, edited by Langdon Jones, Hutchinson, 1969. "The Delhi Division" and "The Tank Trapeze" first appeared in *New Worlds Magazine*, 1968, 1969. "Sea Wolves" first appeared in *Science Against Man*, edited by Anthony Cheetham, Avon, 1970. "The Sunset Perspective" first appeared in *Ronald Reagan: A Magazine of Poetry*, edited by John Sladek and Pamela Zoline, 1971. "Voortrekker" first appeared in *Quark*, No. 4, edited by Samuel R. Delany and Marilyn Hacker, 1971. "The Swastika Set-Up" first appeared in *Corridor*, edited and published by Michael Butterworth, 1972. "The Spencer Inheritance" was first published in *The Edge*, 1997. "The Camus Connection" was first published by Gare du Nord, 1998; "Cheering for the Rockets" was first published in *Interzone*, 1999; and "Firing the Cathedral" was first published by PS Publishing, 2002. The stories appear here in order of writing, and should be read as a continuous narrative.

Published in the United States by:
Four Walls Eight Windows
39 West 14th Street, room 503
New York, N.Y., 10011

Visit our website at http://www.4w8w.com
First printing September 2003.

Library of Congress Cataloging-in-Publication Data

Moorcock, Michael, 1939-
The lives and times of Jerry Cornelius: stories of the comic apocalypse/by Michael Moorcock
p. cm.
ISBN 1-56858-273-0 (pbk.)
1. Cornelius, Jerry (Fictitious character)—Fiction. 2. Fantasy fiction, English.
3. Apocalyptic literature. I. Title.
PR6063.O59A6 2003
823'.914—dc21 CIP

2003054889

10 9 8 7 6 5 4 3 2 1

Typesetting by Pracharak Technologies (P) Ltd.
Printed in Canada

Table of Contents

Introduction: My Times, My Lives

In recent weeks I've been having some pretty terrible dreams. I wake up suddenly with the stink of hot rubble in my nose, my eyes sting with the dust of destroyed buildings, I hear the sounds of falling rockets and the building I'm in shakes violently. I see images of bomb craters making familiar roads impassable. The streets outside are half in ruins. All I don't get is Vera Lynn singing "We'll Meet Again" or "Coming in on a Wing and a Prayer." Which is a bit of a relief.

Perhaps these dreams are my response to our current crises. I know exactly where they come from. I'm remembering my childhood in South London, when the V-2 bombs were rushing down on us and any warning that sounded was always too late. These terrors are a strange experience for me. Until recently I always claimed that I had enjoyed the second world war, that the people who had felt the strain were my parents. Yet it now seems I was successfully repressing the emotions generated by those associations.

I still believe I got the best possible enjoyment out of the times. I grew up in a culture that had laughed its way through the Blitz and learned to make the most of whatever moments of tranquility there were. I think this became pretty much second nature because I remember years later weeping at images of burning children in Vietnam and a few hours later I had turned that grief into comedy in my Jerry Cornelius novel *A Cure for Cancer.* Maybe, after all, that was my way of staying sane.

These stories, which one kind critic called an alternate history of the 20th century, have now slipped naturally into the 21st, where they might have properly belonged all along. Sadly, this has been thanks to a succession of events that to some extent I described, even anticipated. If I hoped, by a sort of shamanistic chemistry, to stop that succession, I've evidently failed, just as ultimately I failed to ground my experiences of the second world war.

The Jerry Cornelius short stories are in several ways complementary to the novels, especially *The Cornelius Quartet*, themselves responses to the political and social events of my own lifetime, including the Vietnam war, the Soviet invasion of Czechoslovakia, South African apartheid, the rise of Thatcherism, the death of Princess Diana, and Clinton's attack on the Sudanese pharmaceutical plant in response to the terrorist bombing of American embassies in Africa.

If I've responded to those events obliquely (for instance, referring to Britain's occupation of Burma while Russian tanks entered Prague) it's in the hope of understanding them better in the context of modern history, especially modern imperial history. For that reason I have, for instance, quoted Cromwell in *Firing the Cathedral,* a story about what I consider to be the Bush faction's unseemly response to the horrible attacks of September 11th, partly because the Bushoviks' aggressive Protestant fundamentalism has so much in common with Northern Ireland's Ian Paisley and his "No Surrender" unionists.

Of course the stories also contain the aforesaid element of black farce, or existential comedy as someone called it, which has a lot to do with human folly and our apparent inability to learn from our mistakes, forever choosing the simple, easy options which always get us into complicated situations. If, too, readers detect a note of contempt for the primitive economic theories which served the corporate world so well when introduced by free market deregulating liberal consumerists like Reagan, Thatcher, Blair and Bush, I make no apologies. They were quite as stupid as Communists who thought a few good slogans and some simple ideas would at a stroke solve the problems of the world. But since I'm not interested in writing polemics as such, I refer you to the economic arguments of David Harvey (who has also written a superb book, *The Problems of Postmodernity*), witty political commentators like Molly Ivins or Jim Hightower or Old American patricians like Senator Robert Byrd.

As a writer of fiction I've used a number of methods to respond to the world around me, including a form of exaggeration not dissimilar to Italian Commedia dell'Arte. In the sixties and seventies of the last century various writers and poets, including William Burroughs, J.G. Ballard, Thomas M. Disch, George MacBeth, John Sladek, Brian Aldiss, James Sallis, D. M. Thomas, B. J. Bayley, M. J. Harrison and myself formed a rough and ready movement around *New Worlds*, a magazine I edited. We rejected conventional modernism as well as the conventions of commercial SF, hoping to discover methods which would help us to deal more effectively in our fiction with the events and idiosyncrasies of modern life. Jerry Cornelius was my response. Not so much a character, as Harrison pointed out, as a technique.

To be fair, I do also think of Jerry as a personality. He's perhaps not wholly reliable or consistent and maybe not entirely politically correct. For me, he's a character combining the endearing and enduring traits of a number of my contemporaries as well as being a latter day Pierrot, Colombine, and Harlequin, responding to the world around him with, if not always appropriate sentimentality, at least an admirable resourcefulness and malleability. An almost limitless good humor. Jerry's a pretty lighthearted existentialist. He once claimed to be too shallow to hold on to his miseries for very long. I think he also said somewhere (or I might have said it for him) that it isn't especially important if all we're doing is dancing forever on the edge of the abyss. It's scarcely worth worrying about. The really important thing, of course, is the dance itself and how we dance it.

So here are what I consider to be the best of the dances Jerry has danced since the 1960s. I hope some of them at least will get your feet tapping. After a while, you might even feel like joining in.

Michael Moorcock,
Lost Pines, Texas
February 2003

The Peking Junction

1

Out of the rich and rolling lands of the West came Jerry Cornelius, with a vibragun holstered at his hip and a generous message in his heart, to China.

Six feet two inches tall, rather fat, dressed in the beard and uniform of a Cuban guerrilla, only his eyes denied his appearance or, when he moved, his movements. Then the uniform was seen for what it was and those who at first had admired him loathed him and those who had at first despised him loved him. He loved them all, for his part, he kissed them all.

On the shores of a wide lake that reflected the full moon stood a tall, ruined pagoda, its walls inlaid with a faded mosaic of red, pale blue and yellow. In the dusty room on the first floor Jerry poured Wakayama Sherry for three disconcerted generals whose decision to meet him in this remote province had been entirely a matter of instinct.

"Substantial," murmured one general, studying the glass.

Jerry watched the pink tongue travel between the lips and disappear in the left-hand corner of the mouth.

"The tension," began a second general carefully. "The tension."

Jerry shrugged and moved about the room very swiftly. He came to rest on the mat in front of them, sat down, folded his legs under him.

A winged shadow crossed the moon. The third general glanced at the disintegrating mosaic of the wall. "Only twice in . . ."

Jerry nodded tolerantly.

For Jerry's sake they were all speaking good Mandarin with a certain amount of apprehensive self-contempt, like collaborators who fear reprisals from their countrymen.

"How is it now, over there?" asked one of the generals, waving towards the west.

"Wild and easy," said Jerry, "as always."

"But the American bombing . . ."

"A distraction, true." Jerry scratched his palm.

The first general's eyes widened. "Paris razed, London gutted, Berlin in ruins . . ."

"You take a lot from your friends before you condemn them."

Now the shadow had vanished. The third general's right hand spread its long fingers wide. "But the destruction . . . Dresden and Coventry were nothing. Thirty days—skies thick with Yankee pirate jets, constant rain of napalm, millions dead." He sipped his sherry. " It must have seemed like the end of the world . . ."

Jerry frowned. "I suppose so." Then he grinned. "There's no point in making a fuss about it, is there? Isn't it all for the best in the long run?"

The general looked exasperated. "You people . . ."

2

Tension, resulting in equilibrium: the gestures of conflict keep the peace. A question of interpretation.

3

Having been Elric, Asquiol, Minos Aquilinus, Clovis Marca, now and forever he was Jerry Cornelius of the noble price, proud prince of ruins, boss of the circuits. Faustaff, Muldoon, the eternal champion . . .

Nothing much was happening in the Time Center that day; phantom horsemen rode on skeletal steeds across worlds as fantastic as those of Bosch or Breughel, and at dawn when clouds of giant scarlet flamingoes rose from their nests of reeds and wheeled through the sky in bizarre ritual dances, a tired, noble figure would go down to the edge of the marsh and stare over the water at the strange configurations of dark lagoons and tawny islands that seemed to him like hieroglyphs in some primeval language (the marsh had once been his home, but now he feared it his tears filled it.).

Cornelius feared only fear and had turned his albino beast from the scene, riding sadly away, his long mane flowing behind him so that from a distance he resembled some golden-haired madonna of the lagoons.

4

Imposition of order upon landscape; the romantic vision of the age of reason, the age of fear. And yet the undeniable rhythm of the spheres, the presence of God. The comforts of tidiness; the almost unbearable agony of uncompromising order. Law and Chaos. The face of God, the core of self:

> For the mind of man alone is free to explore the lofty vastness of the cosmic infinite, to transcend ordinary consciousness, or roam the secret corridors of the brain where past and future melt into one . . . . And universe and individual are linked, the one mirrored in the other, and each contains the other
>
> —*The Chronicle of the Black Sword*

5

It was extremely subtle, he thought, staring out of the window at the waters of the lake. In another room, the generals slept. The appearance of one thing was often almost exactly that of its diametric opposite. The lake resembled a spread of smoothed silver; even the reeds were like wires of pale gold and the sleeping herons could have been carved from white jade. Was this the ultimate mystery? He checked his watch. Time for sleep.

6

In the morning the generals took Cornelius to the site of the crashed F111A. It was in fair condition, with one wing buckled and the tailplane shot away, its ragged pilot still at his controls, a dead hand on the ejector lever. The plane stood in the shadow of the cliff, half-hidden from the air by an overhang. Jerry was reluctant to approach it.

"We shall expect a straight answer," said a general.

"Straight," said Jerry, frowning. It was not his day.

"What was the exact nature of the catastrophe?" enquired one general of another.

Jerry forced himself to climb up onto the plane's fuselage and strike a pose he knew would impress the generals. It was becoming important to speed things up as much as he could.

"What do you mean by that?" The general raised his eyes to him, but Jerry was not sure that he had been addressed. "What does it mean to you, Mr. Cornelius?"

Jerry felt cornered. "Mean?" He ran his hand over the pitted metal, touching the USAF insignia, the star, the disc, the bar.

"It will go in the museum eventually." said the first general, "with the '58 Thunderbird, of course, and the rest. But what of the land?" A gesture towards the blue-green plain which spread away beyond their parked jeeps. "I do not understand."

Jerry pretended to study the cliff. He didn't want the generals to see him weeping.

Later they all piled into the jeep and began to roar away across the dusty plain, protecting their mouths and eyes with their scarves.

Returning to the pagoda by the lake, one of the generals stared thoughtfully back across the flat landscape. "Soon we shall have all this in shape."

The general touched a square object in one uniform pocket. The sound of a raucous Chinese brass band began to squall out. Herons flapped from the reeds and rose into the sky.

"You think we should leave the plane where it is, don't you?" said General Way Hahng.

Cornelius shrugged. But he had made contact, he thought complacently.

7

The heavy and old-fashioned steam locomotive shunted to a stop. Behind it the rickety carriages jostled together for a moment before coming to rest. Steam rose beneath the locomotive and the Chinese engineer stared pointedly over their heads at the plain as they clambered from the jeep and approached the train.

A few peasants occupied the carriages. Only one stared briefly through the window before turning his head away. The peasants, men and women, wore red overalls.

Walking knee-deep through the clammy steam they got into the carriage immediately behind the tender. The locomotive began to move.

Jerry sprawled across the hard bamboo seat and picked a splinter from his sleeve. In the distance he could see hazy mountains. He glanced at General Way Hahng but the general was concentrating on loosening a belt buckle. Jerry craned his head back and spotted the jeep, abandoned beside the rails.

He switched on his visitaper, focusing it on the window. Shadowy figures began to move on the glass, dancing to the music which had filled the carriage. The generals were surprised but said nothing. The tune was "Hello Goodbye," by the Beatles.

It was not appropriate. Jerry turned it off. There again, he thought, perhaps it was appropriate. Every plugged nickel had two sides.

He burst into laughter.

General Way Hahng offered him a swift, disapproving glance, but no more.

"I hear you are called the Raven in the West," said another general.

"Only in Texas," said Jerry, still shaking.

"Aha, in *Texas*."

General Way Hahng got up to go to the lavatory. Jacket removed, the general's tight pants could be seen to stretch over beautifully rounded buttocks. Jerry looked at them feeling ecstatic. He had never seen anything like them. The slightly rumpled material added to their attraction.

"And in Los Angeles?" said another general "What are you called in Elay?"

"Fats," said Jerry.

8

"Even though he was a physicist, he knew that important biological objects come in pairs."

—Watson, *The Double Helix*

"With sinology, as with Chinese food, there are two *kinds* . . ."

—Enright, *Encounter*, July 1968

9

General Lee met them at the station. It was little more than a wooden platform raised between the railroad line and the Yellow River.

He shook hands with Jerry. "My apologies," he said. "But under the circumstances I thought it would be better to meet here, than in Weifang."

"How much time have you got?" Jerry asked.

General Lee smiled and spread his hands. “You know better than that, Mr. Cornelius.” They walked to where the big Phantom IV staff car was parked.

General Way Hahng called from the window as the train moved off. “We will go on to Tientsin and journey back from there. We will wait for you, Mr. Cornelius.”

Jerry waved reassuringly.

General Lee was dressed in a neat Ivy League suit that was a little shiny, a little frayed on one sleeve. He was almost as tall as Jerry, with a round face, moody eyes and black chin whiskers. He returned his driver’s salute as he personally opened the door of the limousine for Jerry. Jerry got in.

They sat in the stationary car and watched the river. General Lee put a hand on Jerry’s shoulder. Jerry smiled back at his friend. “Well,” said the general eventually, “what do you think?”

“I think I might be able to do it. I think I’m building something up there. With Way Hahng.”

Lee rubbed at the corner of his mouth with his index finger. “Yes. I thought it would be Way Hahng.”

“I can’t promise anything,” Jerry said.

“I know.”

“I’ll do my best.”

“Of course. And it will work. For good or ill, it will work.”

“For good and ill, General. I hope so.”

10

“Too much,” said Jerry back in the pagoda, drinking tea from cracked Manchu bowls, eating shortbread from elegant polystyrene ware that had been smuggled from the factories at Shimabara or Kure.

The generals frowned. “Too much?”

“But the logic,” said General Way Hahng, the most beautiful of the three.

“True,” said Jerry, who was now in love with the generals and very much in love with General Way Hahng. For that general in particular he was prepared (temporarily or metatemporally, depending how it grabbed him) to compromise his principles, or at least not speak his mind fully. In a moment of self-exasperation he frowned. “False.”

General Way Hahng’s expression was disappointed. “But you said . . .”

“I meant ‘true’,” said Jerry. It was no good. But the sooner he was out of this one the better. Something had to give shortly. Or, at very least, someone. He suddenly remembered the great upsurge of enthusiasm among American painters immediately after the war and a Pollock came to mind. “Damn.”

“It is a question of mathematics, of history,” said the second general.

Jerry’s breathing had become rapid.

11

“I do not read French,” said General Way Hahng disdainfully handing the piece of paper back to Jerry. This was the first time they had been alone together.

Jerry sighed.

12

A shout.

13

As always it was a question of gestures. He remembered the way in which the wing of the F111A had drooped, hiding the ruin of the undercarriage. Whatever fallacy might exist—and perhaps one did—he was prepared to go along with it. After all, his admiration and enthusiasm had once been generous and it was the sort of thing you couldn’t forget; there was always the sense of loss, no matter what you did to cover it up. Could he not continue to be generous, even though it was much more difficult? He shrugged. He had tried more than once and been rejected too often. A clean break was best.

But the impulse to make yet another gesture—of sympathy, of understanding, of love—was there. He knew no way in which such a gesture would not be safely free of misinterpretation, and he was, after all, the master forger. There was enormous substance there, perhaps more than ever before, but its expression was strangled. Why was he always ultimately considered the aggressor? Was it true? Even General Lee had seen him in that role. Chiefly, he supposed, it was as much as anything a question of equilibrium. Perhaps he simply had to reconcile himself to a long wait.

In the meantime, duty called, a worthy enough substitute for the big search. He stood on the top floor of the pagoda, forcing himself to confront the lake, which seemed to him as vast as the sea and very much deeper.

14

Memory made the martyr hurry; duality. Past was future. Memory was precognition. It was by no means a matter of matter. Karl Glogauer pinioned on a wooden cross by iron spikes through hands and feet.

"But if you would believe the unholy truth—then Time is an agony of Now, and so it will always be."—*The Dreaming City*. Do Not Analyze.

15

Devious notions ashamed the memory of his father's fake Le Corbusier château. But all that was over. It was a great relief.

"It is cool in here now," said General Way Hahng.

"You'd better come out," he said cautiously. "Quick. The eye. While it is open."

They stood together in the room and Jerry's love filled it.

"It is beautiful," said the General.

Weeping with pity. Jerry stroked the general's black hair, bent and kissed the lips. "Soon." The vibragun and the rest of the equipment was handy.

16

A SWEET SHOUT.

17

The voice of the flatworm. Many-named, many-sided, metatemporal operative extraordinary, man of the multiverse, metaphysician metahealed metaselfed. The acid voice.

" 'God,' said Renark and he lived that moment forever."

—*The Sundered Worlds*

18

The flow of the Mandarin, the quality of the Sanskrit that the general spoke in love. It all made sense. Soon. But let the victim call once more, move once more.

19

Jerry went to the window, looked out at the lake, at the black and shining water.

Behind him in the room General Way Hahng lay naked, smoking a powerful dose. The general's eyes were hooded and the general's lips curved in a beatific, almost stupid, smile. The little visitaper by the side of the mattress cast abstract images on the mosaic of the wall, played "What You're Doing," but even that made Jerry impatient. At this moment he rarely wanted complete silence, but now he must have it. He strolled across the room and waved the visitaper into silence. He had the right. The general did not dispute it.

Jerry glanced at his discarded outfit and touched his clean chin. Had he gone too far?

His own heavy intake was making his heart thump as if in passion. There had been his recent meeting with the poet he admired but who denied himself too much. "Irony is often a substitute for real imagination," the poet had said, speaking about a recent interplanetary extravaganza.

But all that was a distraction now. It was time.

Jerry bowed his head before the lake. Sentiment, not the water, had overcome him momentarily. Did it matter?

20

Jerry pointed the vibragun at the general and watched the body shake for several minutes. Then he took the extractor and applied it. Soon the infinitely precious nucleotides were stored and he prepared to leave. He kissed the corpse swiftly, put the box that was now the general under his arm. In Washington there was a chef who would know what to do.

He climbed down through the floors to where the remaining generals were waiting for him.

"Tell General Lee the operation was conducted," he said.

"How will you leave?"

"I have transportation," said Jerry.

21

The lovebeast left China the next morning carrying Jerry Cornelius with it, either as a rider or against his will: those who saw them pass found it impossible to decide. Perhaps even Jerry or the beast itself no longer knew; they had moved about the world together for so long.

Like a dragon it rose into the wind, heading for the ruined, the rich and rolling lands of the West.

The Delhi Division

1

A smoky Indian rain fell through the hills and woods outside Simla and the high roads were slippery. Jerry Cornelius drove his Phantom V down twisting lanes flanked by white fences. The car's violet body was splashed with mud and it was difficult to see through the haze that softened the landscape. In rain, the world became timeless.

Jerry switched on his music, singing along with Jimi Hendrix as he swung around the corners.

Were they finding the stuff? He laughed involuntarily.

Turning into the drive outside his big wooden bungalow, he brought the limousine to a stop. A Sikh servant gave him an umbrella before taking over the car.

Jerry walked through the rain to the veranda; folding the umbrella, he listened to the sound of the water on the leaves of the trees, like the ticking of a thousand watches.

He had come home to Simla and he was moved.

2

In the hut was a small neatly made bed and on the bed an old toy bear. Above it a blown-up picture of Alan Powys had faded in the sun. A word had been scratched into the wall below and to the left of the picture:

ASTRAPHOBIA

By the side of the bed was a copy of *Vogue* from 1952, a Captain Marvel comic book, a clock in a square case. The veneer of the clock case had been badly burned. Propping up the clock at one corner was an empty Pall Mall pack which had faded to a pinkish color and was barely recognizable. Roaches crawled across the gray woollen blankets on the bed.

Rain rattled on the corrugated asbestos roof. Jerry shut and locked the door behind him. For the moment he could not concern himself with the hut. Perhaps it was just as well.

He looked through the waving trees at the ruined mansion. What was the exact difference between synthesis and sensationalism?

3

Jerry stayed in for the rest of the afternoon, oiling his needle rifle. Aggression sustained life, he thought. It had to be so; there were many simpler ways of procreating.

Was this why his son had died before he was born?

A servant brought in a silver tray containing a bottle of Pernod, some ice, a glass. Jerry smiled at it nostalgically, then broke the rifle in order to oil the barrel.

4

The ghost of his unborn son haunted him; though here, in the cool bungalow with its shadowed passages, it was much easier to bear. Of course, it had never been particularly hard to ignore; really a different process altogether. The division between imagination and spirit had not begun to manifest itself until quite late, at about the age of six or seven. Imagination—usually displayed at that age in quite ordinary childish games—had twice led him close to a lethal accident. In escaping, as always, he had almost run over a cliff.

Soon after that first manifestation the nightmares had begun, and then, coupled with the nightmares, the waking visions of twisted, malevolent faces, almost certainly given substance by *Fantasia*, his father's final treat before he had gone away.

Then the horrors increased as puberty came and he at last found a substitute for them in sexual fantasies of a grandiose and sadomasochistic nature. Dreams of jewelled elephants, cowed slaves and lavishly dressed rajahs parading through baroque streets while crowds of people in turbans and loincloths cheered them, jeered at them.

With some distaste Jerry stirred the fire in which burned the collection of religious books for children.

He was distracted by a sound from outside. On the veranda servants were shouting. He went to the window and opened it.

"What is it?"

"Nothing, sahib. A mongoose killing a cobra. See."

The man held up the limp body of the snake.

5

From the wardrobe Jerry took a coat of silk brocade. It was blue, with circles of a slightly lighter blue stitched into it with silver threads. The buttons were diamonds and the cloth was lined with buckram. The high, stiff collar was fixed at the throat by two hidden brass knuckles. Jerry put the coat on over his white silk shirt and trousers. Carefully he did up the buttons and then the collar. His long black hair fell over the shoulders of the coat and his rather dark features, with the imperial beard and moustache, fitted the outfit perfectly.

Crossing the bedroom, he picked up the rifle from the divan. He slotted on the telescopic sight, checked the magazine, cradled the gun in his left arm. A small drop of oil stained the silk.

Pausing by a chest of drawers he took an old-fashioned leather helmet and goggles from the top drawer.

He went outside and watched the ground steam in the sun. The ruined mansion was a bright, sharp white in the distance. Beyond it he could see his servants wheeling the light Tiger Moth biplane on to the small airfield.

6

A journey of return through the clear sky; a dream of flying; wheeling over blue-gray hills and fields of green rice, over villages and towns and winding yellow roads, over herds of cattle; over ancient, faded places, over rivers and hydroelectric plants; a dream of freedom.

In the distance, Delhi looked as graceful as New York.

7

Jerry made his way through the crowd of peons who had come to look at his plane. The late Victorian architecture of this suburb of Delhi blended in perfectly with the new buildings, including a Protestant church, which had been erected in the last ten years.

He pulled the flying goggles on to his forehead, shifted the gun from his left arm to his right and pushed open the doors of the church.

It was quite fancifully decorated, with murals in orange, blue and gold by local artists, showing incidents from the life of Jesus and the Apostles. The windows were narrow and unstained; the only other decoration was the altar and its furnishings. The pulpit was plain, of polished wood.

When Jerry was halfway down the aisle a young Indian priest appeared. He wore a buff-colored linen suit and a dark blue shirt with a white dog collar and he addressed Jerry in Hindi.

"We do not allow guns in the church, sir."

Jerry ignored him. "Where is Sabiha?"

The priest folded his hands on his stomach. "Sabiha is in Gandhinagar, I heard this morning. She left Ahmadabad yesterday. . . ."

"Is the Pakistani with her?"

"I should imagine so." The priest broke into English. "They have a tip-top car—a Rolls-Royce. It will get them there in no time."

Jerry smiled. "Good."

"You know Sabiha, then?" said the priest conversationally, beginning to walk towards Jerry.

Jerry levelled the needle rifle at his hip. "Of course. You don't recognize me?"

"Oh, my god!"

Jerry sighed and tilted the rifle a little. He pulled the trigger and sent a needle up through the priest's open mouth and into his brain.

In the long run, he supposed it was all a problem of equilibrium. But even considering his attitude towards the priest, the job was an unpleasant one. Naturally it would have been far worse if the priest had had an identity of his own. No great harm had been done, however, and on that score everybody would be more or less satisfied.

8

THERE are times in the history of a nation when random news events trickling from an unfriendly neighbor should be viewed not as stray birds but as symbols of a brood, the fingerposts of a frame of mind invested with sinister significance.

WHAT is precisely happening in Pakistan? Is there a gradual preparation, insidiously designed to establish dangerous tensions between the two neighbors?

WHY are the so-called Majahids being enrolled in large

numbers and given guerrilla training? Why have military measures like the setting up of pillboxes and similar offensive-defensive steps on the border been escalated up to an alarming degree?

—*Blitz* news weekly, Bombay, July 27, 1968.

9

Through the half-constructed buildings of Gandhinagar Jerry wandered, his flying helmet and goggles in one hand, his rifle in the other. His silk coat was grubby now and open at the collar. His white trousers were stained with oil and mud and his suede boots were filthy. The Tiger Moth lay where he had crash-landed it, one wheel completely broken off its axle. He wouldn't be able to use it to leave.

It was close to sunset and the muddy streets were full of shadows cast by the skeletons of modern skyscrapers on which little work had been done for months. Jerry reached the tallest building, one that had been planned as the government's chief administration block, and began to climb the ladders which had been placed between the levels of scaffolding. He left his helmet behind, but held the rifle by its trigger guard as he climbed.

When he reached the top and lay flat on the roofless concrete wall he saw that the city seemed to have been planned as a spiral, with this building as its axis. From somewhere on the outskirts of the city a bell began to toll. Jerry pushed off the safety catch.

Out of a sidestreet moved a huge bull elephant with curling tusks embellished with bracelets of gold, silver and bronze. On its head and back were cloths of beautifully embroidered silk, weighted with tassels of red, yellow and green; its howdah was also ornate, the wood inlaid with strips of enamelled brass and silver, with onyx, emeralds and sapphires. In the howdah lay Sabiha and the Pakistani, their clothes disarrayed, making nervous love.

Jerry sighted down the gun's telescope until the back of the Pakistani's head was in the cross hairs, but then the man moved as Sabiha bit his shoulder and a strand of her blue nylon sari was caught by the evening wind, floating up to obscure them both. When the nylon drifted down again Jerry saw that they were both close to orgasm. He put his rifle on the wall and watched. It was over very quickly.

With a wistful smile he picked up his gun by the barrel and dropped it over the wall so that it fell through the interior of the building, striking girders and making them ring like a glockenspiel.

The couple looked up but didn't see Jerry. Shortly afterwards the elephant moved out of sight.

Jerry began to climb slowly back down the scaffolding.

10

As he walked away from the city, he saw the Majahid commandos closing in on the street where he supposed the elephant was. They wore crossed ammunition belts over their chests and carried big Lee-Enfield .303s. The Pakistani would be captured, doubtless, and Sabiha would have to find her own way back to Delhi. He took his spare keys from his trouser pocket and opened the door of the violet Rolls-Royce, climbed in and started the engine. He would have to stop for petrol in Ahmadabad, or perhaps Udaipur if he went that way.

He switched on the headlights and drove carefully until he came to the main highway.

11

In the bath he examined the scar on his inner thigh; he had slipped while getting over a corrugated iron fence cut to jagged spikes at the top so that people wouldn't climb it. He had been seven years old: fascinated at what the gash in his flesh revealed. For hours he had alternately bent and straightened his leg in order to watch the exposed muscles move through the seeping blood.

He got out of the bath and wrapped a robe around his body, walking slowly through the bungalow's passages until he reached his bedroom.

Sabiha had arrived. She gave him a wry smile. "Where's your gun?"

"I left it in Gandhinagar. I was just too late."

"I'm sorry."

He shrugged. "We'll be working together again, I hope."

"This scene's finished now, isn't it?"

"Our bit of it, anyway, I should think." He took a brass box from the dressing table and opened the lid, offering it to her. She looked into his eyes.

When she had taken all she needed, she closed the lid of the box with her long index finger. The sharp nails were painted a deep red.

Exhausted, Jerry fell back on the bed and stared at her vaguely as she changed out of her nylon sari into khaki drill trousers, shirt and sandals. She bunched up her long black hair and pinned it on top of her head.

"Your son . . ." she began, but Jerry closed his eyes, cutting her short.

He watched her turn and leave the room, then he switched out the light and very quickly went to sleep.

12

THE unbridled support given to the Naga rebels by China shows that India has to face alarums and excursions on both sides of her frontier. It is not likely that China would repeat her NEFA adventure of 1962, as she might then have to contend with the united opposition of the USSR and the USA.

THAT is precisely why the stellar role of a cat's paw appears to have been assigned to Pakistan . . . .

OUR Intelligence service should be kept alert so that we get authentic information well in advance of the enemy's intended moves.

AND once we receive Intelligence of any offensive being mounted, we should take the lesson from Israel to strike first and strike hard on several fronts before the enemy gets away with the initial advantages of his blitzkrieg.

—*Blitz*, ibid.

13

"Waterfall" by Jimi Hendrix was playing on the tape as Jerry ate his breakfast on the veranda. He watched a mongoose dart out from under the nearby hut and dash across the lawn towards the trees and the ruined mansion. It was a fine, cool morning.

As soon as the mongoose was safe, Jerry reached down from the table and touched a stud on the floor. The hut disappeared. Jerry took a deep breath and felt much better. He hadn't accomplished everything, but his personal objectives had been tied up very satisfactorily. All that remained was for a woman to die. This had not, after all, been a particularly lighthearted episode.

14

KRISHNAN MOHAN JUNEJA (Ahmadabad): How you have chosen the name BLITZ and what does it mean?

It was started in 1941 at the height of Nazi blitzkrieg against Britain.

—*Blitz*, ibid, correspondence column

15

At least there would be a little less promiscuous violence, which was such a waste of everybody's life and time and which depressed him so much. If the tension had to be sustained, it could be sustained on as abstract a level as possible. And yet, did it finally matter at all? It was so hard to find that particular balance between law and chaos. It was a dangerous game, a difficult decision, perhaps an irreconcilable dichotomy.

16

As he walked through the trees towards the ruined mansion he decided that in this part of the world things were narrowing down too much. He wished that he had not missed his timing where the Pakistani was concerned. If he had killed him, it might have set in motion a whole new series of crosscurrents. He had slipped up and he knew why.

The mansion's roof had fallen in and part of the front wall bulged outwards. All the windows were smashed in the lower stories and the double doors had been broken backwards on their hinges. Had he the courage to enter? The presence of his son was very strong.

If only it had not been here, he thought. Anywhere else and the Pakistani would be dead by now.

Until this moment he had never considered himself to be a coward, but he stopped before he got to the doorway and could not move forward. He wheeled round and began to run, his face moving in terror.

The Phantom V was ready. He got into it and drove it rapidly down the drive and out into the road. He went away from Simla, and he was screaming, his eyes wide with self-hatred. His scream grew louder as he passed Delhi and it only died completely when he reached Bombay and the coast.

He was weeping uncontrollably even when the SS *Kao An* was well out into the Arabian Sea.

The Tank Trapeze

01.00 hours:

Prague Radio announced the move and said the praesidium of the Czechoslovak Communist Party regarded it as a violation of international law, and that Czechoslovak forces had been ordered not to resist.

* * *

Perfection had always been his goal, but a sense of justice had usually hampered him. Jerry Cornelius wouldn't be seeing the burning city again. His only luggage an expensive cricket bag, he rode a scheduled corpse boat to the Dubrovnik depot and boarded the SS *Kao An* bound for Burma, arriving just in time.

After the ship had jostled through the junks to find a berth, Jerry disembarked, making his way to the Rangoon public baths where, in a three-kyat cubicle, he took off his brown serge suit and turban, changing into an elaborately embroidered Russian blouse loose enough to hide his shoulder holster. From his bag he took a pair of white flannels, soft Arabian boots and an old-fashioned astrakhan shako. Disguised to his satisfaction he left the baths and went by pedicab to the checkpoint where the Buddhist monk waited for him.

The monk's moody face was fringed by a black "Bergman" beard making him look like an unfrocked BBC producer. Signing the safe-conduct order with a Pentel pen that had been recharged in some local ink, he blinked at Jerry. "He's here today."

"Too bad." Jerry adjusted his shako with the tips of his fingers then gave the monk his heater. The monk shrugged, looked at it curiously and handed it back. "Okay. Come on. There's a car."

"*Every gun makes its own tune,*" murmured Jerry.

As they headed for the old Bentley tourer parked beyond the guard hut, the monk's woolly saffron cardigan billowed in the breeze.

*   *   *

02.15

All telephone lines between Vienna and Czechoslovakia were cut.

*   *   *

They drove between the green paddy fields and in the distance saw the walls of Mandalay. Jerry rubbed his face. "I hadn't expected it to be so hot."

"Hell, isn't it? It'll be cooler in the temple." The monk's eyes were on the twisting white road.

Jerry wound down the window. Dust spotted his shirt but he didn't bother to brush it off. "Lai's waiting in the temple, is he?"

The monk nodded. "Is that what you call him? Could you kill a child, Mr. Cornelius?"

"I could try."

* * *

03.45

Prague Radio and some of its transmitters were off the air.

* * *

All the roofs of Mandalay were of gold or burnished brass. Jerry put on his dark glasses as they drove through the glazed gates. The architecture was almost primitive and somewhat fierce. Hindu rather than Buddhist in inspiration, it featured as decoration a variety of boldly painted devils, fabulous beasts and minor deities.

"You keep it up nicely."

"We do our best. Most of the buildings, of course, are in the later Pala-Sena style."

"The spires in particular."

"Wait till you see the temple."

The temple was rather like an Anuradhapuran ziggurat, rising in twelve ornate tiers of enamelled metal inlaid with silver, bronze, gold, onyx, ebony and semiprecious stones. Its entrance was over-hung by three arches, each like an inverted V, one upon the other. The building seemed overburdened, like a tree weighted with too much ripe fruit. They went inside, making their way between pillars of carved ivory and teak. Of the gods in the carvings, Ganesh was the one most frequently featured.

"The expense, of course, is enormous," whispered the monk. "Here's where we turn off."

A little light entered the area occupied chiefly by a reclining Buddha of pure gold, resting on a green marble plinth. The

Buddha was twenty feet long and about ten feet high, a decadent copy in the manner of the Siamese school of U Thong. The statue's thick lips were supposed to be curved in a smile but instead seemed fatuously pursed.

From the shadow of the Buddha a man moved into the light. He was fat, the color of oil, with a crimson fez perched on his bald head. His hands were buried in the pockets of his beige jacket. "You're Jeremiah Cornelius? You're pale. Haven't been out east long . . ."

"This is Captain Maxwell," said the monk eagerly.

"I was to meet a Mr. Lai."

"This is Mr. Lai."

"How do you do." Jerry put down his cricket bag.

"How do you do, Mr. Cornelius."

"It depends what you mean."

Captain Maxwell pressed his lips in a red smile. "I find your manner instructive." He waved the monk away and returned to the shadows. "Will it matter, I wonder, if we are not *simpatico*?"

* * *

03.30

Russian troops took up positions outside the Prague Radio building.

* * *

In the bamboo bar of the Mandalay Statler-Hilton Jerry looked through the net curtains at the rickshaws passing rapidly on both sides of the wide street. The bar was faded and poorly stocked and its only other occupants, two German railway technicians on their way through to Laos, crossed the room to the far corner and began a game of bar billiards.

Jerry took the stool next to Captain Maxwell who had registered at the same time, giving his religion as Protestant and his occupation as engineer. Jerry asked the Malayan barman for a Jack Daniels that cost him fourteen kyats and tasted like clock oil.

"This place doesn't change," Maxwell said. His Slavic face was morose as he sipped his sherbet. "I don't know why I come back. Nowhere else, I suppose. Came here first . . ." He rubbed his toothbrush moustache with his finger and used the same finger to push a ridge of sweat from his forehead. Fidgeting for a moment on his stool he dismounted to tug at the material that had stuck to the sweat of his backside. "Don't touch the curries here. They're murder. The other grub's okay though. A bit dull." He picked up his glass and was surprised to find it empty. "You flew in, did you?"

"Boat in. Flying out."

Maxwell rolled his sleeves up over his heavy arms and slapped at a mosquito that had settled among the black hairs and the pink, torn bites. "God almighty. Looking for women?"

Jerry shrugged.

"They're down the street. You can't miss the place."

"See you." Jerry left the bar. He got into a taxi and gave an address in the suburbs beyond the wall.

As they moved slowly through the teeming streets the taxi driver leaned back and studied Jerry's thin face and long blond hair. "Boring now, sir. Worse than the Japs now, sir."

* * *

03.45

Soviet tanks and armored cars surrounded the party Central Committee's building in Prague.

* * *

From the other side of the apartment's oak door Jerry heard the radio, badly tuned to some foreign station, playing the younger Dvořák's lugubrious piano piece, "The Railway Station at Cierna nad Tisov." He rang the bell. Somebody changed the channel and the radio began to play "Alexander's Ragtime Band," obviously performed by one of the many Russian traditional jazz bands that had become so popular in recent years. A small woman in a blue cheongsam, her black hair piled on her head, opened the door and stepped demurely back to let him in. He winked at her.

"You're Anna Ne Win?"

She bowed her head and smiled.

"You're something."

"And so are you."

On the heavy chest in the hallway stood a large Ming vase of crimson roses.

The rest of the apartment was full of the heavy scent of carnations. It was a little overpowering.

* * *

03.47

Prague Radio went off the air completely.

* * *

The child's body was covered from throat to ankles by a gown on to which intricately cut jewels had been stitched so that none of the material showed through. On his shaven head was a similarly worked cap. His skin was a light, soft brown and he seemed a sturdy little boy, grave and good-looking. When Jerry entered the gloomy, scented room, the child let out a huge sigh, as if he had been holding his breath for several minutes. His hands emerged from his long sleeves and he placed one on each arm of the ornate wooden chair over which his legs dangled. "Please sit down."

Jerry took off his shako and looked carefully into the boy's large almond eyes before lowering himself to the cushion near the base of the chair.

"You've seen Lai?"

Jerry grinned. "You could be twins."

The boy smiled and relaxed in the chair. "Do you like children, Mr. Cornelius?"

"I try to like whatever's going."

"Children like me. I am different, you see." The boy unbuttoned his coat, exposing his downy brown chest. "Reach up, Mr. Cornelius, and put your hand on my heart."

Jerry leaned forward and stretched out his hand. He placed his palm against the child's smooth chest. The beat was rapid and irregular. Again he looked into the child's eyes and was interested by the ambiguities he saw in them. For a moment, he was afraid.

"Can I see your gun, Mr. Cornelius?"

Jerry took his hand away and reached under his blouse, tugging his heater from his holster. He gave it to the child who drew it up close to his face to inspect it. "I have never seen a gun like this before."

"It's a side-product," Jerry said, retrieving the weapon, "of the communications industry."

"Ah, of course. What do you think will happen?"

"Who knows? We live in hope."

Anna Ne Win, dressed in beautiful brocade, with her hair hanging free, returned with a tray, picking her way among the cushions that were scattered everywhere on the floor of the gloomy room. "Here is some tea. I hope you'll dally with us."

"I'd love to."

* * *

04.20

The Soviet Tass Agency said that Soviet troops had been called into Czechoslovakia by Czechoslovak leaders.

* * *

In the hotel room Maxwell picked his nails with a splintered chopstick while Jerry checked his kit.

"You'll be playing for the visitors, of course. Hope the weather won't get you down."

"It's got to get hotter before it gets cooler."

"What do you mean by that?" Maxwell lit a Corona from the

butt of a native cheroot he had just dropped in the ashtray, watching Jerry undo the straps of his bag.

Jerry upended the cricket bag. All the equipment tumbled noisily on to the bamboo table and hit the floor. A red cricket ball rolled under the bed. Maxwell was momentarily disconcerted, then leaned down and recovered it. His chair creaked as he tossed the ball to Jerry.

Jerry put the ball in his bag and picked up a protector and a pair of bails. "The smell of brand-new cricket gear. Lovely, isn't it?"

"I've never played cricket."

Jerry laughed. "Neither have I. Not since I had my teeth knocked out when I was five."

"You're considering violence, then?"

"I don't get you."

"What is it you dislike about me?"

"I hadn't noticed. Maybe I'm jealous."

"That's quite likely."

"I've been aboard your yacht, you see. The *Teddy Bear.* In the Pool of London. Registered in Hamburg, isn't she?"

"The *Teddy Bear* isn't my yacht, Mr. Cornelius. If only she were. Is that all . . .?"

"Then it must be Tsarapkin's, eh?"

"You came to Mandalay to do a job for me, Mr. Cornelius, not to discuss the price of flying fish."

Jerry shrugged. "You raised the matter."

"That's rich."

* * *

04.45

Prague radio came back on the air and urged the people of Prague to heed only the legal voice of Czechoslovakia. It repeated the request not to resist. "We are incapable of defending these frontiers," it said.

* * *

Caught at the wicket for sixteen off U Shi Jheon, Jerry now sat in his deckchair watching the game. Things looked sticky for the visitors.

It was the first few months of 1948 that had been crucial. A detailed almanac for that period would reveal a lot. That was when the psychosis had really started to manifest itself. It had been intensifying ever since. There was only a certain amount one could do, after all.

* * *

06.25

Russian troops began shooting at Czechoslovak demonstrators outside the Prague Radio building.

* * *

While Jerry was changing, Captain Maxwell entered the dressing room and stood leaning against a metal locker, rubbing his right foot against his fat left leg while Jerry combed his hair.

"How did the match go?"

"A draw. What did you expect?"

"No less."

"You didn't do too badly out there, old boy. Tough luck, being caught like that."

Jerry blew him a kiss and left the pavilion, carrying his cricket bag across the empty field towards the waiting car that could just be seen through the trees.

* * *

06.30

Machine-gun fire broke out near the Hotel Esplanade.

* * *

Jerry strolled among the pagodas as the sun rose and struck their bright roofs. Shaven-headed monks in saffron moved slowly here and there. Jerry's boots made no sound on the mosaic paths. Looking back, he saw that Anna Ne Win was watching him from the corner of a pagoda. At that moment the child appeared and took her hand, leading her out of sight. Jerry walked on.

*　　*　　*

06.30

Prague television was occupied.

*　　*　　*

Maxwell stared down through the window, trying to smooth the wrinkles in his suit. "Rangoon contacted me last night."

"Ah."

"They said: 'It is better to go out in the street.' " Maxwell removed his fez. "It's all a matter of profits in the long run, I suppose." He chuckled.

"You seem better this morning. The news must have been good."

"Positive. You could call it positive. I must admit I was beginning to get a little nervy. I'm a man of action, you see, like yourself."

*　　*　　*

06.37

Czech National Anthem played.

*　　*　　*

Anna Ne Win moved her soft body against his in the narrow bed, pushing his legs apart with her knee. Raising himself on one elbow he reached out and brushed her black hair from her face. It was almost afternoon. Her delicate eyes opened and she smiled.

He turned away.

"Are you crying, Jerry?"

Peering through the slit in the blind he saw a squadron of L-29 Delfins fly shrieking over the golden rooftops. Were they part of an occupation force? He couldn't make out the markings. For a moment he felt depressed, then he cheered up, anticipating a pleasant event.

* * *

06.36

Prague Radio announced: "When you hear the Czech National Anthem you will know it's all over."

* * *

Jerry hung around the post office the whole day. No reply came to his telegram but that was probably a good sign. He went to a bar in the older part of the city where a Swedish folk-singer drove him out. He took a rickshaw ride around the wall. He bought a necklace and a comb. In Ba Swe Street he was almost hit by a racing tram and while he leaned against a telephone pole two *Kalan cacsa* security policemen made him show them his safe conduct. It impressed them. He watched them saunter through the crowd on the pavement and arrest a shoeshine boy, pushing him aboard the truck which had been crawling behind them. A cathartic act, if not a kindly one.

Jerry found himself in a deserted street. He picked up the brushes and rags and the polish. He fitted them into the box and placed it neatly in a doorway. A few people began to reappear. A tram came down the street. On the opposite pavement, Jerry saw Captain Maxwell. The engineer stared at him suspiciously until he realized Jerry had seen him, then he waved cheerfully. Jerry pretended he hadn't noticed and withdrew into the shade of a tattered awning. The shop itself, like so many in the street, had been closed for some time and its door and shutters were fastened by heavy iron padlocks. A proclamation had been pasted on one door panel. Jerry made out the words *Pyee-Daung-Su Myanma-Nainggan-Daw*. It was an official notice, then. Jerry watched the rickshaws and cars, the trams and the occasional truck pass in the street.

After a while the shoeshine boy returned. Jerry pointed out his equipment. The boy picked it up and walked with it under his arm towards the square where the Statler-Hilton could be seen. Jerry decided he might as well follow him, but the boy began to run and turned hastily into a side street.

Jerry spat into the gutter.

*   *   *

07.00

President Svoboda made a personal appeal over the radio for calm. He said he could offer no explanation for the invasion.

*   *   *

As Jerry checked the heater's transistors, Maxwell lay on the unmade bed watching him. "Have you any other occupation, Mr. Cornelius?"

"I do this and that."

"And what about political persuasions?"

"There you have me, Captain Maxwell."

"Our monk told me you said it was as primitive to hold political convictions as it was to maintain belief in God." Maxwell loosened his cummerbund.

"Is that a fact?"

"Or was he putting words into your mouth?"

Jerry clipped the heater back together. "It's a possibility."

*   *   *

08.20

Pilsen Radio described itself as "the last free radio station in Czechoslovakia".

* * *

A Kamov Ka-15 helicopter was waiting for them on the cricket field near the pavilion. Maxwell offered the pilot seat to Jerry. They clambered in and adjusted their flying helmets.

"You've flown these before," said Maxwell.

"That's right." Jerry lit a cheroot.

"*The gestures of conflict keep the peace*," murmured Maxwell nostalgically.

* * *

10.00

The Czechoslovak agency Četeka said that at least ten ambulances had arrived outside Prague Radio station, where a Soviet tank was on fire.

* * *

When they had crossed the Irrawaddy, Jerry entered the forest and headed for the shrine. He had a map in one hand and a compass in the other.

The atmosphere of the forest was moist and cool. It would begin to rain soon; already the sky was becoming overcast. The air was full of little clusters of flies and mosquitoes, like star systems encircling an invisible sun, and in avoiding them Jerry knocked off his shako several times. His boots were now muddy and his shirt and trousers stained by the bark and foliage. He stumbled on.

About an hour later the birches began to thin out and he knew he was close to the clearing. He breathed heavily, moving more cautiously.

He saw the chipped green tiles of the roof first, then the dirty ivory columns that supported it, then the shrine itself. Under the roof, on a base of rusting steel sheeting, stood a fat Buddha carved from local stone and painted in dark reds, yellows and blues. The statue smiled. Jerry crawled through the damp undergrowth until he could get a good view of the boy.

A few drops of rain fell loudly on the roof. Already the ground surrounding the shrine was churned to mud by a previous rainfall. The boy lay in the mud, face down, arms flung out towards the shrine, legs stiffly together, his jewelled gown covering his body. One ankle was just visible; the brown flesh showing in the gap between the slipper and the hem. Jerry touched his lips with the tip of his finger.

Above his head monkeys flung themselves through the green branches as they looked for cover from the rain. The noise they made helped Jerry creep into the clearing unobserved. He frowned.

The boy lifted his head and smiled up at Jerry. "Do you feel like a woman?"

"You stick to your prayers, I'll stick to mine."

The boy obeyed. Jerry stood looking down at the little figure as it murmured the prayers. He took out his heater and cleared his throat, then he adjusted the beam width and burned a thin hole through the child's anus. He screamed.

Later Maxwell emerged from the undergrowth and began removing the various quarters from the jewelled material. There was hardly any blood, just the stench. He shook out the bits of flesh and folded the parts of the gown across his arm. He put one slipper in his right pocket and the other in his left. Lastly he plucked the cap from the severed head and offered it to Jerry.

"You'd better hurry. The rain's getting worse. We'll be drowned at this rate. That should cover your expenses. You'll be able to convert it fairly easily in Singapore."

"I don't often get expenses," said Jerry.

*   *   *

10.25

Četeka said shooting in the center of Prague had intensified and that the "Rude Pravo" offices had been seized by "occupation units".

* * *

Waiting near the Irrawaddy for the Ka-15 to come back, Jerry watched the rain splash into the river. He was already soaked.

The flying field had only recently been cleared from the jungle and it went right down to the banks of the river. Jerry picked his teeth with his thumbnail and looked at the broad brown water and the forest on the other side. A wooden landing stage had been built out into the river and a family of fishermen were tying up their sampan. Why should crossing this particular river seem so important?

Jerry shook his umbrella and looked up at the sound of the helicopter's engines. He was completely drenched; he felt cold and he felt sorry for himself. The sooner he could reach the Galapagos the better.

* * *

11.50

Pilsen Radio said: "The occupation has already cost twenty-five lives."

* * *

He just got to the post office before it closed. Anna Ne Win was standing inside reading a copy of *Dandy*. She looked up. "You're British, aren't you? Want to hear the Test results?"

Jerry shook his head. It was pointless asking for his telegram now. He no longer had any use for assurances. What he needed most at this stage was a good, solid, undeniable fact; something to get his teeth into.

"A Captain Maxwell was in earlier for some money that was being cabled to him," she said. "Apparently he was disappointed. Have you found it yet—the belt?"

"I'm sorry, no."

"You should have watched where you threw it."

"Yes."

"That Captain Maxwell. He's staying at your hotel, isn't he?"

"Yes. I've got to leave now. Going to Singapore. I'll buy you two new ones there. Send them along." He ran from the post office.

"Cheerio," she called. "Keep smiling."

* * *

12.28

Četeka said Mr. Dubček was under restriction in the Central Committee building.

* * *

Naked, Jerry sat down on his bed and smoked a cheroot. He was fed up with the east. It wasn't doing his identity any good.

The door opened and Maxwell came in with a revolver in his hand and a look of disgust on his fat face. "You're not wearing any damned clothes!"

"I wasn't expecting you."

Maxwell cocked the revolver. "Who do you think you are, anyway?"

"Who do you think?"

Maxwell sneered. "You'd welcome suggestions, eh? I want to puke when I look at you."

"Couldn't I help you get a transfer?"

"I don't need one."

Jerry looked at the disordered bed, at the laddered stockings Anna Ne Win had left behind, at the trousers hanging on the string over the washbasin, at the woollen mat on the floor by the bed, at the cricket bat on top of the wardrobe. "It would make me feel better, though." He drew on his cheroot. "Do you want the hat back?"

"Don't be revolting, Cornelius."

"What do you want, then, Captain Maxwell?"

"Justice."

"I'm with you." Jerry stood up and reached for his flannels. Maxwell raised the Webley and Scott 45 and fired the first bullet. Jerry was thrust against the washbasin and he blinked rapidly as his vision dimmed. There was a bruise five inches in diameter on his right breast and its center was a hole with red, puckered sides; around the edges of the bruise a little blood was beginning to force its way out. "There certainly are some shits in the world," he said.

A couple of shots later, when Jerry was lying on the floor, he had the impression that Maxwell's trousers had fallen down. He grinned. Maxwell's voice was faint but insulting. "Bloody gangster! Murderer! Fucking killer!"

Jerry turned on his side and noticed that Anna Ne Win's cerise suspender belt was hanging on a spring under the bed. He reached out and touched it and a tremor of pleasure ran through his body. The last shot he felt hit the base of his spine.

He shuddered and was vaguely aware of the weight of Maxwell's lumpen body on his, of the insect-bitten wrists, of the warm Webley and Scott still in one hand and the cordite smell on the captain's breath. Then Maxwell whispered something in his ear and reaching around his face carefully folded down his eyelids.

(All quotes from the *Guardian*, August 22, 1968)

The Swastika Set-Up

Introduction

Often Dr. Cornelius has said he should not interfere with the calendar, for he almost invariably removes two sheets at the same time and so produces even more confusion. The young Xaver, however, apparently delights in this pastime and refuses to be denied his pleasure.

—Thomas Mann, *Disorder and Early Sorrow*

The Fix

His early memories were probably no longer reliable: his mother lying on the bed with her well-muscled legs wide apart, her skirt up to her stomach, her cunt smiling.

"You'll have to be quick today. Your father's coming home early."

The school satchel, hastily dumped on the dressing table, contained his homework: the unified field theory that he had eventually destroyed, save for the single copy on a shelf somewhere in the Vatican Library.

Jerry took out his cigar case and selected an Upmann. Time moved swiftly and erratically these days. With the little silver syringe he cut the cigar and lit it, staring through the rain-dappled window at the soft summer landscaping surrounding his isolated Tudor Mansion. It had been some while since he had last visited the West Country.

He adjusted the stiff white shirt cuffs projecting an inch beyond the sleeves of his black car coat, placed his hand near his heart and shifted the shoulder holster slightly to make it lie more comfortably. Even the assassination business was getting complicated.

On the Job

"The conflicting time streams of the 20th century were mirrored in Jerry Cornelius."

—Early reference

At the Time Center

Alvarez, a man of substance, sniggered at Jerry as they climbed into their orange overalls. Jerry pursed his lips good-humoredly. The brightly colored lab was humming with activity and all the screens gleamed. Alvarez winked.

"Will you want the use of the mirror tonight, Mr. Cornelius?"

"No thanks, Alvarez. Enough's enough, right?"

"Whatever you say, though there's not much time left."

"Whichever—we'll get by."

They strolled towards the machine, a shimmering web of crimson and gold, so sophisticated.

With some poise Alvarez adjusted a dial, darting a glance at

Jerry who seated himself, placed the tips of his fingers on his forehead, and stared into the shimmering web.

"How would you like it, Mr. Cornelius?"

"Medium," Jerry said.

As Alvarez busied himself with the little controls he murmured incidentally. "Do you think mouth-to-mouth fertilization will make much difference, sir? What's your bet? How do you fancy their chances?"

Jerry didn't bother to reply. The web was beginning to bulge near N¾E.

"Look to your helm, Mr. Alvarez."

"Aye, eye, sir."

The Dessert

Jerry hated needling a dead man, but it was necessary. He looked down at the twice-killed corpse of Borman, the first Nazi astronaut. The riding britches had been pulled below his thighs. Perhaps it had been a last minute attempt to gain sympathy, Jerry thought, when Borman had unbuttoned the britches to expose the thin white scars on his pelvis and genitals.

The seedy Sherman Oaks apartment was still in semi-darkness. Borman had been watching a cartoon show when Jerry had called. An arsenical Bugs Bunny leapt along a mildew-colored cliff.

Jerry turned off the cheap TV and left.

Tense

Curling his hair with his fingers, Jerry looked quizzically at the mirror. Then he looked hard. But it didn't work.

The mirror.

He pinched the tip of his nose.

Reflecting on the enigma, he got into his purple brocade bell-bottoms, his deep crimson shirt, and delicately strapped on his heater, settling the holster comfortably on his hip.

The room was cool, with white walls, a gold carpet, a low glass table in the middle of the floor.

From the floor, Catty Ley reached smoothly up to stroke his trousers. "You got . . .?"

She wore the bra that showed her nipples, the black stockings, the mauve garters and boots. "You object . . ."

"Oh, yes."

"Darling."

He smiled, began to comb his hair, taking the long strands down so that they framed his face. "There's been a bulge," he said, "and it's still bulging. We're trying to do something about it. Fuck it."

"A rapture?"

"Who's to say?"

"An eruption?"

"Perhaps."

"Will you be needing me for anything?"

"It depends how everything goes."

"Jerry!"

"Catty . . ."

It was time to get back to the Time Center.

Facts

There were two sexes, he thought, *plus permutations. There is death, there is fear, there is time. There is birth, serenity, and time. There is identity, maybe. There is conflict. Robbed of their ambiguities, things cease to exist. Time, as always, was the filter.*

Double Lightning

A whole school of ships lay at anchor in the Bay and the tall cranes on the dockside formed a long wedding arch for Jerry as he walked lightly towards the pier where *Teddy Bear* was berthed. The sun shone on the rainbow oil, on the crisp, white shrouds of the ship, on the schooner's bright brass. She was a beautiful vessel, built in 1920 for Shang Chien, the playboy warlord, who had sailed her regularly from the opium-rich ports of the China seas to Monte Carlo until Mao had paid him off to settle in France where he had recently died.

What was the ship doing in Frisco?

Jerry went aboard.

A tatty jack tar greeted him, rolling along the deck whistling "So Sad."

"Master in the cabin?" Jerry asked. Something was shaping.

The sailor sighed. "Won't be." He went to the rail and ran his fingers along the brasswork. He gave Jerry a secret, sardonic look. "Larger things have come up."

The sailor didn't stop him as he sauntered to the main companionway and descended.

The schooner's fittings were really Edwardian; all guilt and redplush. Jerry's feet sank into the soft carpet. He withdrew them, moving with difficulty. Finding the cabin he walked in, sniffing the musty air. Korean tapestries in the manner of Chong Son covered the walls; ceramics—mainly Yi dynasty—were fixed on all the shelves. He knew at once that, for the moment at least, the action was elsewhere. But where?

As he made his way back he saw that the holes his feet had made were filling with masses of white maggots. He grinned. There was no doubt in his mind: sooner or later the schooner would be scuppered by someone. A woman? He paused, trying to get the feel of it. Yes, possibly a woman. He lit an Upmann. The maggots began to squirm over his shoes. He moved on.

As he reached the gangplank, the sailor reappeared.

"You know what's wrong with you . . ." the sailor began.

"Save it, sailor."

Jerry swung down to the pier, making it fast to where his Phantom III was parked.

He got the big car going. His spirits had risen considerably.

"It's all essential," he laughed.

Facts

It was so elusive. There were events that frightened him; relationships that he could not cope with directly. Were his own actions creating some particular kind of alchemy?

There was birth.

Beckett had written a letter to a friend. "What can I do? Everything I touch turns to art in my hands."

After thirty or forty years, even Duchamp's ready-mades had come to be objects of interest for him.

Tolerance. Tension. Integrity. Why was he running away?

I am tired, he thought; exhausted. But he had to finish the job in hand.

There was murder.

The Map

Jerry studied the map. His father would have known what to do, and he would have done the right or the wrong thing.

The map was a little faded in places, but it offered a clue. Now he had to wait for a phone call.

"*The next great American hero will be a Communist.*"

Jerry grinned as he drove along. The recent discovery of sex and drugs had taken their minds off the essential problems. Time was silting up. Sooner or later there would be the Flood and then, with a spot of luck, everything would be cooler. It was his job to get the muck shifted as fast as possible. It was a dirty but essentially satisfying job.

His car hit an old man with an extraordinary resemblance to Walt Disney's Pinocchio. No, there was an even closer likeness. He got it. Richard Nixon. He roared with laughter.

It had all started to work out nice with the folding, at long last, of *The Saturday Evening Post.*

Development I

Really, one only had to wait for death to kiss the bastards. Those who wouldn't die had to be killed. Kinetically, of course, it was very simple.

He switched on the car radio and got "*Your Mother Should Know*" by the Beatles.

Fact

There was death.

Supposition

You had to keep your eye on the facts.

Falsehood

There was no such thing as falsehood.

Uncomfortable Visions

Toronto was gray, square and solid. The sun wasn't shining and the traffic wasn't moving. There was a crowd in the street.

Andrew Wells was due to speak at and inspire the big Civil Rights Convention in Toronto where all the American exiles (or "yellow bellies" as they were known) had gathered.

True to the spirit of convention, Andrew, dressed in a neat gray business suit, addressed the exiles and their friends from a balcony on the second floor of Rochdale College, the squarest block in the city. From the roof of the building opposite Jerry had an excellent view of the balcony, the crowd below, and the speaker. Jerry was dressed in the full ceremonial uniform of a Royal Canadian Mounted Policeman. The only difference was that the gun in the neat leather holster on his belt was his trusty heater.

As Andrew began his conventional address concerning universal brotherhood, freedom and the New Apocalypse, Jerry drew the heater, levelled it on his crooked left arm, sighted down it and burned Andrew right in the middle of his black mouth, moving the beam about to cauterize the face. Naturally, there wasn't much blood.

He got into the Kamov Ka-15 helicopter and ascended to the clouds where he made a quick getaway, wondering which poor bastard would claim the credit this time.

Muscle Trouble

In mutable times like these, thought Jerry as he walked back into Lionel Himmler's Blue Spot Bar, everything was possible and nothing was likely. His friend Albert the émigré nodded to him from the shadowy corner by the bar, lifting his glass of schnapps in the strobelight, saluting both Jerry and the stripper on the stage.

Jerry flickered to a table, sat down and ordered scotch and milk. Once history ceased to be seen in linear terms, it ceased to be made in linear terms. He glanced at his new watch. It consisted of eight yellow arrows radiating from a purple central hub. There were no figures marked on it, but the arrows went rapidly round and round. He could check the time only in relation to the speed at which the arrows moved. The arrows were moving very rapidly now.

Albert finished his schnapps, wiped his hands over his shaggy, gray beard and staggered towards the Wardour Street exit of the bar, on his way back to his sad little bedsitter decorated from floor to ceiling with dusty old charts, sheets of equations and eccentric geometric figures.

In these days of temporal and social breakdown the human psyche suffered enormously. Jerry felt sorry for the little Jew. History had destroyed him.

The drums stopped beating. The strobe gave way to conventional lighting. Suddenly it seemed he was the only customer. The waiter arrived, put his drink down, tucking the bill under the glass.

"How about that—Symphony Sal," said the MC, coming on clapping. "Give her a big hand," he said quietly, looking around the deserted bar. "Give her a big hand," he told Jerry.

Jerry started to clap.

The MC went away. The bar was silent.

Only in dreams did karma continue to have any meaning, thought Jerry. Or, at least, so it sometimes seemed.

He turned.

She was standing there in the doorway, smiling at him, her wide-brimmed hat like a halo. A Tory woman in garden party good taste.

She came to his table and picked up the tag with her gloved fingers.

"I'll take that, sonny."

The gloves were of blue lace, up to the elbow. She wore a dark blue cotton suit that matched her hat. Her hair was black and her oval face was beautiful. She parted her lips.

"So?" said Jerry.

"Soon," she purred. "I've got some answers for you. Are you interested?"

"What do you think?"

She glanced demurely at her blue shoes. "To stop now would severely complicate things. You and your friends had better call it a day. You could always come in with me."

"In there?" Jerry shook his head.

"It's not so different." She gave him a hard little smile.

"About as different as yin from yang. Sure." Jerry reached out and placed his right palm hard against her stomach. She shrugged.

"It's too late, I think," she said. "We should have got together earlier." With a movement of her hips she took a small step away from him.

"You could always get some new sex stars, couldn't you?" Jerry sipped his scotch and milk.

"Certainly."

"Are the current ones essential?"

She smiled more openly and gave him a candid look. "I see. You know a lot, Mr. Cornelius."

"My job."

"And you want a new one?"

"Maybe."

"I'm Lady Susan Sunday," she said.

"Lady Sue."

She shrugged. "You're out of luck, I think. We're really moving. Frightfully nice to have met you, Mr. Cornelius."

Jerry watched her pay the waiter. He knew her from the file. A close associate of his old enemy Captain Maxwell, from the Burma and China days. The opposition was organizing a freeze, if he wasn't mistaken. She had told him everything. A stasis situation. He sniffed.

When she had gone, he went up to the bar. "Have you a mirror?"

"Lovely for you," said the barman.

The Pieces

When he got back, Catty was still in her uniform. He took her soft shoulders and kissed her on the mouth. He put his hands in her pants.

"Look," she said, waving at the center of the room where an ornate crystal chess set was laid out on a low table. "Want a game?"

"I can't play chess," he said.

"Oh, fuck," she said.

He regarded her with compassionate anticipation. "You'd better fetch me those levitation reports," he said.

The Music of Time

The road was straight and white between avenues of cedars and poplars. Jerry idled along doing forty.

The Inkspots were singing "Beautiful Dreamer" on the Duesenberg's tapes. It amused Jerry to match his tapes to his cars. They finished that one and began "How Deep is the Ocean?"

On the seat beside him Jerry had a Grimshaw guitar with the shaped resonator. They had appeared just too late and had been quickly superseded by the electric guitar. Now George Formby's ukulele thrummed.

In a young lady's bedroom I went by mistake
My intentions were honest you see
But she shouted with laughter,
I know what you're after:
It's me Auntie Maggie's remedy.

1957 had marked the end of the world Jerry had been born into. Adapting was difficult. He had to admit that he had had special advantages. Already people were beginning to talk about him as "The Messiah of the Age of Science" and a lot of apocryphal stories were circulating. He laughed. He wasn't the archetype. He was a stereotype.

Still, he did what he could.

Science, after all, was a much more sophisticated form of superstition than religion.

After this little episode was completed (if "completed" was the word) he would go and relax among that particularly degenerate tribe of headhunters who had adopted him on his last visit to New Guinea.

He smiled as large drops of rain hit the windscreen and were vaporized. On that trip he had been responsible for starting at least eight new cargo cults.

Don't Let Me Down

That great big woman had almost been the death of him. There had been so much of her. A hungry woman who had fed his own greed. He sucked breath through clenched teeth at the memory, expelled a shivering sigh.

He had probably been the last of the really innocent motherfuckers. It had been her slaughter, not society, that had put a stop to it. His funny old father, Dr. Cornelius (a lovable eccentric, a visionary in his own way), had killed her when she got cancer of the cervix, running a white-hot poker into her cunt without so much as a by-your-leave.

His eyes softened nostalgically. He remembered her wit.

Once, when his sister Catherine had come out with a particularly sour remark, his mother had rounded on her from the table where she had been cutting up onions.

"Say that again, love, and I'll carve me fucking name on your womb."

As it turned out, she'd made something of a prophetic retort.

His childhood had been, until his voluntary entry into the Jesuit seminary, an unspoiled and relatively uncomplicated one. But he couldn't complain. It had been much more interesting than many.

He turned the Duesenberg into a side lane. Through the twilight he could see the silhouette of the Tudor Mansion.

He needed a fresh car coat. The brown leather one, in the circumstances.

Get Back

An expectancy of change grew out of the dynamic of a search for the "new politics", a kind of quest-epic which had to end on schedule on November 5. Disappointment followed when the search produced nothing new. All the found objects were cast in old forms. Humphrey's coalition was virtually indistinguishable from Roosevelts's, Truman's or Johnson's—except that crucial sections had fallen away. McCarthy and Nixon were both relying on a Fifties phenomenon—the ascendancy of the surburban elite. John Kennedy had used that class already in 1960. In their separate ways, Nixon and McCarthy both sought its allegiance, and, if they had contested each other directly, 1968 would have been a delayed-replay of 1960. McCarthy would probably have won: precisely because he could recapture the old spirit, not because he could fashion the new.

—Andrew Kopkind, *America: the Mixed Curse*

Pour les originaux

Jerry looked through the mail that had accumulated since he had been away.

Outside the French windows the sky was overcast and rain still swished among the oaks. Softly from the stereo came the Beatles' *Only a Northern Song.*

There was a request to open a local fête. It was from the vicar of the village church and began "I know you have a very full schedule but . . ." He was a month behind on his Telstar rental and there was a final demand from the firm who had supplied the aircraft carrier which he had lost on the abortive Antarctic expedition where they had failed to find the opening to Pellucidar. A pot scheme if ever there had been one.

A folded sheet marked *Plattegrond van Amsterdam.* Several postcards without messages.

At last he found what he'd been expecting. The envelope had been resealed and forwarded from his Ladbroke Grove convent. He opened it and shook out the contents.

A torn envelope. Small brown manilla with the address ripped off and a stamp that said "Join the sun set in Eastbourne this year". A fivepenny stamp, postmarked Eastbourne, Sussex, the date indecipherable. On the back, three words: Assassin—Assassin—Assassin.

An Imperial Reply Coupon stamped Juliasdale, Rhodesia, 23rd Jan. 69: "Valid only for exchange within the British Empire. Southern Rhodesia. Selling 3d price. This coupon may be exchanged in any part of the BRITISH EMPIRE for a postage stamp or stamps representing the postage on a single rate letter to a destination within the Empire. Exceptionally the exchange value in India and Burma is 2½ annas." The engraving, blue on oatmeal, was of a standing Britannia looking out over the sea at a square-rigged sailing ship.

An empty book match folder marked UCS.

A postcard with a fourpenny Concorde stamp postmarked Weston-S-Mare, Somerset, 15 Apr. 1969. It showed a big wave breaking on a rock and the caption read: "The Cornish Seas. A study of the waves breaking on the rocks. There is nothing but the open Atlantic between the Cornish coast and America: A Natural Color Photograph."

The last item was a rather dog-eared sheet of paper, folded several times and secured with a paper clip. Jerry removed the paper clip and unfolded the paper.

There was a message. A single handwritten line in separated upper and lower case letters. "The ship is yours. B."

Jerry frowned and put the various bits and pieces back into the envelope. He sipped his mug of black coffee as the Beatles sang *Altogether Now* and he studied the envelope to see if it gave him any further clues. It had four stamps on it. A fivepenny showing the *Queen Elizabeth II;* a shilling showing the RMS *Mauretania;* another shilling showing the SS *Great Britain.* It bore his Ladbroke Grove address and the forwarding number circled in blue ballpoint—93. In the top left-hand corner was written in black felt pen: Urgent Special Delivery. The fourth stamp was in the bottom right-hand corner. Another fourpenny Concorde.

What was he to make of it?

There was nothing else but to go down to the harbor in the morning and look at the ships.

For the rest of the evening, before he went to bed, he read the comic strip serial in his back issues of *International Times*. The strip was called *The Adventures of Jerry Cornelius. The English Assassin.*

Maybe it would add up to something, after all.

The Golden Apples of the Sun

Dylan and the rest, unable to face the implications of their own subject matter, had beaten a quick retreat. Those few whom they had urged on were left stranded, staring around them in bewilderment.

Now the times, had, indeed, changed. But the prophets had not. They had only been able to predict—not adapt.

Multi-value logic.

Was it logic, in any real sense, at all?

Or was he really only imposing his own vision on reality; a vision so strong that, for a short time, it would seem to be confirmed by the events around him.

Be that as it may, it was time for some action. He stripped and cleaned his needle-gun, drew on his black car coat, his black bell-bottoms, his white shirt with the Bastille-style collar, put the gun in its case, put the case in his pocket, left the Tudor Mansion, locked the doors behind him, looked up at the morning sun slanting through the clouds, and walked on his cuban-heeled feet towards the blue and sparkling sea.

In his dress and his methods of operation he, too, was an anachronism. But he knew no other way. Perhaps there would, in human terms, never be another way. Equilibrium had to be maintained somehow and as far as Jerry was concerned, only the ontologists had any kind of satisfactory answer.

The New Man

Pope Paul turned saint-slayer in the interests of historical accuracy. Out go the saints whose existence is now doubted. St. Barbara, whose name has been given to millions of girls and an American city, is struck off. So are Susanna, Boniface of Tarsus, Ursula and her fellow martyrs. An English saint whose existence cannot be doubted moves into the Calendar . . .

—*Sunday*, May 10, 1969

Capacity

At Harbour Street Jerry paused to rest. His boots weren't suitable for cobbled lanes.

There was hardly anyone about in the little Cornish village. A smell of fish, a few inshore trawlermen mending their nets, white stone walls of the cottages, gray slate roofs, the masts of the boats that had not yet put out to sea.

Looking down the narrow street at the harbour and beyond it, Jerry saw the yacht anchored at the far end of the stone mole that had been built during the village's better days.

It was *Teddy Bear.* The yacht had been given a lick of fresh white paint. A corpse of a boat. Is that where the meeting was to take place?

He began to trudge along the mole. The mole was also cobbled. His feet were killing him.

Development II

The War is Over

The kind of chromosomes a person has is called his genotype, and the appearance of a person is called his phenotype. Thus, males have the genotype XY and the phenotype male. Women have the genotype XX and the phenotype female. . . . In every war in history there must have been a considerable flow of genes one way or another. Whether the genes of the victors or of the vanquished have increased most is a debatable point.

—Papazian, *Modern Genetics*

Miss Brunner

The boat smelled as if she had been fouled by a score of cats. Jerry stood on the rotting deck and waited.

Eventually Miss Brunner emerged from the wheelhouse. She was dressed as severely as ever in a Cardin trouser suit as dated as Jerry's own clothes. She held a baby in her crooked right arm, a Smith & Wesson .44 revolver in her left hand.

She gave him a bent smile. "Good morning, Mr. Cornelius. So our paths come together again."

"I got your note. What's up, Miss Brunner?"

She shook her short red hair in the wind and turned her feline face down to regard the baby.

"Do you like children, Mr. Cornelius?"

"It depends." Jerry moved to look at the baby and was shocked.

"It's got your eyes and mouth, hasn't it?" said Miss Brunner. She offered it to him. "Would you like to hold it?"

He took a wary step backward. She shrugged and tossed the little creature far out over the rail. He heard it hit the water, whine, gurgle.

"I only hung on to it in case you'd want to have it," she said apologetically. "Okay, Mr. Cornelius. Let's get down to business."

"I might have kept it," Jerry said feelingly. "You didn't give me much of a chance to consider."

"Oh, really, Mr. Cornelius. You should be able to make up your mind more quickly than that. Are you going soft?"

"Just crumbling a little, at the moment."

"Ah well, it's all written in the quasars, I suppose. Come along."

He followed her down the companionway, along the passage and into the cabin decorated with the Korean tapestries.

"Could we have a porthole open?" Jerry asked.

Pettishly Miss Brunner flung open a porthole. "I didn't know you cared that much for fresh air."

"It's to do with my upbringing." Jerry saw that there were charts unfolded on the ornate mother-of-pearl chart table. He gave them the once-over. A cockroach crawled across a big detailed plan of Hyde Park.

"I suppose you know it's Maxwell and his gang," Miss Brunner said. "Trying the old diversion game again. I don't know who that woman thinks she is . . ." She glared at Jerry and turned her head to stare out of the porthole. "They're building up a sex scene that could set us back by I don't know how long. Essentially a red herring—but we'll have to nip it in the bud, if we can. Fight fire with fire. I'm not unsympathetic, Mr. Cornelius . . ."

"Any clues?" Jerry lit an Upmann in the hope that it would overlay some of the stink.

Miss Brunner made an agitated gesture.

He gave her a cool, slightly contemptuous look. She couldn't work that one on him. There was no background.

She crossed rapidly to a locker set high in the bulkhead near the door. Taking something from the locker she tossed it to him. "Recognize that?"

Jerry turned the dildo in his hands. It had a crude, unaesthetic feel to it. "Don't know. It looks slightly familiar, but . . ."

"Have a look at the stem."

Jerry stared closely at the stem. A brand name. *Maxwell's Deviant Devices, London, W.8.*

"Overloaded. He's not happy in his work. That links it with the captain, all right," Jerry agreed.

She brought something else out of the locker and put it on the chart table. It was a vial of processed DNA.

"Makes sense," said Jerry. "They're attempting to slow down the transmogrification by fucking about with identity—concentrating on the heaviest sex angles they can find. It's the easiest way, of course. But crude. I can't believe that anyone these days . . . Such an old trick . . ."

"But it could be an effective one. You know how unstable things have been getting since 1965. These people are pre-1950!"

They laughed together.

"I'm serious, though," added Miss Brunner, sitting down. "They won't even use chrono-barometers."

"Bugger me. How do they tell the Time?"

"They don't admit it's here. It's our main advantage, of course."

Fact

There were a great many instincts in common between *homo sapiens* and the other animals.

As Barrington Bayley had pointed out in his book *Structural Dynamism,* man was not an intelligent animal. He was an animal with intelligence that he could apply to some, not all, of his activities.

Supposition

$E = mc^2$

Falsehood

Truth is absolute.

Cutting the Mustard

Miss Brunner handed him a beef sandwich. He bit it and grimaced. "It tastes of grass."

"It's all a question of how you process it, I suppose," she said.

She began to strap on her underclothes. "Well, that's our pact sealed. Where do you intend to go from here?"

"Back to London first. Then I'll start sniffing around."

She darted him an admiring look.

"You're coarse, darling—but you know how to get down to the nitty gritty."

"I don't suppose you'll be around when the shit hits the fan."

"You never know. But we'd better say goodbye, just in case."

She handed him a cardboard carton full of old Beatles singles and a photograph. "Don't lose it. It's our only contact."

"You anticipate a wax situation?"

"Maybe something a little more sophisticated than that. Is your equipment okay?"

"Ready to go."

"Oh, sweetie . . ."

She fell on his erection.

Electric Ladyland

Jerry took the Kamov Ka-15 to London. From there he would call Oxford.

The sound of the 'copter's rotors drummed in his ears. The fields fled by below. He didn't care for this sort of backtracking operation.

He would need Catty. And he would need one of them. A particular one.

He'd better check his circuits and get in any chemicals he was short on. He sighed, knowing that he would soon be immersed, but not relishing the prospect.

Reaching to the far side of the cockpit, he adjusted the Ellison meter.

Ladbroke Grove lay ahead. He began to drop her down.

If his mother hadn't taken it into her head that he should have a hobby, he wouldn't be in this situation now. He supposed he was grateful, really.

Consequences

When he had made the phone call, Jerry looked through his mother's recipe books to refresh his memory.

Then he made a list of ingredients.

Captain Maxwell

Captain Maxwell left the Austin Princess and crossed the grass verge at the agreed point. They were meeting on the banks of the

Cam, just to the north east of Cambridge. The tow-path was lined with fishermen. The river was full of punts. It was a lovely day.

"I thought this would constitute neutral territory, old boy." Maxwell smiled as he came briskly up to where Jerry was standing watching an angler.

"Neutral territory?" Jerry looked up absently.

Maxwell had lost weight since Jerry had last seen him. He wore a Harris Tweed jacket with leather patches on the sleeves and leather bands round the cuffs, cream cricket flannels, an old Etonian tie. His lips were as red as ever, his round face as bland. "How are you, old chap? I thought you were dead!" He insinuated a smile on to his features. "What can I do for you? Say the word."

"I felt like a chat," said Jerry. Although the day was warm, he wore his double-breasted black car coat buttoned up and his hands were in his pockets. "You seem to have done well for yourself since Burma."

"I can't complain, old sport."

"You've expanded your business interests, I hear. Getting the export market."

"You could put it like that. The American tie-up with Hunt seems to be working all right."

Maxwell put his hand on Jerry's elbow and they began to trudge along the tow-path, side by side. The air was full of sweet summer smells. Crickets chirped and bees buzzed.

"I was talking to the bishop about you only the other day," continued Maxwell. "He doesn't approve of you at all, old son." He gave a short, plummy laugh. "I told him it was nothing more than high spirits. 'Spawn of the Antichrist', indeed!"

Jerry grinned.

Maxwell glanced at him, looked disconcerted, cleared his throat. "You know the bishop. A bit of a romantic. A bit High Church, too, for my taste. Since I became PM, I've had to think about things like that."

"How is the government?"

"Oh, well—it's *small,* y'know, but generally pretty effective in what it tries to do, I think."

"I haven't seen much about it recently."

"We don't often get into the media these days, of course. But we remain realistic. In the meantime we're thinking of building a smaller House of Commons. The one we're using now can accommodate over a hundred members. It's far too big for us to manage." Maxwell stopped by the river and kicked at a stone. "But we'll see, we'll see . . ."

"You're hoping people will get interested in politics again?"

"I *am* rather hoping that, old boy, yes." Maxwell tried to cover up a sudden secretive expression.

"But for politics, they need surrogates . . ."

Maxwell looked up sharply. "If you mean *issues*—I think we can find *issues* for them all right."

Jerry nodded. "On the other hand, captain, you can't turn back the clock, can you?"

"Don't intend to, old boy. I'm thinking of the future. The swing of the pendulum, you know."

Jerry began to giggle uncontrollably.

He stepped into a passing punt. "Well, so long, captain."

"TTFN, old chap. Hope I could assist . . ."

Jerry developed hiccups. He fell backwards into the water.

"Oh, shit!" he laughed. He signalled for his helicopter to come down and pick him up.

The only depressing thing about the encounter was that briefly, at any rate, he had to take the captain's plans seriously.

Popcorn

Jerry tuned his guitar to modal G and played "Old Macdonald Had a Farm" with a Far Eastern feeling.

He looked through the leaded and barred window of the converted convent that was his Ladbroke Grove HQ. Maxwell's opium business was booming. The captain disguised his consignments as penicillin and anti-tetanus serum and shipped them mainly to underdeveloped nations. They were, in fact, developing rapidly with the captain's help.

The sun went in. It began to rain.

Jerry got up and put on his coat. Then he went down the long, dark staircase to the front door and out into the courtyard where he climbed into his Phantom VI.

As he drove down Ladbroke Grove, he pulled out the dusty drawer in the dashboard containing the .45 player and stacked the old Beatles singles on to it. "The Inner Light" began to play. Jerry smiled, taking a hand-rolled from the nearby tray and sticking the liquorice paper between his lips. It was all such a long time ago. But he had to go through with it.

He remembered the Burma days.

Every gun makes its own tune . . .

It wasn't the first time Maxwell had succeeded in buggering the equilibrium. But in those days he hadn't liked working with women.

Jerry cheered up at the prospect of his next action.

Cause and Effect

The three men who took the Apollo 8 spaceship on its Christmas journey round the moon were awarded a trophy in London yesterday—for providing "the most memorable color TV moment of the past year or any other year." . . . Others who were honored for the year's best achievements in color TV were comedian Marty Feldman and actress Suzanne Neeve. Derek Nimmo, famous for his parts in "Oh Brother" and "All Gas and Gaiters" won the Royal Television Society's silver medal for "outstanding artistic achievement in front of the camera."

—*Sunday*, May 10, 1969

Sweet Child

Jerry got what he needed. It was the last thing on his list.

In Holland Park he wandered hand in hand with Helen who was happy. Her long blonde hair was thick and delicate and her little mini-dress had a gold chain around the waist. Her breasts were sixteen years old and full and she was just plump enough all over. She had a great big red mouth and delicious teeth and huge dark eyes that were full of surprises.

It was a silent summer day and all the trees were green and still and Jerry sang and sprang along the leafy paths.

Helen, behind him, gave a slightly condescending smile.

Jerry shrugged and folded his arms across his chest, turning. He narrowed his eyes and said softly, "Do you love me, Helen?"

"More or less."

"More or less?"

"Oh, Jerry!" She laughed.

He looked about him, through the trees. The park was deserted.

He drew his needle-gun.

Helen looked at it curiously. "You are silly, Jerry."

He gestured with his weapon.

"Come here, Helen."

She stepped lightly towards him. With his left hand he reached out and felt below her pelvis. He shook his head.

"Is that yours?"

"Of course it's mine."

"I mean real or false?"

"Who can say?"

"Take it off."

She pulled up her skirt and undid the little pin that released it into her hand. She gave it to him. "I feel funny now," she said. "More or less."

"You'd better go ahead of me," said Jerry, replacing his needle-gun.

Resolution

Because man is an animal, movement is most important for him . . . Long distance running is particularly good training in perseverance.

—Mao Tse-Tung, *Hsin ch'ing-nien,* April 1917

Customs

His mouth was full of blood. He popped the last of the liver down his throat and sucked his lower lip, appraising Helen, who stood shivering in the center of the pentagram. Then he took the speakers and placed one on each of the star's five points, turned to the console on the wall and switched on.

Sparks leapt from point to point and settled into a blue-green flow. Helen hugged her naked breasts.

"Keep your arms at your sides, please," said Miss Brunner from the darkness on the other side of the lab.

"It's only a temporal circuit. There's nothing to worry about yet."

Jerry turned a dial. Softly, at first, the music issued from the speakers. Jimi Hendrix's "Still Raining, Still Dreaming." Helen began to sway to the sound.

Jerry switched tracks, studying the girl carefully. He got The Deep Fix and *Laughing Gods.* She jerked, her eyes glazing.

Jerry gave Miss Brunner the thumbs up sign, turned off the power for a moment to let her into the pentagram, switched on and increased the volume.

His eyes stopped blinking. His face was bathed in the blue-green glow as he watched Miss Brunner move in on the girl.

Grand Guignol

It was telekinesis of a sort, Jerry supposed. You had to act it all out. That was the drag, sometimes. Still—desperate days, desperate measures.

When the drums started to beat, you had to dance.

Na Chia

Delicately Jerry removed Catty's lights and threw them steaming into the kidney dish. Miss Brunner picked up the dish and left the room. "I'll be getting on with these."

"Okay," said Jerry. His job involved much more precise surgery, for he was attempting nothing less than necromancy.

And there wasn't much time.

T'si i

He pumped Catty's corpse full of methane wishing that Miss

Brunner had not used up Helen so completely. This was the dark period. The low point. Even if they were successful in cleaning up the Maxwell problem, there was still much to do.

A kalpa, after all, was a kalpa. It sometimes seemed it would last forever. Nonetheless, he would be glad when this particular job was wound up.

The drums were beating faster now. His pulse-rate rose, his temperature increased. In the strobe light his face was flushed, his eyes burning, and there was a rim of blood around his lips. The lab was in chaos where he had ransacked it in his haste, searching out the equipment and chemicals he needed.

Squatting by the gas cylinder, he howled along with The Deep Fix.

Scream

"Belphegor!" shrieked Maxwell as Jerry appeared in the window, his car coat unbuttoned and flapping in the sudden wind, his heater in his hand.

Jerry was incapable of speech now. His glowing eyes scanned the opulent room and he remained stock-still, framed against the full moon.

He would never know if Maxwell had identified him as Belphegor or whether that was who the captain had called for. He crouched.

He sprang.

The prime minister ran across the room. From somewhere the Beatles began to sing "Sexy Sadie." Maxwell touched the door handle and whimpered.

Jerry burned him.

Then, while Maxwell was still hot, he bit off everything he could find.

This was politics with a vengeance.

Baby's in Black

Jerry flattened the accelerator. The world swam with blood.

Walpurgis Eve. Trees and houses flashed past.

The breath hissed in through his tight fangs.

Gradually the drums slowed their tempo and Jerry cooled, dropped down to sixty and began to pick his teeth.

A nervous tick. He couldn't help laughing.

Anarchists in Love

He stopped off at the tenement in Robert Street on the borders of Soho. The house was empty now. It had been condemned for years. He pushed open the broken door and entered the damp darkness, treading the worm-eaten boards. His mother had claimed that this was where he had been born, with thick hair down to his shoulders and a full set of teeth, dragged feet first into the world. But towards the end his memory had been better than hers, though by no means reliable.

He struck a match, frowning, trod the groaning stairs to the first floor and found two tall black candles in bronze holders screwed on either side of the entrance to the room he had come to see. He lit the candles.

The place was being used. Neat symbols had been carved in the walls and there were signs of recent occupation. Rats had been crucified near the candles. Some of them were still alive, moving feebly. An early portrait of himself, framed between two sheets of dark glass, hung on the door.

So the place had already become a shrine of some kind.

Below the portrait was a row of equations, quoted from one of his books. Jerry felt sick. Standing by the room he might have been born in, he bent and vomited out the blood that had bloated his stomach.

Weakly, he stumbled down the stairs and into the festering street.

They had taken the hub caps off his car. He glanced around, conscious of eyes peering at him. He buttoned his coat about his body, got into the driving seat and started the engine.

Perhaps the future would forget him. It had better for its own sake. He was, after all, only standing in until something better turned up.

Mrs. Cornelius

After his mother's death they had moved, finally, to his father's fake Le Corbusier château. Somehow Jerry had always identified the house with his misfortune, though there was no particular evidence to support the idea.

The brain and the womb. Which had created him?

Perhaps neither.

She had begun to claim, as the cancer became more painful, that he had not been conceived by his father. His father had denied this.

"Who else would want to fuck you?" he used to say.

This of course had amused Jerry.

There had been a lot of laughter in the family in those days. Catherine, his brother Frank, his mother and father. Each had a particular kind of humor which had complemented that of the others.

But enough of the past.

He saw Miss Brunner bathed in his headlights and stopped the car.

"Perhaps you could drop me off at the coast," she said as she climbed in beside him. "The rest is up to you."

He smiled sweetly.

"Maxwell's out of it for the time being, I take it," said Miss Brunner. "There's only the residual bits and pieces to tidy up. Then the job's over."

"I suppose so."

The drums had started up again.

His and Hers

Then is there no such thing as justice? . . . His scientific mind is irradiated by this idea. Yet surely the question is, in itself, scientific, psychological, moral, and can therefore be accepted without bias, however disturbing? Lost in these deliberations Dr. Cornelius discovers he has arrived back at his own door.

— Thomas Mann, *Disorder and Early Sorrow*

The Sex Complex

Holland House was a sixteenth-century manor reconstructed as a façade in 1966. On the white battlements stood guards in yellow leather.

"Helen?" called one.

"Okay, Herschel."

They went through the iron doors and the floor began to sink under their feet, taking them down and down through crawling light.

At the bottom Jerry drew his heater and pushed what was left of the fake Helen through the opening into the huge hall where the freaks turned to glance at them before looking back at Lady Sue Sunday, still in her Tory set, who stood in an ornate pulpit at the far end.

"Helen!" Lady Sue looked prim.

"It was inconclusive," said what was left of the fake Helen defensively. "Really."

"S . . ."

Jerry glimmed Lady Sue's freaks. "Jesus," he said. There were little boys dressed as little girls. There were men dressed as women and women decked out like men in almost every detail. There were androgynes and hermaphrodites. There were little girls dressed as little boys. There were hugely muscled women and tiny, soft men.

"Irony, Lady Sue, is no substitute for imagination."

He shook his head and unbuttoned his car coat with his free hand.

Lady Sue put a glove to her lips.

"You're a naughty boy, Jerry. Naughty, naughty, naughty boy . . ."

Jerry laughed. "Evidently you never knew my mother."

Lady Sue scowled.

"Maxwell's had it," Jerry said. "I only dropped in to let you know. You can go home. It's all over."

"Naughty . . ."

"Oh, shut up." He raised his gun.

She licked her lips.

Jerry watched the urine as it began to drip from the floor of the pulpit. Lady Sue looked uncomfortable. She spread her arms to indicate her creatures.

Jerry sighed. "If you hadn't been so damned literal-minded . . ."

"You can accuse . . ." With an impatient gesture she touched a button on the pulpit's console. Little Richard music began to roar about the hall.

Jerry relaxed. No good getting excited.

"This is a one-way ticket," he called, waving his heater at the scene. "A line. Just a line."

"Who needs angles, you little horror?" She picked up her wide-brimmed blue hat and adjusted it on her head.

"At best a spiral," Jerry murmured wearily.

"A chain!" she cried. "A chain! Vitality! Don't you get it?"

"Off you go, Lady Sue."

Little Richard changed to James Brown. It was too much for Jerry. He began to race through the freaks towards the pulpit. The freaks kept touching him.

Lady Sue picked up a small vanity bag. "Well . . ." She was defeated. "Back to Hampstead, I suppose. Or . . ."

"You get a passage on a boat," he said. "The *Teddy Bear.* She's in the Pool of London now. Hurry up . . ."

"Why . . .?"

"Off you go. I might see you later."

She stepped out of the pulpit and walked towards the elevator immediately behind her—a golden cage. She got into the cage. It began to rise. Through the glass bottom Jerry could see right up her skirt, saw the damp pants.

When she had disappeared, he took his heater and burned down the pulpit. The lights began to fade, one by one.

The flaming pulpit gave him enough light to work. He cleaned up Lady Sue's mess, much more in sorrow than in anger. The mess recoiled then rushed at him. It was shouting. He backed away. Normally he would have used his heater, but he was now too full of melancholy. He had been very busy, after all.

They were never grateful.

The freaks pursued him to the lift; he got there first and went up fast.

He left Holland House and the guards shot at him as he raced through the door and out into the park. He ducked behind a statue and burned his initials into the chest of each of them.

That did it.

It was one for mother.

A Cure for Cancer

Jerry watched the *Teddy Bear* sail out into the calm oil of the Pool and start to sink.

Lady Sue leaned moodily on the rail, staring at him as the ship went down. Soon only her hat and the topmast were visible.

Jerry looked at his watch. It had almost stopped.

As he made his way back through the decrepit warehouses on the quayside he became aware of groups of figures standing in the shadows staring at him. Each of the figures was dressed in a moth-eaten black car coat he recognized as one of his cast-offs.

He shuddered and climbed into the Phantom VI.

His tongue was sweating. His heart was cold.

It had been a much tougher job that he expected.

Time off Time

"Adjustment okay," said Alvarez, coughing cheerfully. "Well, well, well . . ."

Jerry sat tired in his chair and inspected the shimmering web of crimson and gold. Apart from tiny and perfectly logical fluctuations in the outer strands, it was sweet and perfect.

"Aquilinus on tomorrow, isn't he?" Alvarez said as he tidied up.

Jerry nodded. He took a deep breath. "I'll have that mirror now. I'm looking forward to the change."

"That's a fact," said Alvarez.

The Sunset Perspective

A Moral Tale

1

MOGADISCIO, Somalia, Oct. 15—President Abirashid Ali Shermarke of Somalia was assassinated today by a member of the police force, an official announcement said here. The announcement said that a man had been arrested and accused of the murder at Las Anod in northern Somalia, where the President was touring an area stricken by drought. No reason for the assassination was suggested.

—*New York Times,* October 16, 1969

Energy Quotient

Jerry Cornelius lay on his back in the sweet warm grass and looked across the sunny fields, down the hill towards the bright, smart sea. Overhead a flight of friendly Westland Whirlwinds chattered past, full of news. Soon it was silent again.

Jerry stretched and smiled.

A small fox terrier wriggled through the stile at the bottom of the hill and paused, wagging its tail at him.

A cloud moved in front of the sun and the day chilled. Jerry first watched the cloud and then watched the dog. He listened to the grasshoppers. They were scraping their legs together in the long grass by the hedge. He sniffed the wind.

It was all a matter of how you looked at it, thought Jerry, getting tired of waiting for the cloud to pass. He took a deep breath and sprang to his feet, dusting off his brown velvet bell-bottoms. The dog started to bark at him. On the other side of the hedge a cow's heavy body shook the leaves. In the distance a woman's voice called the dog. Things were moving in on him.

Time to be off.

Jerry buttoned up his black car coat and adjusted the collar to frame his pale face. He tramped along the footpath towards the village.

Seagulls screamed on the cliffs.

The church bell began to clank.

Jerry sighed. He reached the field where his Gates Twinjet was parked. He climbed in, revved the chopper's engine, and buzzed up into the relative peace of the skies over Cornwall, heading for London.

One was allowed such short periods of rest.

2

There was something in that blind, scarred face that was terrifying . . . He did not seem quite human.

—W. Somerset Maugham, Preface, *Ashenden*

Time Quotient

When Jerry got to the Time Center only Alvarez was on duty. He was boredly watching the chronographs, his bearded face a pale green in the light from the machines. He heard the footsteps and turned large, liquid brown eyes to regard Jerry.

"Looks salty," Jerry quipped, indicating the web model in the centre of the operations room. The web bulged badly along one of its straights.

"Miss Brunner said she'd see to the adjustments," Alvarez told him pettishly. Morale seemed to have declined since Jerry had been away. "But between you and me, Mr. C., I think the whole bloody structure's going out of phase."

"Oh, come now . . ." Jerry made a few minor adjustments to Number Six 'graph, studied the results for a moment and then shrugged. "You haven't located the central cause of the bulge?"

"Miss Brunner's gone a bit funny, if you ask me."

Alvarez began to pick his teeth. "*On* the quiet," he added, "I'm pissed off with that bird."

"We all have our ups and downs, Mr. Alvarez."

He went into the computing room. Miss Brunner's handbag was on her desk. There were some sheets of calculations near it, but they hadn't gone very far. The face of each wall was a section of the huge computer she had built. But the machine was dormant.

Miss Brunner had turned off the power.

That meant something. She was probably having another identity crisis.

But what had caused it?

3

Life proceeds amid an incessant network of signals . . .

—George Steiner

Rise of the Total Energy Concept

Jerry finally managed to track Miss Brunner down. She was burying a goat in the Hyde Park crater and didn't see him come up and stand looking over the rim at her.

He watched as she mumbled to herself, hitching her Biba maxi-skirt up to her thighs and urinating on the new mound of earth.

"Well, you're really in a bad way, aren't you, Miss B.?"

She raised her head. The red hair fell over her foxy face; the eyes were glassy. She hissed and smoothed down her muddy clothes. "It's a difficult situation, Mr. Cornelius. We've got to try everything."

"Isn't this a bit dodgy?"

She picked up a stick and began to draw her usual mandala in the steaming earth. "If I can't be allowed to do my own job in my own way . . ."

"You've been working too hard."

"I've got eight toads and four newts buried around here!" She glared at him. "If you think I'm going to go round digging them up for you or anybody else . . ."

"Not necessary. Anyway, Alvarez obviously thinks we'll have to rephase."

"Bugger off."

"Look at yourself. You always revert to type in a crisis."

She paused, pushing back her hair and offering him a pitying smile. "Electricity's all you ever think about, isn't it? There are other methods, you know, which . . ."

Jerry dug inside his black car coat and took the needler from the shoulder holster. He waved it at her. "Come up out of there. You'll ruin your clothes."

She sniffed and began to climb, the loose earth falling away behind her.

He nudged her in the ribs with the needler and marched her to the Lear Steamer. Alvarez was in the driving seat. He had already got up enough pressure to start moving. Jerry sat beside Miss Brunner in the back seats of the car as it drove towards Bayswater Road.

"You reckoned the emanations vectored back to New York, didn't you?" he asked her. She had calmed down a bit now. "I read your initial calculations."

"New York was just involved in the first phase. I could have told you much more if you'd've let me finish with the goat . . . "

"I don't think goats are very efficient, Miss B."

"Well, what can we do about New York, anyway? We can't sort one AA Factor out from that lot there!"

"But the factor might sort us out."

4

WASHINGTON, Oct. 15—Congress voted today to coin a new dollar that would honor former President, Dwight D. Eisenhower, but the Senate and the House of Representatives differed on whether it should be a silver dollar. Flourishing a letter from Mrs. Eisenhower, a group of Western legislators got the Senate to override the Administration's proposal to produce a copper and nickel coin. A similar effort, backed by the same letter, failed in the House, which opted for the Administration's non-silver dollar. Mrs. Eisenhower's letter disclosed that the former President had loved to collect and distribute silver dollars as mementos.

—*New York Times,* October 16,1969

Horror Rape of the Kidnapped Teenage Beauty

Jerry pared the black mixture of oil and blood from the nail of the little finger of his right hand and carefully licked his upper lip. Then he put both hands back on the steering wheel of the wavering Cadillac limousine. The car was as hard to control as a hovercraft. The sooner it was used up the better. He saw the toll barrier ahead on the multilane highway and brought the car down to seventy.

Cars pulled into the sides of the road as his siren sounded. Jerry's six outriders, in red and orange leather, moved into position at front and back of the Cadillac, their arms stretched on the crucifixes of their apehanger bars.

Jerry pressed a switch.

The Who began to sing "Christmas." The sign hanging over the highway said DRIVERS WITH CORRECT CHANGE—THIS LANE.

Jerry paid his twenty-five cents at the turnpike and drove into New Jersey.

This was a noisy situation. There were either too many facts, or no facts at all—he couldn't be sure at this stage. But he had the feel of it. There was no doubt about one thing—it was a morality syndrome of the worst sort.

He checked his watch. The arrows whirled rapidly round the dial. Not much longer now.

The car lolloped along between the overgrown subsidy fields and the ramshackle internment centers.

Jerry lit a brown Sherman's Queen-Size Cigarettello.

Why Homosexuals Seek Jobs in Mental Hospitals

On the George Washington Bridge Jerry decided to change the Cadillac for one of his outriders' BMW 750s. He stopped. The riders got off their bikes and parked them neatly in a line along the rail. Drivers behind them on the highway hooted, their horns dying as they approached, pulled up, looked elsewhere.

He slid from the car, was passed the leather helmet and mirror goggles by the blond who took his place in the driving seat.

Jerry tucked his black flare pants into the tops of his ornate Cherokee boots, buckled up and mounted the vacated bike. He kicked the starter and had reached eighty by the time he hit Manhattan and entered the island's thick haze of incense.

The Holy City

The babble of the charm-sellers, the fortune-tellers, the fakirs, the diviners, the oracles, the astrologers, the astromancers and necromancers mingled with the squeal of the tires, the wail of the sirens, the caterwauling of the horns.

Corpses swayed on steel gibbets spanning the streets.

Broadsheets pasted on the sides of buildings advertized spectacular entertainments, while on the roofs little parties of marauders crept among the chimneys and the collapsing neon signs.

The popping of distant gunfire occasionally signified a clash.

Shacked up for Slaughter!

Jerry and his riders got all the way down Seventh Avenue to West Ninth Street before they were blocked by a twelve-foot-high pile-up and had to abandon their bikes.

From what Jerry could see, the pile-up went down as far as Sheridan Square and West 4th St. The faggots had probably closed off the area again and were defending their territory. They had had a lot of bad luck up to now. Maybe this time they would be successful.

Jerry took out his glasses and scanned the fire escapes—sure enough, the faggots, sporting the stolen uniforms of the Tactical Riot Police, were lobbing B-H5 gas grenades into the tangled heaps of automobiles.

Sheltering under a sign saying DOLLARS BOUGHT AT COMPETITIVE PRICES, Jerry watched for a few seconds.

It looked like a mince-over for the faggots.

My God, Wild Dogs Are Attacking the Kids!

Eventually Jerry reached his headquarters at the Hotel Merle on St. Mark's Place—the other side of the battle area. He had bought the hotel cheap when the Mafia had moved out to Salt Lake City.

Leaving his riders to go to the aid of their comrades on West Fourth, he entered the seedy gloom of the lobby.

Shaky Mo Collier was on the desk. His black face was caked with white clay and his expression was unusually surly. He cheered up when he saw Jerry.

"Mornin', Guv. Vere's a bloke waitin' fer yer in 506."

"What's his name?"

Mo screwed up his eyes in the poor light and his lips moved as he tried to read something he had scribbled on a checking-in card. "Robin—nar—Reuben—nar—Robert—de—Fate? Nar! Rob. . ."

"Robert de Fete." Jerry felt relieved. His trip hadn't been wasted. He recognized the "whimsical" pseudonym. "Foreign Office."

Mo sniffed and picked at the clay on his face. "I'll buy it, won' I?"

Jerry chucked him under his chin. "We bought it."

He took the groaning elevator to the fifth floor. The warren of narrow corridors was everywhere painted the same chocolate brown. Jerry found 506.

Cautiously, he opened the door.

The darkened room contained a bed without sheets and blankets. It had a striped, stained mattress. On the floor was a worn green carpet. A bedside table, lamp and secretaire were all coated with several layers of the same brown paint. The blind had been pulled down. On the secretaire stood a half-full bottle of Booth's Gin and a plastic cup.

Jerry opened the door into the bathroom. The pipes gurgled and shook, but the room was empty. He checked the shower-stall just the same.

He went back into the bedroom and looked at the bottle of gin. Obviously, his visitor had left it as a message.

It made sense.

The trip had paid off.

5

> The New York Mets moved to within one victory of the pot of gold yesterday when they defeated the Baltimore Orioles 2–1, in 10 innings and took a lead of three games to one in the World Series. The victory was the third straight for the underdog Mets over the champions of the American League and it was laced with potent doses of the "magic" that has marked their fantastic surge to the top in 1969.
>
> —*New York Times*, October 16, 1969

Upset or Equilibrium in the Balance of Terror?

Miss Brunner appeared to have cooled down the reversion process somewhat when Jerry returned to the Center. She was still mumbling, half the doodles on her pads were astrological equations she was either feeding into or receiving from her computer, but the worst part of her work was over now Jerry had isolated the key mark's identity type.

She licked her lips when he handed her the paper with the name on it.

"So it's a morality syndrome?"

"Yes, the poor sod." Jerry rubbed the back of his neck. "I'll have to take him out as soon as possible. No time for a transmogrification. This'll have to be a termination. Unless . . ." He narrowed his eyes as he looked at her. "Are you sure you're all right?"

"Yes, of course. It's this bloody pattern. You know what it does to me."

"Okay. Well, can you pin him down in a hurry? We had a break in that he's evidently going 'guilty' on us, like a lot of them. They do half our work for us. Very few are ever one hundred percent sure of themselves. That's why they say they are."

She started to sort through her notes, stopped and picked up a bottle of cologne. She unscrewed the cap, upended the bottle and dabbed some of the cologne on her forehead.

Jerry rocked on the balls of his feet.

"At least it's a familiar pattern," she said. "A standard British resurrection plan of the old type. With 'conscience' overtones. What does Alvarez say?"

Jerry went into the next room. "How's it shaping, Mr. Alvarez?"

Alvarez shrugged and spread his hands helplessly. "Most of the Middle East's breaking up. Complete temporal entropy in many areas. It'll be South East Asia next, and you know what that means."

Jerry frowned.

Almost shyly, Alvarez glanced at Jerry. "It's never been this bad, has it, Mr. Cornelius?"

Jerry scratched his left hand with his right hand. "How about other sectors?"

Alvarez made a radio call. He listened to the headphones for a while and then swivelled to face Jerry who was now leaning against a console smoking an Upmann Exquisitos.

"Moscow's completely out. New York more or less the same. Half of Peking's down—its southern and western districts. Singapore's completely untouched. No trouble in Shanghai. None in Sydney or Toronto. No trouble in Calcutta, but New Delhi's had it . . . "

Jerry dropped his cigar on the floor and stood on it.

The factor was overplaying his hand.

He went back into Miss Brunner's room and told her the news.

She spoke distantly. "I've got it down to eight localities." She started to tap out a fresh program and then stopped.

She went to her handbag, picked it up, squatted on the floor of the computing room. She was breathing heavily.

Jerry watched her as she took something from her bag and threw it on the ground. It was a handful of chicken bones. Miss Brunner was casting the runes.

"For God's sake, Miss Brunner!" Jerry took a step towards her. "The whole balance is gone and you're fucking about with bones . . ."

She raised her head and cackled. "You've got to have faith, Mr. C."

"Oh, Christ!"

"Exactly," she mumbled. "It's a sort of progress report on the Second Coming, isn't it? You ought to know after all!"

"Mother of God!"

He pressed the button marked POWER OFF and the computer went dead.

Sometimes he would admit that one form of superstition was as good as another, but he still preferred to rely on the forms he knew. He flung himself on top of Miss Brunner and began to molest her.

They were all operating on instinct at the moment.

Systems Theory and Central Government

Jerry was running.

The backlash was bound to hit London soon and the whole

equilibrium would be thrown. Alvarez's dark suggestions about rephasing might have to be implemented. That meant a great deal of work—a long job involving a lot of risks. He wasn't sure he was up to it at the moment.

He would have to play his hunch, picking one locality from the list of eight Miss Brunner had shown him before she reverted.

He ran through a deserted Holland Park. The autumn leaves slapped his face. He headed for the Commonwealth Institute.

Whither ESRO?

The sun had set by the time Jerry arrived outside the Institute where a few lights were burning.

He turned up the collar of his black car coat, walked under the flags, past the pool and into the main hall. It was deserted. He crossed the hall and opened a door at the back. It led into a small corridor. At the end of the corridor was another door. Jerry approached it and read the name on it:

COLONEL MOON

The name seemed right.

Jerry turned the handle of the door. It was unlocked. He walked into absolute blackness.

An electric light went on.

He was in a steel office. There were steel filing cabinets, steel shelves and a steel desk. At the desk sat Colonel Moon, a stiff-backed man, no longer young. A cigarette in a black plastic holder was clamped between his teeth. He had a square, healthy face, a little touched by drink. His eyes were blue and slightly watery. He wore the tweed jacket of a minor Civil Service poet.

As Jerry entered, Colonel Moon closed a boxfile with one hand. His other hand was still by the light switch on the wall near the desk.

"Miss Brunner is dead, eh? It was just as well, Mr. Cornelius. We couldn't have her running wild."

"So you're the Great Terror." Jerry rubbed his left eyelid with his left index finger. He looked casually about. "They don't give you much room."

Moon presented Jerry with a patronizing smile. "It serves my simple needs. Won't you sit down?"

Jerry crossed to the far wall and seated himself in the wicker rocker. "Where did you pick this up?"

"Calcutta. Where else?"

Jerry nodded. "I got your message in New York."

"Jolly good."

"I'm not really up to this, but what was it—'guilt' or something?"

"Sense of fair play, old boy."

Jerry burst out laughing.

"I'll be seeing *you,* Colonel."

6

While the strategic importance of large air-launched weapons declines in the age of ICBMs and submarine-launched ballistic missiles, airborne guided weapons for tactical use grow in importance. Vietnam has become a "testing ground" for a wide range of weapons from the Walleye TV-guided bomb to Bullpup and the radar-homing Shrike. The lessons learned from actual operations are rapidly being applied to new weapons systems such as the AGM-80A Viper and the AGM-79A Blue Eye, both conceived as Bullpup replacements.

—*Flying Review International,* November 1969

Emotion and the Psychologist

In mutable times like these, thought Jerry as he walked into Lionel Himmler's Blue Spot Bar, everything was possible and nothing was likely. His friend Albert the émigré nodded to him from the shadowy corner by the bar, lifting his glass of schnapps in the strobelight, saluting both Jerry and the stripper on the stage.

Jerry flickered to a table, sat down and ordered scotch and milk. Once history ceased to be seen in linear terms, it ceased to be made in linear terms. He glanced at his new watch.

Moon's machinery could be useful if used in conjunction with their own. He was sorry that he'd have to blow up Bhubaneswar, though.

The problems, of course, would be "psychological" rather than "moral"—if "moral" meant what he thought it did. That was, he admitted, one of his blind spots. It was a pity Miss Brunner wasn't herself (or, rather, was too much herself). She had a much better grasp of that sort of thing.

From behind the curtain a record of Mozart's 41st Symphony began to play.

Jerry settled back in his chair and watched the act.

7

> Peace rallies drew throngs to the city's streets, parks, campuses and churches yesterday in an outpouring of protest against the Vietnam war. The Times Square area was hit by a colossal traffic jam during rush hour as tens of thousands of demonstrators marched to the culminating event of the day—a rally in Bryant Park, west of the New York Public Library. The park was saturated with people, many of them unable to see the speakers' stand or hear the denunciations of war . . . Mayor Lindsay had decreed a day of mourning. His involvement was bitterly assailed by his political opponents and by many who felt that the nationwide demonstrations were not only embarrassing President Nixon's efforts to negotiate an honorable peace but were giving aid and comfort to the enemy as well.
>
> —*New York Times*, October 16, 1969

Technology Review

Miss Brunner would be a complete write-off soon, if she wasn't saved.

She was up to her old tricks. She had constructed a pentagram circuit on the floor of the computer room and she had dug up her goat. It lay in the center of the pentagram, its liver missing.

Jerry watched for a moment and then closed the door with a sigh. He'd have to deal with Moon himself—and what's more it wouldn't now be a simple take-out.

Moon had known what he was doing when he had arranged events so that Miss Brunner's logic patterns would be scattered. He had doubtless hoped that with Miss Brunner's reversion, the whole Time Center would be immobilised. It had been a clever move—introducing massive chaos factors into twelve major cities, like that. Moon must have been working on the job a long time.

Now Miss Brunner was doing the only thing she could, under the circumstances.

He turned to Alvarez who was sipping a cup of hot Ribena.

"They keep turning up, don't they?"

Alvarez's tone was sardonic. "Will it ever end?"

Westminster Scene

Jerry needed sleep. Miss Brunner could get by on a drop or two of blood at the moment, but it wouldn't do for him. Moon would make a good substitute, of course, if he wasn't now needed as an antidote, but that would anyway mean rushing things, probably buggering them up altogether. It was something of a vicious circle.

He went back to his Ladbroke Grove HQ and took the lift up to the tower where he had his private apartments. He switched on the stereo and soothed himself down with a rather mannered version of Beethoven's Ninth, conducted by von Karajan. He typed his notes on the IBM 2000 and made a hundred copies on his Xerox 3600. It wasn't like the old days, when the Center had only needed one chronograph and the entire works could be run by a single operator. Perhaps the whole thing should be folded. It was becoming a large randomizing feature in its own right.

He followed the Beethoven with a Del Reeves album, after considering a Stones LP. There were some perversions left in the world, but he didn't feel up to that one at present. It would have been like drinking Wild Turkey bourbon in an Austin Princess.

He lay down on the leather ottoman by the window.

He dozed until Alvarez called.

"Absolute Crisis Situation just about to break," Alvarez told him. "I'd say you have three hours. After that, there won't even be a chance of rephasing, if I'm any judge."

"Check," said Jerry and winked at his reflection in the mirror.

Tantalizer

It had to be this way. Jerry couldn't have managed it alone, otherwise. He had been forced to wait for the moment when the feedback would start to hit Moon.

He found him in his office, completely naked, sitting in the middle of a huge and tattered Union Jack, the empty cigarette holder between his teeth. It was the flag that had been missing from the pole Jerry had passed on his way in.

Moon's well-preserved body was pale and knotted with muscle. He was remarkably hairy. He saw Jerry and got up.

"Nice to see you, dear boy. As a matter of interest, how did you find me, originally?"

"Originally? The only person sentimental enough to look after those old outposts was you. I knew you would have left NY. I had a hunch you'd be here."

Moon pursed his lips.

"Coffee?" he said at length. He crossed to a gas-ring set up on one of the steel filing cabinets. He put the kettle on and measured spoonfuls of Camp coffee into orange plastic cups.

"No, thanks," said Jerry.

Moon began to pour the coffee back into the bottle. It flooded over the neck and ran down the sides, staining the label.

"It's a shame you refused to fall back on the old methods," he said. "I thought you would when Miss Brunner went."

"They aren't suitable, in this case," Jerry told him. "Anyway, I've been in a funny mood for some time."

"You've got jolly moralistic all of a sudden, haven't you?" Colonel Moon raised his eyebrows in his "quizzical" expression.

"You shouldn't have done that, Colonel." Jerry began to tremble. "I've never understood the death-wish you people have."

"Ah, well, you see—you're younger than me."

"We'll have to wipe out most of your bloody logic sequence. That's not a 'moralistic' reaction. I'm just annoyed."

Again the "quizzical" expression. "So you say."

Jerry smacked his lips.

"I would have thought," Moon added, "that in your terms my sequence was a fairly simple one."

Jerry couldn't answer. He knew Moon was right.

"Everything's so boringly complicated these days, isn't it?" Moon put his hand on the handle of the kettle and winced. He stiffened his lips and began to pour the water into the cup.

Jerry stopped trembling. He felt quite sympathetic towards Moon now. "It's a question of attitude, I suppose."

Moon looked surprised. There were tears in his eyes; just a few. "Yes, I suppose so."

"Shall we be off?" Jerry removed his black gloves and put one in each pocket of his car coat. He reached inside the coat, pulling his needler free of its holster.

"Mind if I finish my coffee?"

"I'd appreciate it if you'd hurry up, though." Jerry glanced at his watch. "After all, there's Miss Brunner to think of."

8

> Today as an extensive auto trip has confirmed, the only danger along Route 4 is the traffic, which is dreadful, and the potholes, which can shatter an axle. The improved security along the road is one of the more visible examples of the progress achieved over the last year by the allied pacification program.
>
> —*New York Times*, October 16, 1969

People

Jerry took Colonel Moon to the basement of the Ladbroke Grove HQ.

The colonel smoothed his iron-grey hair and looked around the bare room. "I thought—well—Miss Brunner?"

"That's next. We're going to have to soften you up a bit first. Jimi Hendrix, I'm afraid."

Jerry went to the hidden panel and opened it. He flipped a toggle switch to turn on the power.

Colonel Moon said: "Couldn't you make it George Formby?"

Jerry thought for a moment and then shook his head. "I'll tell you what. I'll make it early Hendrix."

"Very well. I suppose there isn't much time left. You can't blame me for trying, eh?"

Jerry's eyes were glazed as he waltzed over to Colonel Moon and positioned him. "Time? Trying?"

Colonel Moon put his head in his hands and began to sob.

Jerry took aim with the needler, pulled the trigger. The needles passed through the hands and through the eyes and into the brain. Jerry pulled his little transmogrifier from his pocket and stuck the electrodes on Moon's skull.

Then he switched on the music.

Books

It was *And the Gods Made Love* that did it.

His hands rigid over his eyes, Colonel Moon fell down. He murmured one word: Loyalty. And then was supine.

Jerry reduced the volume and picked up a wrist. It was completely limp.

Thoroughly into it now, Jerry licked his lips, heaved the body on to his back, and left for the Time Center.

9

ROME, Oct. 15—Cardinal Cooke, Archbishop of New York, urged the Roman Catholic Synod of Bishops today to consider the present period of "stress and strain" in the church "frankly and positively, with great charity."

—*New York Times,* October 16, 1969

He Smashed the "Death Valley" Terror Trap

Jerry stumbled through the door with the body over his shoulder. "All ready. Where's Miss B.?"

Alvarez was chewing a beef sandwich. "Still in there. She locked the door a while ago."

"Use the emergency lock to open it, will you?"

"You haven't given yourself much margin." Alvarez spoke accusingly as he operated the lock. The computing room door sank into the floor.

Jerry stepped through. "Close it up again, Mr. A."

"Aye, aye, Mr. C."

Alvarez was getting very edgy about the whole thing. Jerry wondered if he would have to go.

Blue lights flickered on five points. Red lights, close together, shifted on the far side of the room. The red lights were Miss Brunner's beautiful eyes.

"I've come to help you." Jerry grinned and his teeth felt very sharp.

She screamed.

"Oh, do shut up, Miss B. We're going to break the spell together."

"*BELPHEGOR!*"

"Anything you say."

We Survived the Cave of the 10,000 Crazed Bats

Jerry sucked his lower lip.

Colonel Moon now stood shivering in the center of the pentagram, an inane grin on his face.

Jerry took the speakers and placed one on each of the five points, then turned the computer to FULL INPUT and switched on the rest of the equipment.

Sparks leapt from point to point and settled into a blue-green flow. It was all very familiar. Colonel Moon's mouth went slack.

"Cheer up, Colonel. You never saw an act like this at the Empire!"

From the darkness, Miss Brunner cackled stupidly.

Jerry turned a dial. The music came out softly at first, but it got to the colonel in no time. It was the Mothers of Invention and "Let's Make the Water Turn Black."

He heard Miss Brunner through it all. "Tasty," she was saying. At least she was responding a bit.

"In you go, Miss B."

He watched her scrawny, naked body in silhouette as it moved through the blue-green glow into the pentagram.

Colonel Moon hissed as Miss Brunner took her first nip.

Jerry's part of it was over. He slipped from the room.

The antidote had been administered, but there was still a lot of tidying up to do.

Sex Habits of Bonnie Parker and the Women Who Kill

Alvarez was smiling now. He looked up from his headphones. "The situation's static. We've got a silly season on our hands by the smell of it."

Jerry was worn out. "Reset all the chronographs, will you. It's not over yet."

Miss Brunner could be a great asset, but her habits sometimes put him off her.

He yawned. "Poor old Moon."

"Hoist by his own petard, eh?" grinned Alvarez.

"Silly bugger. He didn't really believe in what he was doing."

"But Miss Brunner did."

"Well, Moon felt he ought to have a 'sense of purpose', you see. It lets them all down in the end."

10

It would be foolish to speculate further.

—George Steiner

Facts by Request

Miss Brunner and Jerry Cornelius walked hand in hand through Hyde Park and paused where the crater had been.

"It's very hazy," she said. "So I did it again."

"Moon set you up. You knocked him down."

"*C'est la vie!*"

"You could put it like that."

She stopped and removed her hand from his. "Really, Mr. Cornelius, you do seem *down*."

"Well, it's all over now. Here's your transport."

He pointed through the trees at the Sikorsky SH-3D which began to rev up, blowing the last of the leaves from the branches, blowing the other leaves up into the air. The day was cold and sunny.

She paused, looking in her handbag for something and not finding it. "You sympathize with them, yet you'll never understand their morality. It was such a long while ago. You're a kind little chap, aren't you?"

Jerry folded his arms and closed his face.

He watched her walk towards the helicopter, her red hair ruffled by the wind. She was full of bounce. Moon had agreed with her.

He thought she called something out, but he couldn't hear her above the whine of the rotors.

The helicopter shuddered and lumbered into the sky.

Soon it was gone.

Jerry looked at his watch. The arrows were revolving at a moderate speed. It was all he could hope for.

The gestures of conflict keep the peace.

It was a motto that even Moon had understood, but he had chosen to ignore it. Those old men of action. They were the ones you had to watch.

Jerry lay down on the grass and closed his eyes. He listened to the lazy sound of the distant traffic, he sniffed the scents of autumn.

It had been a rotten little caper, all in all.

Other texts consulted include:
Real Detective Yearbook, No. 101,1969
Confidential Detective Cases, March 1969
Women in Crime, May 1969
Male, June 1969
Encounter, August 1969
New Scientist, November 13, 1969

Sea Wolves

Your computer needs you

It occurs to us that while we've been saying "you need your computer" we'd also like to emphasise something equally important.

"Your computer needs you."

You see, without you your computer is nothing.

In fact it's people like yourself that have made the computer what it is today.

It's people like you that have made their computer do some pretty exciting things.

Like help them keep on top of sales trends.

Or design a bridge.

Or keep track of all the parts that go into a giant whirlybird.

To do things like that, your computer needs some help.

It needs you to get more involved with it. So you can use it to help you do more than just the payroll and the billing.

And it needs some terminals.

Terminals let you get information in and out of your computer fast.

They let you get up close to your computer.

Even though you might be miles away . . .

But terminals are nothing unless something happens between you and your computer.

Unless you get involved with your computer.

You need your computer.

Your computer needs you.

KNOW YOUR BUSINESS.
KNOW YOUR COMPUTER.
IBM

1

Running, grinning, aping the movements of the mammals milling about him, Jerry Cornelius made tracks from the menagerie that was My Lai, the monster tourist attraction of the season, and threw his Kamov Ka-15 into the sky, flew over the tops of the tall hotels and novelty factories, away from there; away to the high privacy of Bangkok's Hotel Maxwell where, panting, he froze his limbs in the angles of sleep.

A posture, after all, was a posture.

2

Jerry's uniform was that of the infamous Brigade of St Basil. These Osaka-based White Cossack Mercenaries had recently changed from the Chinese to the American side; a half-hearted move; a compromise. But the uniform—cream, gold and fawn—overrode most other considerations.

Meanwhile revolutionary troops continued to march on the great automated factories of Angkor Wat and Anuradhapura. It would all be over by the Festival of Drakupolo.

A week passed. Jerry continued to sleep, his well-cut jacket and jodhpurs uncrumpled, for he did not stir and his breathing was minimal, neither did he perspire. There was a complete absence of REMs.

3

The war ended with a complete victory for the factories. The defected revolutionaries made their way back to Simla and Ulan Bator. Jerry woke up and listened to the news on Radio Thai. He frowned.

A fine balance had to be maintained between man and machine, just as between man and man, man and woman, man and environment.

It was as good as it was bad.

Regretfully he stripped off his uniform. He was not sure he looked forward to civvy street.

4

The gestures of conflict keep the peace. The descendants of Tompion and Babbage toyed with inaccurate engines while their enemies entertained impossible debates concerning the notion that an electronic calculating device could not possess a "soul". The old arguments perpetuated themselves: resolved in the ancient formulae of warfare.

5

When Jerry arrived in Phnôm Penh the streets were full of bunting. Rickshaws, bicycles, cars and trams were hung with paper banners, streamers and posters. The Central Information Building shuddered with bright flame. The factories had won, but others were suffering for them. It was as it should be, thought Jerry.

Cheerfully he mounted an abandoned British-made Royal Albert gent's black roadster and pedalled along with the procession, avoiding the wreckage of cash-registers and adding machines that had been hurled from shops and offices that morning, heading for the suburbs where his bungalow housed a Leo VII cryogenic storage computer which he had, before the war, been programming on behalf of the monks at the new temple on Kas Rong. But the anti-religious riots had not only been directed at the machines. The monastery had been hastily disbanded by the authorities in the hope that this measure would save the new research wing of the Hospital of the Secret Heart at Chanthaburi. It had not.

6

Jerry entered the bungalow and shivered. The temperature was almost at zero. He pushed back the steel sliding doors of the inner room. The computer glistened under a thick coating of ice.

Was entropy setting in again?

Turning up the collar of his black car coat he inspected the power inputs. Something had overloaded Leo VII.

Jerry sniffed the sharp air. A problem of cardinal importance. He twitched his lips. Time to be moving.

He paused, studying the computer. It trembled under its sheathing of ice. He went to wall and took his kid gloves from his pocket. He pulled them on, pressed the DESTRUCT button, but it would not move. It was frozen solid.

Jerry reached inside his coat and brought out his needle-gun. With the butt he hammered the button home.

He left the computer room. In the living-room ice had formed traceries on the walls and windows, whorls and lines spelling out equations of dubious importance. A little bile came into his throat.

All the signs pointed West.

He went to the garage at the side of the bungalow, wheeled his big BMW 750cc hog on to the path, put it between his legs, kicked the starter and whisked wild and easy off down the concrete road towards the jungle.

Yellow sun.
Blue sky.
Green trees.
Monkeys screaming.

7

Zut alors!
Maxim's in Paris
buys its fish
from a machine.

Part of the reason that fish at Maxim's is so fabulous is because it's so fresh. Fresh from General Electric data-processing equipment. When a French fisherman unloads his catch at the port of Sète, a unique data-gathering and display system takes over . . .

Progress is our most important product
GENERAL ELECTRIC

8

A loud shriek.

9

The Dnieper flowed slowly, its muddy waters churned by the wind. In the brown land some snow remained. The great sky was low and gray over the steppe. A small wooden landing stage had moored to it a carved fishing boat, its sail reefed.

On the landing stood three Cossacks. They had long moustaches, smoked large pipes, wore big fur caps on the sides of their shaven heads. Heavy burkas swathed their burly bodies and they wore baggy trousers of blue or green silk, boots of red or yellow morocco leather. There were sabres at their sides, rifles on their backs. They watched the horseman as he galloped nearer on his shaggy, unshod pony.

The rider had bandoliers of cartridges crossing his chest, an M-60 on his back. He wore the Red Army uniform of the "Razin" 11th Don Cossack Cavalry and he carried the horsehair standard of an ataman. He was young, with long pale hair and sharp blue eyes. He drew his horse to a skidding halt and saluted the three men whose expressions remained set.

"Cossacks of the Zaporozhian Sech, greetings from your brothers of the Don, the Yaik and the Kukan." He spoke with a strong Ukrainian accent, driving the standard into the hard ground.

The nearest Zaporozhian reached down and picked up a sack that lay at his feet. "The Sech is no more," he said. "We and this is all that remains. The great horde came four days ago from the East." He upended the sack and emptied it.

Jerry dismounted and went to stare at the collection of small metal cogs, transistors and tapes.

"The krug is dead." Tears came to the leading Zaporozhian's hard, gray eyes. "The Khan rules. This is the end of our ancient freedom."

Jerry got back on to his horse and rode away. He left the horsehair standard waving in the wind. He left the Cossacks weeping. He left the bank of the muddy Dnieper and headed out across the steppe, riding South again, towards the Black Sea.

10

The anthropomorphic view:

The Bug Slayer

No computer stamps out program bugs like RCA's Octoputer. It boosts programming efficiency up to 40%. Programming is already one-third of computer costs, and going up faster than any other cost in the industry. A lot of that money is eaten up by bugs . . .

11

He wandered along the grassy paths between the ancient ruins. Everywhere was litter. Broken tape-spools crunched beneath his boots, printouts snagged his feet; he was forced to make detours around buckled integrator cabinets. A few white-coated technicians tried to clean up the mess, haul the torn bodies away. They ignored Jerry, who went past them and hit the jungle once more. In his hand he held an ice-pick.

One of the technicians jerked his thumb as Jerry disappeared. "Asesino …" he said.

Jerry was glad to be out of Villahermosa.

12

He was cleaning his heat in his hut when the pale young man came in, shut the flimsy door and shuddered. Outside, the jungle stirred.

Jerry replaced rod, rag and oil in their case and carefully closed the lid.

The young man was dressed in a brown tropical suit with sweat-stains under arms and crotch. He had noticed the three weapons in the case: the needler, the heater, the vibragun. He crossed himself.

Jerry nodded and drew on his black leather Norfolk jacket. From the tops of his dark Fry boots he untucked his pink bell-bottomed Levis and smoothed them down with the tips of his fingers, watching the pale young man with amused, moody eyes.

An Aeroflot VC 10 began its approach to the nearby Mowming drome. The windows vibrated shrilly and then subsided.

"The sense of oneness known to the Ancients." The young man waved his hands vaguely in all directions. "At last it is within our grasp."

Jerry rubbed his nose with his case.

"I'm sorry, Mr. Cornelius, I am, of course, Cyril Tome." A smile of apologetic patronage. "What a nightmare this world is. But the tide is turning . . ."

Jerry began vigorously to brush his fine blond hair, settling it on his shoulders. "I wasn't expecting you, Mr. Tome."

"I left a message. In Kiev."

"I didn't get it."

"You mean you didn't receive it?"

"If you like."

"Mr. Cornelius, I gathered from a mutual acquaintance that we were of a similar mind. 'Science is only a more sophisticated form of superstition'—didn't you say that?"

"I'm told so. Who was the acquaintance?"

"Malcolm." He raised his eyebrows. "Beesley? But don't you agree that in place of the old certainties, rooted in the supreme reality of existence, we have transferred our faith to science, the explanation for everything which explains nothing, the ever more fragmented picture of reality which becomes ever more unreal . . ."

"How is Bishop Beesley?"

"Carrying on the fight as best he can. He is very tired."

"He is indeed."

"Then you don't agree . . ."

"It's a question of attitude, Mr. Tome." Jerry walked to the washstand and picking up a carton of Swedish milk poured out half a saucer for the half-grown black and white cat which now rubbed itself against his leathered leg. "Still, we don't need emotional rapport, you know, to do business."

"I'm not sure . . ."

"Who is, Mr. Tome?"

"I am sure . . ."

"Naturally."

Tome began to pace about the floor of the hut. "These machines. They're inhuman. But so far only the fringes have been touched."

Jerry sat down on the bed again, opening his gun case. He began to fit the vibragun together, snapping the power unit into place.

Tome looked distastefully on. "I suppose one must fight fire with fire."

Jerry picked his teeth with his thumbnail, his brows furrowed. He did not look at Tome.

"What's the pattern?" he murmured, stroking the cat.

"Is there a pattern to anarchy?"

"The clearest of all, I'd have thought." Jerry slipped the vibragun into his shoulder holster. "In Leo VII all things are possible, after all."

"A machine is — "

"—a machine is a machine." Jerry smiled involuntarily.

"I don't understand you."

"That's what I was afraid of."

"Afraid?"

"Fear, Mr. Tome. I think we might have to book you."

"But I thought you were on my side."

"Christ! Of course I am. And their side. And all the other sides. Of course I am!"

"But didn't you start the machine riots in Yokohama? When I was there?"

Tome burst into tears.

Jerry rubbed at his face in puzzlement.

"There's been a lot of that."

Tome made for the door. He had started to scream.

Some beastly instinct in Jerry responded to the movement and the sound. His vibragun was slipped from its holster and aimed at Tome as the pale young man fumbled with the catch.

Tome's teeth began to chatter.

He broke up.

All but insensate, Jerry fell back on the bed, his mad eyes staring at the ceiling.

Eventually they cooled.

Jerry left the hut and struck off through the jungle again. He had an overwhelming sense of *déjà vu*.

13

The mechanistic view:

Horace is Hornblower's remarkable new computer system. And what he does with confirmations is a Hornblower exclusive . . .

Only Horace prints complete confirmations in Seconds

14

Jerry was lost and depressed. Thanks to Tome, Beesley and their fellow spirits, a monstrous diffusion process was taking place.

He stumbled on through the jungle, followed at a safe distance by a cloud of red and blue macaws. They were calling out phrases he could not quite recognize. They seemed malevolent, triumphant.

A man dressed in the tropical kit of an Indian Army NCO emerged from behind a tree. His small eyes were almost as confused as Jerry's.

"Come along, sir. This way. I'll help."

For a moment Jerry prepared to follow the man, then he shook his head. "No, thank you, Corporal Powell, I'll find my own way."

"It's too late for that, Mr. Cornelius."

"Nonetheless . . ."

"This jungle's full of natives."

Jerry aimed a shot at the NCO, but the little man scurried into the forest and disappeared.

Several small furry mammals skittered out into the open, blinking red eyes in the direct sunlight. Their tiny thumbs were opposable. Jerry smiled down indulgently.

Around him the Mesozoic foliage whispered in the new, warm wind.

15

He had reached the sea.

He stood on the yellow shore and looked out over the flat, blue water. Irresolutely he stopped as his boots sank into the sand. The sea frightened him. He reached inside his coat and fingered the butt of his gun.

A white yacht was anchoring about a quarter of a mile away.

Soon he heard the sound of a motorboat as it swept towards him through the surf.

He recognized the yacht as the *Teddy Bear.* It had had several owners, none of them particularly friendly. He turned to run, but he was too weak. He fell down. Seamen jumped from the boat and pulled him aboard.

"Don't worry, son," one of them said. "You'll soon be back in Blighty."

"Poor bastard."

Jerry whimpered.

They'd be playing brag for his gear soon.

Because of the sins which ye have committed before God, ye shall be led away captives into Babylon by Nabuchodonosor king of the Babylonians.—*Baruch* 6:2

He was feeling sorry for himself. He'd really blown this little scene.

16

Need to improve customer service? Salesman productivity? Here's your answer—Computone's portable computer terminal, the world's smartest briefcase. It weighs only 8¾ pounds, and it costs as little as $20 per month. Through a telephone in the prospect's home or office, your salesman can communicate directly with a computer, enter orders and receive answers to inquiries within seconds. The terminal converts your salesman into a team of experts who bring to the point of sale the vast memory of a computer and its ability to solve problems immediately and accurately.

—COMPUTONE SYSTEMS INC. *the company that put the computer in a briefcase*

17

Jerry was dumped outside the Time Center's Ladbroke Grove HQ. He got up, found his front door, tried to open it. The door was frozen solid. The Leo VII had spread its cryogenic bounty throughout the citadel.

Jerry sighed and leaned against the brick wall. Above his head someone had painted a new slogan in bright orange paint:

NO POPERY

There were only two people who could help him now and neither was particularly sympathetic to him.

Was he being set up for something?

18

Hans Smith of Hampstead, the Last of the Left-wing Intellectuals, was having a party to which Jerry had not been invited.

Because of his interest in the statistics of interracial marriage in Vietnam in the period 1969/70, Hans Smith had not heard about the war. There had been few signs of it on Parliament Hill. Late one night he had seen a fat, long-haired man in a tweed suit urinating against a tree. The man had turned, exposing himself to Smith, grinning and leering. There had also been some trouble with his Smith-Corona. But the incidents seemed unrelated.

Balding, bearded, pot-bellied and very careful, Hans Smith had codified and systemized his sex-life (marital, extra-marital and inter-marital) to the point where most discomfort and enjoyment was excluded. His wife filed his love-letters and typed his replies for him and she kept his bedroom library of pornography and sex-manuals in strict alphabetical order. Instead of pleasure, Smith received what he called "a healthy release". The sexual act itself had been promoted into the same category as a successful operation for severe constipation. Disturbed by the Unpleasant, Smith belonged to a large number of institutions devoted to its extinction. He lived a smooth existence.

Jerry opened the front door with one of the keys from his kit and walked up the stairs. Somewhere The Chants were singing "Progress."

He was late for the party. Most of the remaining guests had joined their liberal hosts in the bedroom, but Smith, dressed in a red and gold kimono that did much to emphasize the pale obscenity of his body, came to the door at his knock, a vibro-massager clutched in one thin hand. He recognized Jerry and made a Church Army smile through his frown.

"I'm sorry, bah, but . . ."

But Jerry's business was urgent and it was with another guest.

"Could I have a word with Bishop Beesley, do you think?"

"I'm not sure he's . . ."

Jerry drew out his heater.

"There's no need to be boorish." Smith backed into the bedroom. Unseen middle-aged flesh made strange, dry sounds. "Bishop. Someone to see you . . ." He fingered his goatee.

Mrs. Hans Smith's wail: "Oh, no, Hans. Tell them to fiddle off."

Smith made another of his practised smiles. "It's Cornelius, kitten."

"You said you'd never invite—"

"I didn't, lovie . . ."

Jerry didn't want to look inside, but he moved a step nearer. "Hurry up, Bishop."

Naked but for his gaiters and miter, the gross white form of Bishop Beesley appeared behind Hans Smith. "What is it?"

"A religious matter, Bishop."

"Ah, in that case." The bishop bundled up his clothes and stepped out. "Well, Mr. Cornelius?"

"It's the Leo VII cryogenics. They seem to be trying to convert. I can't make it out. They're freezing up."

"Good God! I'll come at once. A clearing needed, eh? An exorcism?"

Jerry's hunch had been a good one. The bishop had been expecting him. "You'd know better than I, Bishop."

"Yes, yes." Beesley gave Jerry's shoulder a friendly pat.

"Well, the shit's certainly hit the fan," said Jerry. He winked at Smith as he left.

"I'm very glad you called me in, dear boy." Bishop Beesley hopped into his trousers, licking his lips. "Better late than never, eh?"

Jerry shivered.

"It's your baby now. Bishop."

He had another old friend to look up.

19

"One down, eight letters, *To Lucasta, faithful unto death . . .*" Jerry shrugged and put the newspaper aside. They had arrived. He tapped the pilot on the shoulder. "Let's descend, Byron."

As the cumbersome Sikorsky shuddered towards the ground, Jerry had an excellent view of the ruins on the headland. All that remained of the castle was grass-grown walls a foot or two high, resembling, from this perspective, a simplified circuit marked out in stones—a message to an extraterran astronomer. The archaeologists had been at work again in Tintagel.

Beyond the headland the jade sea boomed, washing the ebony beach. The Sikorsky hovered over the ocean for a moment before sweeping backwards and coming to rest near Site B, the monastery.

Dressed in his wire-rimmed Diane Logan black corduroy hat, a heavy brown Dannimac cord coat, dark orange trousers from Portugal, and near-black Fry boots, Jerry jumped from the Sikorsky and walked across the lawn to sit on a wall and watch the helicopter take off again. He unbuttoned his coat to reveal his yellow Sachs cord shirt and the Lynn Stuart yellow and black sash he wore in place of a tie. He was feeling light in his gear but he was still bothered.

In the hot winter sunshine, he pranced along the footpath that led to the Computer Research Institute—a series of geodesic domes stained in bright colors.

"A meaning is a meaning," he sang, "is a meaning is a meaning."

He was not altogether himself, these days.

Outside the gates he grinned inanely at the guard and displayed his pass. He was waved through.

The Institute was a private establishment. The red moving pavement took him to the main admin building and the chrome doors opened to admit him. He stood in the white-tiled lobby.

"Mr. Cornelius!"

From a blue door marked DIRECTOR came Miss Brunner, her auburn hair drawn back in a bun, her stiff body clothed in a St. Laurent tweed suit. She stretched her long fingers at him. He grasped them.

"And what's your interest in our little establishment, Mr. C?" Now she led him into her cool office. "Thinking of giving us a hand?" She studied a tank of small carp.

"I'm not sure I know the exact nature of your research." Jerry glanced around at all the overfilled ashtrays.

She shrugged. "The usual thing. This and that. We're checking analogies at present—mainly forebrain functions. Amazing how similar the human brain is to our more complex machines. They can teach us a lot about people. The little buggers."

He looked at the graphs and charts on her walls. "I see what you mean." He rubbed a weary eye and winced. He had a sty there.

"It's all very precise," she said.

"Get away."

Jerry sighed. Didn't they know there was a war on?

20

"Sweet young stuff," said Miss Brunner. "Tender. Only the best goes into our machines."

Jerry looked at the conveyor, at the aluminium dishes on the belt, at the brains in the dishes.

"They feel nothing," she said, "it's all done by electronics these days."

Jerry watched the battery brains slipping like oysters into the gullets of the storage registers.

"You will try it, won't you?"

"It works both ways," she said defensively.

"I bet it does."

Miss Brunner smiled affectionately. "It's beautifully integrated. Everything automatic. Even the pentagrams are powered."

"This isn't religion," said Jerry, "it's bloody sorcery!"

"I never claimed to be perfect, Mr. Cornelius. Besides, compared with my methods the narrow processes of the orthodox . . ."

"You've been driving the whole bloody system crazy, you silly bitch! You and that bastard Beesley. I thought there were only two polarities. And all the while . . ."

"You've been having a bad time, have you? You bloody puritans . . ."

Jerry pursed his lips. She knew how to reach him.

21

When he got back to Ladbroke Grove he found the door open. It was freezing inside.

"Bishop Beesley?" His voice echoed through the dark passages.

The cold reached his bones.

"Bishop?"

Time was speeding. Perhaps his counter-attack had failed.

He found Beesley in the library. The bishop had never got to the computer. His round, flabby face peered sadly out of the block of ice encasing him. Jerry drew his heater and thawed him out.

Beesley grunted and sat down. "I suppose it was a joke. Doubtful taste . . ."

"Sorry you were bothered, Bishop . . ."

"Is that all . . .?"

"Yes. I must admit I was desperate, but that's over now, for what it was worth."

"You treacherous little oik. I thought you had made a genuine repentance."

Jerry had been triggered off again. His eyes were glowing a deep red now and his lips were curled back over his sharp teeth. His body radiated such heat that the air steamed around it. He waved his gun.

"Shall we press on into the computer room?"

Beesley grumbled but stumbled ahead until they stood before the iced-up Leo VII.

"What point is there in my presence here," Beesley chattered, "when your claims—or its—were plainly insincere?"

"The logic's changed." Jerry's nostrils widened. "We're having a sacrifice instead."

Jerry thought he smelled damp autumn leaves on the air.

He snarled and chuckled and forced the bishop towards the appropriate input.

"Sacrilege!" howled Beesley.

"Sacrosanct!" sniggered Jerry.

Then, with his Fry boot, he kicked Beesley's bottom.

The clergyman yelled, gurgled and disappeared into the machine.

There was a sucking sound, a purr, and almost immediately the ice began to melt.

"It's the price we pay for progress," said Jerry. "Your attitudes, Bishop, not mine, created the situation, after all."

The computer rumbled and began a short printout. Jerry tore it off.

A single word:

TASTY.

22

Like it or not, the Brunner program had set the tone to the situation, but at least it meant things would calm down for a bit . . . Time to work on a fresh equation.

These alchemical notions were, he would admit, very commonplace. The pattern had been begun years before by describing machines in terms of human desires and activities, by describing human behavior in terms of machines. Now the price of that particular logic escalation was being paid. Beesley had paid it. The sweet young stuff was paying it. The mystical view of science had declined from vague superstition into positive necromancy. The sole purpose of the machines was confined to the raising of dead spirits. The polarities had been the Anthropomorphic View and the Mechanistic View. Now they had merged, producing something even more sinister: the Pathological View.

A machine is a machine is a machine . . . But that was no longer the case. A machine was anything the neurotic imagination desired it to be.

At last the computer had superseded the automobile as the focus for mankind's hopes and fears. It was the death of ancient freedoms.

23

It was raining as Jerry picked his way over the Belgrade bomb-sites followed by crowds of crippled children and the soft, pleading voices of the eleven- and twelve-year-old prostitutes of both sexes.

His clothes were stained and faded. Behind him were the remains of the crashed Sikorsky which had run out of fuel.

On foot he made for Dubrovnik, through a world ruled by bad poets who spoke the rhetoric of tabloid apocrypha and schemed for the fruition of a dozen seedy apocalypses.

At Dubrovnik the corpse-boats were being loaded up. Fuel for the automated factories of Anuradhapura and Angkor Wat. On one of them, if he was lucky, he might obtain a passage East.

Meanwhile machines grew skeletons and were fed with blood and men adopted metal limbs and plastic organs. A synthesis he found unwelcome.

24

Out of the West fled Jerry Cornelius, away from Miss Brunner's morbid Eden, away from warm steel and cool flesh, on a tanker crammed with the dead, to Bombay and from there to the interior, to rest, to wait, to draw breath, to pray for new strength and the resurrection of the Antichrist.

A posture, after all, was a posture.

You won't make an important decision in the 70s without it
Your own personal desk-top computer terminal

Remember the 1970s are just around the corner. A call to Mr. A. A. Barnett, Vice President—Marketing, Bunker-Ramo, could be your most important decision for the new decade.

(All ad quotes from *Business Week*, December 6, 1969)

Voortrekker

A Tale of Empire

My Country 'Tis of Thee

> Mr. Smith said that the new Constitution would take Rhodesia further along the road of racial separate development—although he preferred to call it "community development and provincialisation." He agreed that, initially, this policy would not improve Rhodesia's chances of international recognition, but added: I believe and I sincerely hope that the world is coming to its senses and that this position will change, that the free world will wake up to what international communism is doing.
>
> —*Guardian*, April 14, 1970

Think It Over

The group was working and Jerry Cornelius, feeling nostalgic, drew on a stick of tea. He stood in the shadows at the back of the stage, plucking out a basic pattern on his Futurama bass.

"She's the girl in the red blue jeans,

She's the queen of all the teens . . ."

Although The Deep Fix hadn't been together for some time Shaky Mo Collier was in good form. He turned to the console, shifting the mike from his right hand to his left, and gave himself a touch more echo for the refrain. Be-bop-a-lula. Jerry admired the way Mo had his foot twisted just right.

But it was getting cold.

Savoring the old discomfort, Jerry peered into the darkness at the floor where the shapes moved. Outside the first Banning cannon of the evening were beginning to go off. The basement shook.

Jerry's numb fingers muffed a chord. A whiff of entropy.

The sound began to decay. The players blinked at each other. With a graceful, rocking pace Jerry took to his heels.

None too soon. As he climbed into his Silver Cloud he saw the first figure descend the steps to the club. A woman. A flat-foot.

It was happening all over again.

All over again.

He put the car into gear and rippled away. Really, there was hardly any peace. Or was he looking in the wrong places?

London faded.

He was having a thin time and no mistake. He shivered. And turned up the collar of his black car coat.

Hopes for US vanish, he thought. If he wasn't getting older then he wasn't getting any younger, either. He pressed the button and the stereo started playing "Sergeant Pepper". How soon harmony collapsed. She never stumbles. There was no time left for irony. A Paolozzi screenprint. She likes it like that. Rain fingered his windscreen.

Was it just bad memory?

Apple crumble. Fleeting scene. Streaming screen. Despair.

At the head of that infinitely long black corridor the faceless man was beckoning to him.

Not yet.

But why not?

Would the time ever be right?

He depressed the accelerator.

Diffusion rediffused.

Breaking up baby.

Jump back . . .

He was crying, his hands limp on the wheel as the car went over the ton.

All the old men and children were dying at once.

HANG ON

"NO!"

Screaming, he pressed his quaking foot right down and flung his hands away from the wheel, stretching his arms along the back of the seat.

It wouldn't take long.

I Love You Because

What the Soviet Union wants in Eastern Europe is peace and quiet . . .

—Hungarian editor quoted, *Guardian*, April 13, 1970

Clearwater

"How's the head, Mr. Cornelius?"

Miss Brunner's sharp face grinned over him. She snapped her teeth, stroked his cheek with her hard fingers.

He hugged at his body, closed his eyes.

"Just a case of the shakes," she said. "Nothing serious. You've got a long way to go yet."

There was a stale smell in his nostrils. The smell of a dirty needle. Her hands had left his face. His eyes sprang open. He glared suspiciously as she passed the chipped enamel kidney dish to Shaky Mo who winked sympathetically at him and shrugged. Mo had a grubby white coat over his gear.

Miss Brunner straightened her severe tweed jacket on her hips. "Nothing serious . . ."

It was still cold.

"Brrrr . . ." He shut his mouth.

"What?" She whirled suddenly, green eyes alert.

"Breaking up."

"We've been through too much together."

"Breaking up."

"Nonsense. It all fits." From her large black patent leather satchel she took a paper wallet. She straightened her . . . "Here are your tickets. You'll sail tomorrow on the *Robert D. Fete.*"

Shaky Mo put his head back round the tatty door. The surgery belonged to the last backstreet abortionist in England, a creature of habits. "Any further conclusions. Miss Brunner?"

She tossed her red locks. "Oh, a million. But they can wait."

Heartbreak Hotel

Refugees fleeing from Svey Rieng province speak of increasing violence in Cambodia against the Vietnamese population. Some who have arrived here in the past 24 hours tell stories of eviction and even massacre at the hands of Cambodian soldiers sent from Phnôm Penh.

—*Guardian*, April 13, 1970

Midnight Special

The *Robert D. Fete* was wallowing down the Mediterranean coast. She was a clapped out old merchantman and this would be her last voyage. Jerry stood by the greasy rail looking out at a sea of jade and jet.

So he was going back. Not that it made any difference. You always got to the same place in the end.

He remembered the faces of Auchinek and Newman. Their faces were calm now.

Afrika lay ahead. His first stop.

That's When Your Heartaches Begin

Four rockets were fired into the center of Saigon this evening and, according to first reports, killed at least four people and injured 37.

. . . When used as they are here, in built-up areas, rockets are a psychological rather than a tactical weapon.

—*Guardian*, April 14, 1970

Don't Be Cruel

Could the gestures of conflict continue to keep the peace? Was the fire dying in Europe? "Ravaged, at last, by the formless terror called Time, Melniboné fell and newer nations succeeded her: Ilmiora, Sheegoth, Maidahk, S'aaleem. All these came after Melniboné. But none lasted ten thousand years." (The Dreaming City.) *In the flames he watched the shape of a teenage girl as she ran about dying. He turned away. Why did the old territorial impulses maintain themselves ("sphere of influence") so far past their time of usefulness? There was no question about it in his mind. The entropy factor was increasing, no matter what he did. The waste didn't matter, but the misery, surprisingly, moved him. Een Schmidt, so Wolenski had said, now had more personal power than Hitler or Mussolini. Was it take-out time again? No need to report back to the Time Center. The answer, as usual, was written in the hieroglyphs of the landscape. He smiled a rotten smile.*

The Facts of Death

"Name your poison, Mr. Cornelius."

Jerry raised distant eyes to look into the mad, Boer face of Van Markus, proprietor of the Bloemfontein *Drankie-a-Snel-Snel.* Van Markus had the red, pear-shaped lumps under the eyes, the slow rate of blinking, the flushed neck common to all Afrikaners.

Things were hardening up already. At least for the moment he knew where he was.

"Black velvet," he said. "Easy on the black."

Van Markus grinned and wagged a finger, returning to the bar. "*Skaam jou!*" He took a bottle of Guinness from beneath the counter and half-filled a pint glass. In another glass he added soda water to three fingers of gin. He mixed the two up.

It was eleven o'clock in the morning and the bar was otherwise deserted. Its red flock fleur-de-lis wallpaper was studded with the dusty heads of gnu, hippo, aardvark and warthog. A large fan in the center of the ceiling rattled rapidly round and round.

Van Markus brought the drink and Jerry paid him, took a sip and crossed to the juke-box to select the new version of *Recessional* sung by the boys of the Reformed Dutch Church School at Heidelberg. Only last week it had toppled The Jo'burg Jazz Flutes' *Cocoa Beans* from number one spot.

The tjumelt end the shouwting days;
The ceptens end the kengs dep'haht:
Stell stends Thine incient secrefize,
En umble end e contriteart.
Loard Goed ev Osts, be with us yit,
List we fergit—list we fergit!

Jerry sighed and checked his watches. He could still make it across Basutoland and reach Bethlehem before nightfall. Originally he had only meant to tank-up here, but it seemed the Republik was running out of the more refined kinds of fuel.

If things went slow then he knew a kopje where he could stay until morning.

Van Markus waved at him as he made for the door.

"Christ, man—I almost forgot."

He rang No Sale on the till and removed something from beneath the cash tray. A gray envelope. Jerry took it, placed it inside his white car coat.

The Silver Cloud was parked opposite the *Drankie-a-Snel-Snel.* Jerry got into the car, closed the door and raised the top. He fingered the envelope, frowning.

On it was written: *Mr. Cornelius. The Items.*

He opened it slowly, as a man might defuse a bomb.

A sheet of cheap Russian notepaper with the phrase *Hand in hand with horror: side by side with death* written in green with a felt pen. A place mat from an American restaurant decorated with a map of Vietnam and a short article describing the flora and fauna. Not much of either left, thought Jerry with a smile. A page torn from an English bondage magazine of the mid-50s period. Scrawled on this in black ballpoint: *Love me tender, love me sweet!!!* Although the face of the girl in the picture was half-obscured by her complicated harness, he was almost sure that it was Miss Brunner. A somewhat untypical pose.

The handwriting on envelope, notepaper and picture were all completely different.

Jerry put the items back into the envelope.

They added up to a change of direction. And a warning, too? He wasn't sure.

He opened the glove compartment and removed his box of chessmen—ivory and ebony, made by Tanzanian lepers, and the most beautiful pieces in the world. He took out the slender white king and a delicate black pawn, held them tightly together in his hand.

Which way to switch?

Not Fade Away

> SIR: I noticed on page three of the *Post* last week an alleged Monday Club member quoted as follows: "I have listened with increasing boredom to your streams of so-called facts, and I would like to know what you hope to achieve by stirring up people against colored immigrants."
>
> In order that there should be no doubt whatsoever in the minds of your readers as to the position of the Monday Club in this matter, I would quote from *The New Battle of Britain* on immigration: "Immigration must be drastically reduced and a scheme launched for large-scale voluntary repatriation. The Race Relations Acts are blows against the traditional British right to freedom of expression. They exacerbate rather than lessen racial disharmony. They must be repealed."

In a letter from the Chairman of the Monday Club to Mr. Anthony Barber, Chairman of the Conservative Party, it is stated: "Our fourth finding, and it would be foolish to brush this under the carpet, was that references to immigration were thought to be inadequate. In view of the very deep concern felt about this matter throughout the country, failure to come out courageously in the interests of the indigenous population could threaten the very existence of the party . . . However, it was thought there was no good reason to restrict the entry of those people whose forefathers had originally come from these islands . . ."

It would be quite wrong to leave anybody with the impression that the Monday Club was not wholly in support of the interests of the indigenous . . . population . . . of these islands.

—D. R. Bramwell
(letter to *Kensington Post*, March 27, 1970)

That'll Be The Day

Sebastian Auchinek was a miserable sod, thought Jerry absently as he laid the last brick he would lay for the duration.

Removing his coolie hat he stood back from the half-built wall and looked beyond at the expanse of craters which stretched to the horizon.

All the craters were full of muddy water mixed with defoliants. Not far from his wall a crippled kid in a blue cotton smock was playing in one of the holes.

She gave him a beautiful smile, leaning on her crutch and splashing water at him. Her leg-stump, pink and smooth, moved in a kicking motion.

Smiling back at her Jerry reflected that racialism and imperialism were interdependent but that one could sometimes flourish without the other.

The town had been called Ho Thoung. American destroyers had shelled it all down.

But now, as Jerry walked back towards the camp, it was quiet.

"If the world is to be consumed by horror," Auchinek had told him that morning, "if evil is to sweep the globe and death engulf it, I wish to *be* that horror, that evil, that death. I'll be on the winning side, won't I? Which side are you on?"

Auchinek was a terrible old bit of medieval Europe, really. Doubtless that was why he'd joined the USAF. And yet he was the only prisoner in Ho Thoung Jerry could talk to. Besides, as an ex-dentist, Auchinek had fixed Jerry's teeth better than even the Australian who used to have a surgery in Notting Hill.

Several large tents had been erected amongst the ruins of the town which had had 16,000 citizens and now had about 200. Jerry saw Auchinek emerge from one of these tents, his long body clothed in stained olive drab and his thin, pasty Jewish face as morose as ever. He nodded to Jerry. He was being led to the latrine area by his guard, a boy of fourteen holding a big M60.

Jerry joined Auchinek at the pit and they pissed in it together.

"And how is it out there?" Auchinek asked again. "Any news?"

"Much the same."

Jerry had taken the Trans-Siberian Express from Leningrad to Vladivostok and made the rest of his journey on an old Yugoslavian freighter now owned by the Chinese. It had been the only way to approach the zone.

"Israel?" Auchinek buttoned his faded fly.

"Doing okay. Moving."

"Out or in?"

"A little of both. You know how it goes."

"Natural boundaries." Auchinek accepted a cigarette from his guard as they walked back to the compound. "Vietnam and Korea. The old Manchu Empire. It's the same everywhere."

"Much the same."

"Pathetic. Childlike. Did you get what you came for?"

"I think so."

"Still killing your own thing, I see. Well, well. Keep it up."

"Take it easy." Jerry heard the sound of the Kamov Ka-15's rotors in the cloudy sky. "Here's my transport."

"Thank you," said Auchinek's guard softly. "Each brick brings victory a little closer."

"Sez you."

It's So Easy

"That's quite a knockout, Dr. Talbot," agreed Alar. "But how do you draw a parallel between Assyria and America Imperial?"

"There are certain infallible guides. In Toynbeean parlance they're called 'failure of self-determination', 'schism in the body social' and 'schism in the soul'. These phases of course all follow the 'time of troubles', 'universal state' and the 'universal peace'. These latter two, paradoxically, mark every civilization for death when it is apparently at its strongest."

. . . Donnan remained unconvinced. "You long-haired boys are always getting lost in what happened in ancient times. This is here and now—America Imperial, June Sixth, Two Thousand One Hundred Seventy-seven. We got the Indian sign on the world."

Dr. Talbot signed. "I hope to God you're right, Senator."

Juana-Maria said, "If I may interrupt . . ."

The group bowed.

—Charles L. Harness. *The Paradox Men*, 1953

Rave On

In Prague he watched while the clocks rang out.

In Havana he studied the foreign liberals fighting each other in the park.

In Calcutta he had a bath.

In Seoul he found his old portable taper and played his late, great Buddy Holly cassettes, but nothing happened.

In Pyongyang he found that his metabolism had slowed so much that he had to take the third fix of the operation a good two months early. Where those two months would come from when he needed them next he had no idea.

When he recovered he saw that his watches were moving at a reasonable rate, but his lips were cold and needed massaging.

In El Paso he began to realize that the alternatives were narrowing down as the situation hardened. He bought himself a second-hand Browning M35 and a new suede-lined belt holster. With ammunition he had to pay $81.50 plus tax. It worked out, as far as he could judge at that moment, to about £1 per person at the current exchange rate. Not particularly cheap, but he didn't have time to shop around.

It Doesn't Matter Any More

It was raining on the gray, deserted dockyard. The warehouses were all boarded up and there were no ships moored any more beneath the rusting cranes. Oily water received the rain. Sodden Heinz and Campbell cartons lurked just above the surface. Broken crates clung to the edge. Save for the sound of the rain there was silence.

Empires came and empires went, thought Jerry.

He sucked a peardrop, raised his wretched face to the sky so that the cold water fell into his eyes. His blue crushed-velvet toreador hipsters were soaked and soiled. His black car coat had a tear in the right vent, a torn pocket, worn elbows. Buttoned tight, it pressed the Browning hard against his hip.

It was natural. It was inevitable. And the children went on burning—sometimes a few, sometimes a lot. He could almost smell them burning.

A figure emerged from an alley between Number Eight and Number Nine sheds and began to walk towards him with a peculiar, rolling, flatfooted gait. He wore a cream trenchcoat and a light brown fedora, light check wide-bottomed trousers with turnups, tan shoes. The trenchcoat was tied at the waist with a yellow paisley scarf. The man had four or five days' beard. It was the man Jerry was waiting for—Sebastian Newman, the dead astronaut.

A week earlier Jerry had watched the last ship steam out of the Port of London. There would be none coming back.

Newman smiled when he saw Jerry. Rotten teeth appeared and were covered up again.

"So you found me at last," Newman said. He felt in the pocket of his coat and came out with a pack of German-made Players. He lit the cigarette with a Zippo. "As they say."

Jerry wasn't elated. It would be a long while before he re-engaged with his old obsessions. Perhaps the time had passed or was still to come. He'd lost even the basic Greenwich bearings. Simple notions of Time, like simple notions of politics, had destroyed many a better man.

"What d'you want out of me?" Newman asked. He sat down on the base of the nearest crane. Jerry leaned against the corrugated door of the shed. There was twenty feet separating them and, although both men spoke quietly, they could easily hear each other.

"I'm not sure," Jerry crunched the last of his peardrop and swallowed it. "I've had a hard trip, Col. Newman. Maybe I'm prepared to give in . . ."

"Cop out?"

"Go for a certainty."

"I thought you only went for outsiders."

"I didn't say that. I've never said that. Do you think this is the Phoney War?"

"Could be."

"I've killed twenty-nine people since El Paso and nothing's happened. That's unusual."

"Is it? These days?"

"What are 'these days'?"

"Since I came back I've never known that. Sorry. That wasn't 'cool', eh?" A little spark came and went in the astronaut's pale eyes.

Jerry tightened his face. "It never stops."

Newman nodded. "You can almost smell them burning, can't you?"

"If this is entropy, I'll try the other."

"Law and order?"

"Why not?"

Newman removed his fedora and scratched his balding head. "Maybe the scientists will come up with something . . ."

He began to laugh when he saw the gun in Jerry's hands. The last 9mm slug left the gun and cordite stank. Newman rose from his seat and bent double, as if convulsed with laughter. He fell smoothly into the filthy water. When Jerry went to look there were no ripples in the oil, but half an orange box was gently rocking.

Bang.

Listen To Me

Europe undertook the leadership of the world with ardor, cynicism and violence. Look at how the shadow of her palaces stretches out ever farther! Every one of her movements has burst the bounds of space and thought. Europe has declined all humility and all modesty; but she has also set her face against all solicitude and all tenderness.

She has only shown herself parsimonious and niggardly where men are concerned; it is only men that she has killed and devoured.

So, my brothers, how is it that we do not understand that we have better things to do than to follow that same Europe? Come, then, comrades, the European game has finally ended; we must find something different. We today can do everything, so long as we do not imitate Europe, so long as we are not obsessed by the desire to catch up with Europe . . .

Two centuries ago, a former European colony decided to catch up with Europe. It succeeded so well that the United States of America became a monster, in which the taints, the sickness and the inhumanity of Europe have grown to appalling dimensions.

Comrades, have we not other work to do than to create a third Europe? The West saw itself as a spiritual adventure. It is in the name of the spirit in the name of the spirit of Europe, that Europe has made her encroachments, that she has justified her crimes and legitimized the slavery in which she holds four-fifths of humanity . . .

The Third World today faces Europe like a colossal mass

whose aim should be to try to resolve the problems to which Europe has not been able to find the answers . . .

—Frantz Fanon, *The Wretched of the Earth*, 1961

I Forgot to Remember to Forget

The references were all tangled up. But wasn't his job really over? Or had Newman been taken out too soon? Maybe too late. He rode his black Royal Albert gent's roadster bicycle down the hill into Portobello Road. He needed to make better speed than this. He pedalled faster.

The Portobello Road became impassable. It was cluttered by huge piles of garbage, overturned stalls, the corpses of West Indians, Malays, Chinese, Indians, Irish, Hungarians, Cape Coloreds, Poles, Ghanaians, mounds of antiques.

The bike's brakes failed. Jerry left the saddle and flew towards the garbage.

DNA (do not analyze).

As he swam through the stinking air he thought that really he deserved a more up-to-date time machine than that bloody bike. Who was he anyway?

Back to Africa.

Everyday

At the rear of the company of Peuhl knights Jerry Cornelius crossed the border from Chad to Nigeria. The horsemen were retreating over the yellow landscape after their raid on the Foreign Legion garrison at Fort Lamy where they had picked up a good number of grenades. Though they would not normally ride with the Chad National Liberation Front, this time the sense of nostalgia had been too attractive to resist.

Along with their lances, scimitars, fancifully decorated helmets and horse-armor the Peuhl had .303s and belts of ammo crossed over the chainmail which glinted beneath their flowing white surcoats. Dressed like them, and wearing a bird-crested iron helmet painted in blues, reds, yellows and greens, Jerry revealed by his white hands that he was not a Peuhl.

The big Arab horses were coated by the dust of the wilderness and were as tired as their masters. Rocks and scrub stretched on all sides and it would be sunset before they reached the hills and the cavern where they would join their brother knights of the Rey Bouba in Cameroon.

Seigneur Samory, who led the company, turned in his saddle and shouted back. "Better than your old John Ford movies, eh, M. Cornelius?"

"Yes and no." Jerry removed his helmet and wiped his face on his sleeve. "What time is it?"

They both spoke French. They had met in Paris. Samory had had a different name then and had studied Law, doing the odd review for the French edition of *Box Office—Cashiers du Cinema.*

"Exactly? I don't know."

Samory dropped back to ride beside Jerry. His dark eyes glittered in his helmet. "You're always so anxious about the time. It doesn't bother me." He waved his arm to indicate the barren landscape. "My Garamante ancestors protected their huge Saharan empire from the empire of Rome two and a half millennia ago. Then the Sahara became a desert and buried our chariots and our cities, but we fought the Vandals, Byzantium, Arabia, Germany and France."

"And now you're on your way to fight the Federals. A bit of a come down, isn't it?"

"It's something to do."

They were nearing the hills and their shadows stretched away over the crumbling earth.

"You can take our Land Rover to Port Harcourt if you like," Samory told him. The tall Peuhl blew him a kiss through his helmet and went back to the head of the company.

I Love You Because

SIRS: I'm so disgusted with the so-called "American" citizen who knows little or nothing about the Vietnam war yet is so ready to condemn our gov't and soldiers for its actions. Did any of these people that are condemning us ever see their closest friend blown apart by a homemade grenade made by a woman that looks like an "ordinary villager"? Or did they ever see their buddy get shot by a woman or 10-year-old boy carrying a Communist rifle? These people were known VC and Mylai was an NVA and VC village. If I had been there I probably would of killed every one of those goddamned Communists myself.

—SP4 Kurt Jacoboni, *Life*, March 2, 1970

I'll Never Let You Go

Sometimes it was quite possible to think that the solution lay in black Africa. Lots of space. Lots of time.

But when he reached Onitsha he was beginning to change his mind. It was night and they were saving on street lighting. He had seen the huts burning all the way from Awka.

A couple of soldiers stopped him at the outskirts of the town but, seeing he was white, waved him on.

They stood on the road listening to the sound of his engine and his laughter as they faded away.

Jerry remembered a line from Camus's *Caligula*, but then he forgot it again.

Moving slowly against the streams of refugees, he arrived in Port Harcourt and found Miss Brunner at the Civil Administration Building. She was taking tiffin with Colonel Ohachi, the local governor, and she was evidently embarrassed by Jerry's dishevelled appearance.

"Really, Mr. Cornelius!"

He dusted his white car coat. "So it seems, Miss B. Afternoon, Colonel."

Ohachi glared at him, then told his Ibo houseboy to fetch another cup.

"It's happening all over again, I see." Jerry indicated the street outside.

"That's a matter of opinion, Captain Cornelius."

The colonel clapped his hands.

Can't Believe You Wanna Leave

Calcutta has had a pretty rough ride in the past twelve months and at the moment everyone is wondering just where the hell it goes from here. There aren't many foreigners who would allow the possibility of movement in any other direction. And, in truth, the problems of Calcutta, compounded by its recent vicious politics, are still of such a towering order as to defeat imagination; you have to sit for a little while in the middle of them to grasp what it is to have a great city and its seven million people tottering on the brink of disaster. But that is the vital point about Calcutta. It has been tottering for the best part of a generation now, but it hasn't yet fallen.

—*Guardian*, April 14, 1970

True Love Ways

"I thought you were in Rumania," she said. "Are you off schedule or what?"

She came right into the room and locked the door behind her. She watched him through the mosquito netting.

He smoked the last of his Nat Sherman's Queen-Size brown Cigarettellos. There was nothing like them. There would be nothing like them again.

She wrinkled her nose. "What's that bloody smell?"

He put the cigarette in the ashtray and sighed, moving over to his own half of the bed and watching her undress. She was all silk and rubber and trick underwear. He reached under the pillow and drew out what he had found there. It was a necklace of dried human ears.

"Where did you get this?"

"Jealous?" She turned, saw it, shrugged. "Not mine. It belonged to a GI."

"Where is he now?"

Her smile was juicy. "He just passed through."

I Want You, I Need You, I Love You

"Relying on U.S. imperialism as its prop and working hand in glove with it, Japanese militarism is vainly trying to realize its old dream of a 'Greater East Asia Co-Prosperity Sphere' and has openly embarked on the road of aggression against the people of Asia."—Communiqué issued jointly from Chouen-Lai and Kim-il-Sung (President of North Korea) quoted in *Newsweek*, April 20, 1970

Maybe Baby

Jerry's color vision was shot. Everything was in black and white when he arrived in Wenceslas Square and studied the fading wreaths which lay by the monument. Well-dressed Czechs moved about with brief-cases under their arms. Some got into cars. Others boarded trams. It was like watching a film.

He was disturbed by the fact that he could feel and smell the objects he saw. He blinked rapidly but it didn't help.

He wasn't quite sure why he had come back to Prague. May be he was looking for peace. Prague was peaceful.

He turned in the direction of the Hotel Esplanade.

He realized that Law and Order were not particularly compatible.

But where did he go from here?

And why was he crying?

It's So Easy

Weeping parents gathered in the hospital and mortuary of the Nile Delta farming towns of Huseiniya last night as Egypt denounced Israel for an air attack in which 30 children died. The bombs were reported to have fallen on a primary school at Bahr el Bakar, nearby, shortly after lessons had begun for the day. A teacher also died, and 40 children were injured.

In Tel-Aviv, however, the Israeli Defense Minister, General Dayan, accused Egypt of causing the children's deaths by putting them inside an Egyptian army base. The installations hit, he said, were definitely military. "If the Egyptians installed classrooms inside a military installation, this, in my opinion, is highly irresponsible."

—*Guardian*, April 9,1970

All Shook Up

Back to Dubrovnik, where the corpse-boats left from. As he waited in his hotel room he looked out of the window at the festering night. At least some things were consistent. Down by the docks they were loading the bodies of the White South Afrikan cricket team. Victims of history? Or was history their victim? His nostalgia for the fifties was as artificial as his boyish nostalgia, in the fifties, for the twenties.

What was going on?

Time was the enemy of identity.

Peggy Sue Got Married

Jerry was in Guatemala City when Auchinek came in at the head of his People's Liberation Army, his tanned face sticking out of the top of a Scammel light-armored car. The sun hurt Jerry's eyes as he stared.

Auchinek left the car like toothpaste from a tube. He slid down the side and stood with his Thompson in his hand while the photographers took his picture. He was grinning.

He saw Jerry and danced towards him.

"We did it!"

"You changed sides?"

"You must be joking."

The troops spread out along the avenues and into the plazas, clearing up the last of the government troops and the American advisers. Machine guns sniggered.

"Where can I get a drink?" Auchinek slung his Thompson behind him.

Jerry nodded his head back in the direction of the pension he had been staying in. "They've got a cantina."

Auchinek walked into the gloom, reached over the bar and took two bottles of Ballantine from the cold shelf. He offered one to Jerry who shook his head.

"Free beer for all the workers." The thin Jew broke the top off the bottles and poured their contents into a large schooner. "Where's the service around here?"

"Dead," said Jerry. "It was fucking peaceful . . ." Warily, Jerry touched his lower lip.

Auchinek drew his dark brows together, opened his own lips and grinned. "You can't stay in the middle forever. Join up with me. Maxwell's boys are with us now." He looked at the bar mirror and adjusted his Che-style beret, stroked his thin beard. "Oh, that's nice."

Jerry couldn't help sharing his laughter. "It's time I got back to Ladbroke Grove, though," he said.

"You used to be a fun lover.

Jerry glanced at the broken beer bottles. "I know."

Auchinek saluted him with the schooner. "Death to Life, eh? Remember?"

"I didn't know this would happen. The whole shitty fabric in tatters. Still, at least you've cheered up . . ."

"For crying out loud!" Auchinek drank down his beer and wiped the foam from his moustache. "Whatever else you do, don't get dull. Jerry!"

Jerry heard the retreating forces' boobytraps begin to go off. Dust drifted through the door and swirled in the cone of sunlight. Miss Brunner followed it in. She was wearing her stylish battle-dress.

"Revolution, Mr. Cornelius! 'Get with it, kiddo!' What do you think?" She stretched her arms and twirled. "It's all the rage."

"Oh, Jesus!"

Helpless with mirth, Jerry accepted the glass Auchinek put in his hand and; spluttering, tried to swallow the aquavit.

"Give him your gun, Herr Auchinek." Miss Brunner patted him on the back and slid her hands down his thighs. Jerry fired a burst into the ceiling.

They were all laughing now.

Any Way You Want Me

Thirty heads with thirty holes and God knew how many hours or minutes or seconds. The groaning old hovercraft dropped him off at Folkestone and he made his way back to London in an abandoned Ford Popular. Nothing had changed.

Black smoke hung over London, drifting across a red sun.

Time was petering out.

When you thought about it, things weren't too bad.

Oh, Boy

He walked down the steps into the club. A couple of cleaners were mopping the floor and the group was tuning up on the stage.

Shaky Mo grinned at him, hefted the Futurama. "Good to see you back in one piece, Mr. C."

Jerry took the bass. He put his head through the strap.

"Cheer up, Mr. C. It's not the end of the world. Maybe nothing's real."

"I'm not sure it's as simple as that." He screwed the volume control to maximum. He could still smell the kids. He plucked a simple progression. Everything was drowned. He saw that Mo had begun to sing.

The 1500 watt amp roared and rocked. The drummer leaned over his kit and offered Jerry the roll of charge. Jerry accepted it, took a deep drag.

He began to build up the feedback.

That was life.

Other references:
Buddy Holly's Greatest Hits (Coral)
This is James Brown (Polydor)
Elvis's Golden Records (RCA)
Little Richard All-time Hits (Specialty)

The Spencer Inheritance

ONE

"Leave Me Alone"

> "I mean, once or twice I've heard people say to me that you know Diana's out to destroy the monarchy . . . Why would I want to destroy something that is my children's future?"
>
> —Diana, Princess of Wales, Television Interview, November 1995

"Oh, cool! This—" With all his old enthusiasm, Shaky Mo bit into his footlong. "— is what I *call* a hot dog." His bearded lips winked with mustard, ketchup and gelatinous cucumber. "Things are looking up."

Close enough, in the cramped confines of the Ford Flamefang MK IV, to suffer the worst of Mo's fallout, Jerry Cornelius still felt a surge of affection for his little pard. Mo was back on form, an MK 55 on his hip and righteous mayhem in his eyes. He was all relish again. Mounting the ruins of the St. Johns Wood Wottaburger, their armored half-track rounded a tank-trap, bounced over a speed-bump and turned erratically into Abbey Road. "Bugger." Mo's dog had gone all over the place.

"It's chaos out there."

Major Nye fixed a pale and amiable blue eye on the middle distance. Neat gray hairs ran like furrows across his tanned old scalp. His sinewy body had been so long in the sun it was half mummified. They were heading for Hampstead where they hoped to liaise with some allies and carry on up the M1 to liberate their holy relics in the name of their dead liege, who had died reluctantly at Lavender Hill. The old soldier's steering was light and flexible, but sometimes it threatened to overturn them. Glancing back across his shoulder he voiced all their thoughts.

"This is going to be a good war, what?"

"At least we got a chance to lay some mines this time." Colonel Hira brushed a scarlet crumb from his chocolate fatigues and adjusted his yellow turban. Only Hira wore the official uniform of the UPS. The United Patriotic Squadrons (of The Blessed Diana) (Armored Vehicles Division) were famous for their eccentric but influential style, their elaborate flags. "Those Caroline bastards will think twice before taking their holidays in Dorset again."

A saccharine tear graced Bishop Beesley's flurried cheek. Seemingly independent, like toon characters, his fingers grazed at random over his face. From time to time he drew the tips to his lips and tasted them. "Surely this is no time for cynicism?" His wobbling miter gave clerical emphasis to his plea. "We are experiencing the influence of the world-will. We are helpless before a massive new mythology being created around us and of which we could almost be part. This is the race-mind expressing itself." His massive jowls drooped with sincerity. "Can't we share a little common sentiment?" He squeezed at his right eye to taste another tear. "Our sweet patroness died for our right to plant those mines."

"And so her effing siblings could spray us with AIDs virus in the name of preserving national unity." This was Mo's chief grievance. He was afraid he would turn out positive and everyone would think he was an effing fudge-packer like Jerry and the rest of them half-tuned pianos. "Don't go forgetting that." He added, a little mysteriously: "Private money blows us up. Public money patches us up. Only an idiot of a capitalist would want to change that status quo. This is an old-fashioned civil-war. A class war."

Major Nye disagreed. "We're learning to live in a world without poles."

"Anti-semitic bastards." Mo frowned down at his weapon. "They deserved all they got."

"Are we there yet?" The cramped cab was making Jerry claustrophobic. "I think I'm going to be sick."

TWO

"Our grief is so deep . . ."

> ". . . when people are dying they're much more open and more vulnerable, and much more real than other people. And I appreciate that."
>
> —As above

The convoy managed to get as far as Swiss Cottage before a half-dozen of the latest 10×10 extra-sampled Morris Wolverines came surfing over the rubble towards them.

The hulls of the pocket landcruisers shone like pewter. The style leaders in all sides of the conflict, their streamlining was pure 1940s futurist. Their firepower, from the single pointed muzzle of a Niecke 450 LS, was the classiest ordnance available. Those laser-shells could go up your arse and take out a particular pile if they wanted to. It was just that kind of aggressive precision styling which people were looking for these days.

"But can it last, Mr. C?" Shaky Mo was taking the opportunity to retouch some of their burned paint. The fresh cerise against the camouflage gave the car the look of a drunk in the last stages of cirrhosis. Mo ignored the approaching squadron until almost the final moment. Then, nonchalant, he swung into his gunnery perch, pulled the safety lid down behind him, settled himself into the orange innertube he used to ease his lower back, flipped a few toggles, swung his twin Lewis's from side to side with the heel of his hand to check their readiness, pushed up the sights, tested the belts, and put his thumbs to the firing button. A precise and antique burst. The rubble between their Ford and the rank of savvy Morrises suddenly erupted and clouds billowed. A wall of debris rose for at least twenty feet and then began to settle in simple geometric patterns.

"Here's some we laid earlier, pards!"

Mo began to cackle and shriek.

Following this precedent, ash rained across Kelmscott and all the Morris memorials. Ancient Pre-Raphaelites were torn apart for scrap, their bones ground for color, their blood feeding the sand. It became the fashion to dig up poets and painters and own a piece of them. No grave was safe. Everyone now knew that such gorgeous paint was wasted in the cement of heritage. Heritage parks.

"Cementaries?" Jerry did his best with his associations. Why was it wrong to resist their well-meaning intentions?

What secrets could they possibly learn? Nothing which would embarrass me, of course, for I am dead. But secrets of the fields and hedges, eh? Yes, I've found them. It's easy with my eyes. Or was. Secrets in old stones, weakened by the carving of their own runes and the casting of dissipate magic. Desolate churches standing on cold ground which once raced with energy. Why is there such a cooling of this deconsecrated earth? Has the ether been leeched of its goodness by swaggering corporate capital, easing and wheezing its fat bodies through the corridors of privilege, the ratholes of power. Help me, help me, help me. Are you incapable of ordinary human emotion?

Or has that been simulated, too? Or stimulated you by its very nearness. Yet somewhere I can still hear your despairing leitmotifs.

Messages addressed to limbo. Your yearning for oblivion. You sang such lovely, unrepeatable songs. You sank such puritan hopes.

But you were never held to account.
Blameless,
  you were blemished
only
in the minds
of the impure
Of the impure, I said,
but not the unworthy.
For this is Babylon,
  where we live.
Babylon,
  where we live.
This is Babylon, said
  mr big.
What, mr b?
Did you speak?
Only inside, these days,
  mrs c,
for I am dead and my
loyalties are to the dead
I no longer have desire
to commune with the living
  Only you
  mrs c.
  Only good
  old mrs
  c.

Murdering the opposition:
  It is a last
  resort.
  He came up
  that morning
  He said
  From Scunthorpe

or was it Skegness.
You know, don't
you?
The last resort.

Don't blame me:
You're on
your own
in this one
I said
Nobody
calls on
me
for a report.

Oh, good lord.
Sweet lord.
Let me go.
There's work to be done, yet:
You don't know
the meaning
of pain,
she looked over my head
she looked over my head
the whole time she spoke
Her eyes and voice were
in the distance.
You may never know it,
she said.
You could die
and never know it.
And that's my prayer.
Loud enough for you, Jerry?
Loud enough?
She asked.
There's an aesthetic
in loudness itself.

    Or so we think.
    Can you hear me, Jerry?
    Jerry?
An anaesthetic?
    he said.
Oh, this turning multiverse
    is in reverse
And whirling chaos sounds
    familiar patterns
in the shifting
    round
Yet still,
    they take the essence from
    our common ground
    They take our public
    spirit
    from
    our common ground.
We become subject
    to chills and bronchial
    seizures
Now we are paying that price
    Given that prize
    Severed those ties
    Those hampering
        second thoughts
    Those night rides
        down to where
    the conscience still pipes
    a piccolo
    still finds a little resonance
    among the ailing reeds.
    Some unrooted truth
        left to die
    down there.
    Can you hear it?
    Loyal to the end.

Loyal to your well-being.
Wanting nothing else.
Can you hear it?
Still piping a
hopeful note
or two.
All for you.
"You must be
fucking
desperate,"
she said.

The SciFi Channel:

Our ministers are proud
to announce the
restoration of the English
car industry
Record sales of light
armored vehicles
has made this a boom year
for our
auto-makers.
Bonuses all round,
says Toney Flair
our golden age PM.
Let's give ourselves
A pat
on the back.

The domestic arms trade
has stimulated the
domestic car trade
The economy
has never been
stronger.

We are killing

two bards
with one
stone.

Look at America.
That's their
lifeblood,
right?
You
know
what
I
mean?

You
know what I mean?
I mean
what
have
I
done?
I mean
why?
I mean
you
know
why?
I mean
you know.
Came out of the West
Out of the gray West
Where the sea runs
And my blood is at ease.
And this is where I rest.

THREE

Was Diana Murdered?

> International crime syndicates are cheating Princess Diana's memorial fund with pirate versions of Elton John's "Candle in the Wind" . . . Illegal copies of the song, performed at the Princess's funeral, are undercut by up to £2.50 and have been found in Italy, Hong Kong, Singapore and Paraguay. Profits will fund the drugs and arms trade.
>
> —*Daily Bulletin*, Majorca, September 26, 1997

"Gun carriages." Major Nye lowered puzzled glasses. "Dozens of them. Piled across Fitzjohns Avenue. Where on earth are they getting them?"

Behind their battered Ford the smoking aluminium of the Morrises fused and seethed, buckling into complex parodies of Paolozzi sculptures. Abandoning his Lewises, Mo had used a musical strategy aimed at their attackers' over-refined navigational circuits. A few Gene Vincent singles in the right registers and the enemy had auto-destructed.

"It used to be glamorous, dying in a crash. But the nineties did with auto-death what Oasis did with the Beatles. They took an idiom to its dullest place. This wasn't suicide. It wasn't even assassination. It was ritual murder. How can they confuse the three? It was the triumph of the lowest common denominator. The public aren't fools. Don't you think we all sensed it?"

Finchley's trees had gone for fuel. Its leafy authority removed, the Avenue had the air of an exposed anthill. Ankle-deep in sawdust, people clustered around the stumps, holding branches and leaves as if through osmosis they might somehow restore their cover. They had no spiritual leadership. As Jerry & Co. rumbled past, waving, playing snatches of patriotic music and distributing leprous bars of recovered Toblerone, they lifted their rustling limbs in dazed salute.

"These places are nothing without their foliage." Mo lit his last Sherman's.

The deadly oils released their aromatic smoke into the cab. Everyone but Jerry took an appreciative sniff. Jerry was still having trouble with his convulsions.

He had developed a range of allergies with symptoms so unusual they had not yet hit the catalogues. This made him a valuable target for drug company goons, always on the lookout for the clinically exceptional. New diseases needed new cures. But he was not prepared to sell his new diseases just to anyone. There were ethical considerations. This was, after all, the cusp of a millennium. There were matters of public interest to consider. The Golden Age of corporate piracy was gone. We were all developing appropriate pieties.

Mournfully Bishop Beesley saw that he was on his last Mars Megapak. Yet compulsively he continued to eat. Rhythmically, the chocolate disappeared into his mouth, leaving only the faintest trails. They slipped like blood down his troubled jowls.

"Seen anything from the old baroness at all?"

Mo scarcely heard him. He was buried in some distant song.

"You made
the Age
of the
Predatory Lad.
It paid you
well.

"What price victory now, Mr. C?"

"Eh?"

Jerry was still preoccupied with his physical feelings.

He lifted his legs and howled.

FOUR

Das War Diana

> "I'm not a political animal but I think the biggest disease this world suffers from in this day and age is the disease of people feeling unloved."
>
> —As above

Hampstead Heath was a chaos of churned mud and tortured metal given exotic beauty by the movement of evening sunlight through lazy gray smoke. In the silence a few bustling ravens cawed. Hunched on blasted trees they seemed profoundly uneasy. Perhaps the character of the feast upset their sense of the natural order. They were old, conservative birds who still saw some kind of virtue in harmony.

The house the team occupied had a wonderful view all the way across the main battlefield. Its back wall had received two precise hits from an LB7. The body of the soldier who had been hiding behind the wall was now under the rubble. Only his feet remained exposed. Mo had already removed the boots and was polishing them appreciatively, with the previous owner's Cherry Blossom. He held them up to the shifty light. "Look at the quality of that leather. The bastards."

He was upset. He had been convinced that the boots would fit him.

"You turn people into fiction you get shocked when they die real deaths." Little Trixiebell Brunner, never less than smart, had agreed to meet them here with the remains of her squadron.

"Bastards!" Clinging vaguely, her mother drooled viciously at her side. Lady Brunner was having some trouble staying alive.

Trixie lifted disapproving lips. "Mum!"

The infusions weren't working any more. Uncomfortably wired, Lady B muttered and buzzed to herself, every so often fixing her bleak eyes upon some imagined threat. Maybe Death himself.

Jerry was trembling as usual. His mouth opened and closed rapidly. Lady Brunner smiled suddenly to herself as if recalling her old power. "Eh?" She began to cackle.

Trixie let out a sigh of irritated piety. "Mother!"

Until a month ago Trixie had been Toney Flair's Chief Consorte and tipped for the premiership when her leader and paramour took the Big Step, which he had promised to do if he had not brought the nations of Britain to peace by the end of the year. He would join his predecessors in US exile. It was the kind of example the British people now habitually demanded.

Trixie, growing disapproving of Toney's policies, had uttered some significant leaks before siding with the Dianistas whom she had condemned as upstart pretenders a week earlier. But at heart, she told them, she was still a Flairite. She was hoping her actions would bring Toney or his deputy Danny to their senses. Until the Rift of Peckham they had supported the Dianist cause. She would still be a keen Dianista if those twin fools the Earls of Spencer and of Marks, claiming Welsh heritage, hadn't allied themselves with the Black Stuarts and thus brought anarchy to Scotland. Rather than listen to all these heresies, her mother had stood in a corner putting pieces of Kleenex into her ears. One of her last acts in power was to make them both Knights of St Michael.

A shadow darkened the garden.

Jerry was compelled to go outside and look up. Limping over low was the old *Princess of Essex*, her gold, black and fumed oak finish showing the scars of recent combat.

Mo joined him. He gazed approvingly at the ship. "She always had style, didn't she?" he said reverently.

Jerry blinked uncertainly. "Style?"

"Class." Mo nodded slowly, confirming his own wise judgement.

"Class." Jerry's attention was wandering again. He had found a faded *¡Hola!* and began to leaf through it. "*Which*?" For the last couple of centuries Britain had seen her monarchs identify their fortunes first with the aristocracy, then with the upper middle class, then with the middle class and ultimately with the petite bourgeoisie, depending who had the most power. No doubt they would soon appear on the screen adopting the costumes and language of *East Enders*. They were so adaptable they'd be virtually invisible by the middle of the century. "Style? Where?"

"*Essex*." Mo pointed up.

As if in response, the *Princess* shimmied girlishly in the air.

FIVE

Dodi's Psychiatrist Tells All

> Those of us who met Diana can vouch for it, and the rest of us know it's true:
>
> She brought magic into all our lives and we loved her for it. She'll always be what she wanted to be the Queen of our Hearts.
>
> —*Diana, Queen of Our Hearts, News of the World* Special Souvenir Photo Album, September 1997

"It was then," Major Nye told Trixie Brunner, "that I realized a lifetime ambition and bought myself a good quality telescope with the object of fulfilling those two fundamental human needs—to spy on my neighbors and to look at the stars. But Simla seems a long time ago. I often wonder why they resented us so. After all, they didn't have a nation until we made them one. It was either us or some native Bismarck. Much better we should get the blame."

"I believe they used to call that paternalism." Trixie could not help liking this sweet old soldier.

"Quite right," Major Nye squared his jaw approvingly.

His nasty locks bouncing, Mo swung round on the swivel gunseat. "Can I ask you a personal question?"

Trixie adopted that open and agreeable expression which had become so fashionable just before the outbreak of armed hostilities. "Of course," she said brightly.

"How much time do you spend actually making up?"

"Not that long." She smiled as if she took a joke against her. "It gets easier with practice."

"But about how long?"

"Why do you ask?"

"It would take me hours."

"Hardly half-an-hour." She softened.

"What about retouches?"

"I really don't know. Say another half-hour or so."

"What about clothes? I mean, you're always very nicely turned out."

"You mean getting dressed?"

"And deciding what to wear and everything. Say you change two or three times a day."

"Well, it's not that long. You get used to it."

"An hour? Two hours?"

"Some days I hardly get out of my shirt and jeans."

"How long is a break in St. Tropez?"

"What do you mean? For me? A couple of weeks at a stretch at best."

"And how much time a day do you spend working for others?"

Trixie frowned. "What do you mean 'others'?"

"Well, you know, lepers and all that."

"That's hardly work," said Trixie. "But it does involve turning up and posing."

Major Nye patted her gentle shoulder. "The public is very generous in its approval of the rich," he said.

"It's the poor they can't stand," said Mo. "What I want to know is how many big-eyed children will starve to death just because Kim the Stump got all the photo-opportunities? Why isn't there more fucking anger? There's only so much charity to go round!"

"And nothing like enough justice." Major Nye turned his chair towards the car's tiny microwave. "Anyone fancy a cup of tea?"

He peered through one of the observation slits. A gentle mist was rolling over the picturesque ruins of Highgate. Marx's monument had sustained some ironic shelling. You could see all the way across the cemetery to Tufnell Park and beyond it to Camden, Somers Town, Soho and the Thames. It was a quiet morning. The gunfire was distant, lazy.

"Do you think it's safe to lower our armor?"

SIX

Now You Belong To Heaven

> Then, amazingly, the masses who had prayed and sung the hymns, wept deeply as the service floated over London, began to applaud . . . Once the hearse had passed, each and every one of us went home alone.
>
> —Leslie Thomas, *News of the World*, September 7, 1977

Something in Jerry was reviving. He flipped through the latest auto catalogues. He felt a twitch where his genitals might be.

Rover Revenges, Jaguar Snarlers, Austin Attackers, Morris Wolverines, Hillman Hunters and Riley Reliants all sported the latest tasty fashions in firepower. Their rounded carapaces and tapering guns gave them the appearance of mobile phones crossed with surgical instruments. They were loaded with features. They were being exported everywhere. It made you proud to be British again. This was, after all, what you did best.

But the politics of fashion was once again giving way to the politics of precedent. Jerry felt his stomach turn over. Was there any easy way of getting out of the past?

SEVEN

Diana's Smile Lit Up Wembley

> The world is mourning Princess Diana—but nowhere are the tears falling more relentlessly than in Bosnia . . . She met limbless victims of the landmines . . . but she did much more than add another victim to her global crusade . . . She made a despairing people smile again.
>
> —*News of the World*, September 7, 1997

"Thirty years and all these fuckers will be footnotes!" Mo stood knee-deep in rubble running his fingers over the keyboard of a Compaq he had found. The screen had beeped and razzled but had eventually given him the Net. Taking a swig from his gemini, he lit himself a reefer and flipped his way through *The Sunday Times*. "Do they only exist on Sundays?"

"For Sundays." Jerry was frowning down at a drop of machine oil which had fallen onto his cuff and was being absorbed into the linen. "Do they exist for Sundays or do they appear any other days?" He was still having a little trouble with existence.

"We shouldn't have left him alone in the prozac vault." Trixie Brunner brushed white powder from her perfect pants. "You only need one a day."

"I was looking for extra balance," Jerry explained. He smiled sweetly through his wrinkling flesh. "This isn't right, is it?"

Major Nye shook his head and pointed. Across the heaped bricks and slabs of broken concrete came a group of irregulars. They wore bandannas and fatigues clearly influenced by *Apocalypse Now*. This made them dangerous enemies and flaky friends. Virtual Nam had taken them over. Jerry sized them up. Those people always went for the flashiest ordnance. He had never seen so many customized Burberrys and pre-bloodstained Berber flak jackets.

They had stopped and in the accents of Staines and Haywards Heath were calling a familiar challenge.

"For or Against!"

They were Dianistas. But not necessarily of the same division.

Mo cupped his hands and shouted.

"For!"

Major Nye looked around vaguely, as if for a ball.

With lowered weapons, the group began to advance.

Major Nye thought he recognized one of their number.

"Mrs. Persson?"

Carefully he checked his watches.

EIGHT

Princes Teach Charles To Love Again

> Princess Diana was named yesterday as the most inspirational figure for Britain's gay community. *The Pink Paper*, a gay newspaper, said a poll of its readers placed Diana way ahead of people such as 19th century playwright Oscar Wilde who was jailed for being homosexual or tennis star Martina Navratilova.
>
> —*Daily Bulletin*, September 26, 1997

"You never get a free ride, Mr. C. Sooner or later the bill turns up. As with our own blessed Madonna, for instance. All that unearned approval! Phew! Makes you think, eh?"

"I was his valet, you know." 'Flash' Gordon's lips formed soft, unhappy words. He was an interpreter attached to the Sloane Square squadron. His raincoat was secure to the neck and padlocked. They had found him in some provincial prison. "Up there. He was a gent through and through but not exactly an intellectual. She was twice as bright as he and she wasn't any Andrea Dworkin, either. I 'wore the bonnet' as we say in Tannochbrae. Some days you could go mad with boredom. Being a flunkey is a lot more taxing than people think. At least, it was for me."

"Weren't you afraid they'd find out about your past?" Mo noted several old acquaintances amongst the newcomers, not all of them yuppies.

"Well, I was a victim too you know." Flash understood best how to comfort himself.

Una Persson, stylish as ever in her military coat and dark, divided pants, straddled the fire, warming her hands. Her pale oval face, framed by a brunette pageboy, brooded into the middle distance. "Don't buy any of that cheap American shit," she told Major Nye. "Their tanks fall apart as soon as their own crappy guns start firing. Get a French one, if you can. Here's a picture," she reached into her jacket, "from *Interavia*. All the specifications are there. Oh, and nothing Chinese."

"What's wrong with Chinese?" asked Jerry. He lay beside the fire staring curiously at her boot.

"Don't start that," she said firmly.

But she answered him, addressing Mo. "It's totally naff, these days. Jerry never could keep in step."

"No free lunches," said Jerry proudly, as if remembering a lesson.

"No free lunches." Una Persson unslung her MK-50 and gave the firing mechanism her intense attention. "Only what you can steal."

NINE

Sign Your Name in Our Book of Condolence

> As Mr. Blair's voice echoes into silence, Elton John gives his biggest ever performance. He opens with the words—Goodbye England's Rose—of his rewritten version of one of Diana's favorite songs, "Candle in the Wind." Billions around the world sing with him and remember the "loveliness we've lost." In Hyde Park, many watching on giant videos weep uncontrollably.
>
> —*News of the World*, September 7, 1997

"It's not the speed that kills you it's what's in the speed, right?" Sagely Shaky Mo contemplated his adulterated stash. "You want to do something about that nose, Mr. C."

Jerry dabbed at his face with the wet Kleenex Trixie had given him. For a few moments he had bled spontaneously from all orifices.

"Better now?" Bishop C looked up from the month old *Mirror* he had found. It was his first chance to read one of his own columns, *God the Pal*. He was getting along famously with the newcomers. They understood all about Christian Relativism, Consumer Faith and Fast Track Salvation. They had read his *Choice In Faith* and other pamphlets. They were considering tempting him to transfer and become their padre. Trixie was even now involved in negotiations with her opposite number. They used the *can* as their unit of currency.

Not having the stomach to finish them off, the Dianistas had brought a few of their better looking prisoners with them. The allies now stood shoulder to shoulder, staring down at the foxhole they had filled with the cringing youngsters.

Mo felt about inside his coat and came out with a small, clear glass medicine bottle whose top had been carefully sealed with wax.

"See that?" He brandished the vial at the baffled prisoners. "See that?"

"You know what that is? Do you? You fucking wouldn't know, would you? That, my dirty little republican friends, is one of HER tears." With his other hand he unslung his weapon.

As they heard his safeties click off, the half-starved boys and girls began to move anxiously in the trench, as if they might escape the inevitable.

"She fucking wept for you, you fuckers." Mo's eyes shone with reciprocal salt. "You fucking don't deserve this. But *SHE* understood compassion, even if you don't."

The big multifire MKO made deep, throaty noises as it sent explosive shells neatly into each tender body. They arced, twitched, were still. Nobody had had to spend much energy on it. It was a ritual everyone had come to understand.

Mo slung the smoking gun onto his back again.

"You want to search them?" He winked at Trixie. "I haven't touched the pockets."

His visionary eyes looked away into the distance. Killing always heightened his sense of time.

Bishop Beesley murmured over the corpses while Trixie slipped into the trench and collected what she wanted. "It was a culture of self-deception," he said.

Trixie pulled herself up through the clay. "Isn't that the definition of a culture?"

Apologizing for the effect of the cold weather, Bishop Beesley urinated discretely into the pit.

Jerry turned away. He was asking himself a novel question. Was everything going too far?

TEN

Reflexivity

> Last Sunday a light went out that illuminated the world. Nothing would turn it back on. The death of Princess Di, the fairytale princess, the human royal, left us all totally stunned.
>
> I am not a Johnny-come-lately to sing the praises of our magical princess. Unlike many others who now describe her in such glowing terms but certainly did not during her life, I have again and again expressed my love for Diana.
>
> When I got some readers' letters knocking her I was saddened. I wonder how they and all the gray men who put her down feel now? The people have spoken.
>
> —Michael Winner, *News of the World*, September 7, 1997

"Islands within islands, that's the British for you." The Hon. Trixiebell had long since given up on her race. It was her one regret that she had not been born a Continental. Her mother still shuddered if the word was mentioned.

Their convoy had broken through to the M1. Although heavily pitted and badly repaired, the motorway was still navigable. It left them more exposed, but it had been a while since any kind of aircraft had been over. Several friendly and unfriendly airforces were abroad, on hire to continental corporations. It was the only way to raise enough money to pay for the quality of artillery they demanded.

"We have had to learn," PM Flair had announced over the radio, " that we only have so many options. Economics is, after all, the root of most warfare. We can have guns and butter, but we can't have aircraft carriers *and* the latest laser-scopes. It makes sense, really. Only you, the warriors in this great cause, can decide what you need most. And if you tell us what you need, *we will listen*. I guarantee that. Unfortunately, I am not responsible for the failings of my predecessors, who set up the supply systems and who were as unrighteous as I am righteous. But we'll soon have the engine overhauled and back on the road, as it were, before Christmas. I have long preached the gospel of personal responsibility. So you may rest assured that I will keep this promise or take the Big Step in the attempt. Thank you. God bless."

There were seven weeks left to go. By now the people's PM would probably be praying for a miracle. Ladbroke's and the Stock Exchange were setting all kinds of unhelpful odds.

Jerry himself had not ruled out Divine Intervention. Surely something was in control?

"It's not that long since you were collateral yourself, Mr. C." Mo attempted to revive his friend's self-respect. "Remember when your corpse was the hottest commodity on the market?"

"Long ago." The old assassin contemplated his own silver age. "Far away. Obsolete icons. Failed providers. Lost servers. Scarcely an elegy, Miss Scarlett. Hardly worth blacking up for. Government by lowest common denominator. A true market government. Poets have been mourning this century ever since it began. Anyway, how would I remember? I was dead."

"As good as." Una Persson settled a slim, perfect reefer into her holder and fished her Meredith from her top pocket. Her elegant brown bob swung to the rhythm of the half-track's rolling motion and Jerry had a flash, a memory of passion. But it hurt him too much to hang on to it. He let it go. Bile rose into his mouth and he leaned again over the purple Liberty's bag. Something was breaking up inside him, mirroring the social fractures in the nation. He was nothing without his guidelines. This disintegration had been going on for many years and was now accelerating as everyone had predicted. Was he the only one who had planned for this? Had all the others lost their nerve in the end? He stared around him, trying to smile.

"Either stop that," said Una, "or pass me your bag."

"Here we go!"

Ignoring the twisted and buckled signs which sought to misdirect them, they turned towards Long Buckby and their ideal. At some time in the past couple of years some vast caravan of traffic had come this way, flattening the borders and turning the slip-road into a crude highway, reminding Jerry of the deep reindeer paths he had once followed in Lapland, when he had still thought he could find his father.

He had found only an abandoned meteorological post, with some photographs of his mother when she had been in the chorus. Her confident eyes, meeting Jerry's across half a century, had made him weep.

A relatively unblemished sign ahead read:

WELCOME TO THE SHERWOOD EXPERIENCE
Sheriff of Nottingham Security Posts Next 3 Miles.
No admittance without Merry Man guide.
ROBIN HOOD'S FOREST and FEUDAL FEUDING VR
(one-price family ticket value)

"I told you we were near Nottingham." Mo sniffed. "There's nothing like that smell anywhere else in the world. God it makes you hungry!"

"Takes you back a bit, eh?" said Major Nye. "Now this, of course, is where an off-road vehicle proves herself." The delicate veins on his hands quivered and tensed as he found his gears.

"Isn't it still relatively unspoiled?" Trixiebell tried to take the bib from her mother who clung to it, glaring and mumbling. Lady Brunner's lunchtime pap was caked all over her face and chest. "The heartland of England. Where our most potent legends were nurtured."

"That's crap, dear," said Una. "The only thing nurtured around here is two thousand years of ignorance and prejudice."

"So she's right," Colonel Hira rubbed softly at his buttocks. "The heartland of England."

"Fucking tories," said Mo.

"Right on!" Colonel Hira's chubby fist jabbed the overhead air.

"Haven't you forgotten how fucking concerned, caring and multi-cultural the conservatives really were, colonel?" The Hon. Trixiebell was furious. "One more crack like that and you'll be whistling 'Mammy.' "

"I thought you were with the other lot." Major Nye was puzzled.

Trixie made an edgy gesture. She hated argument. It was so

hard to tell who really had the power these days.

"That doesn't mean I can't see all sides."

Laughing, Jerry coughed something up.

As best they could, the others shifted away from him.

It was getting crowded in the steel-plated cab. The heat was unseasonal. What was going wrong with the weather?

"Greenhouse!" Jerry was reading his phlegm. "We have to get back to Kew. Kew."

"Kew?" Mo cheered up. He had always tried to avoid the Midlands.

"Queue?" Trixie shook a vehement head. "Queue? Never again."

"Kew," said Jerry. "Kew. Kew."

"You should get that looked at." From the shadows under the instrument panel Bishop Beesley surfaced. "You could infect us all."

Everyone was staring at him. They had believed him gone off with the renegades.

He adjusted his miter. He shrugged his cassock straight and took a firm grip on his crook. "There were small, unsettled differences," he explained. "In the end I could not in conscience take another appointment. My place is with you."

"But you've wolfed the supplies," said Mo.

"There was hardly anything left." The bishop was all reassurance. "Hardly a bite. Not a sniff. I wish I could tell you otherwise. A little jam would have been welcome, but no. These are harsh conditions and the Church must find the resources to meet them. I suggest that we pick up our holy charge and proceed directly to Coventry where negotiations are already in progress. They're well-known to have enormous stockpiles." His mouth foamed with anticipatory juices. "Rowntrees. Cadbury's. Terry's. Everything. Warehouses worthy of Joseph!"

"Coventry's the soft option." Mo found the butt of his Monteverdi. Contemptuously he stuck it into his mouth. "You want chocs, the bishop, we should go to York. It's the obvious place. They always make the highest bids on this stuff."

"Stuff?" Bishop Beesley was outraged. "Is that any way to speak of such holy remains? The Church's motives, Mr. Collier, if not yours, are of the highest. Coventry is much closer. Moreover the bishop there is well-disposed towards us. Did you hear what the Bishop of York had to say. Idolatry, he says! Step into the 21st century, divine colleague, I say. But when all the dust settles, security is our chief concern. As I am sure it's yours. We should never forget that ours is above all a profoundly spiritual quest."

"Oh, for God's sake! Oh, Christ!"

Accidentally, Trixie had put her hand into Jerry's jerking crotch.

Jerry's lips gave an odd spasm. "Come again?"

ELEVEN

Prince Harry to Meet the Spice Girls

> Earlier, just outside London, the hearse had to stop before it joined the motorway so police could take away blooms from the windscreen. The flowers made a poignant mound on the hard shoulder. Once inside the Althorp estate Diana was laid to rest quietly and privately on an island set in a lake. Her day was over.
>
> —*News of the World*, September 7, 1997

There were now some forty armored cars, in various states of repair, and about a hundred mixed troops on rickshaws, mopeds, bicycles, motorbikes, invalid carriages and milkfloats. Fifteen horsemen wore the tattered uniforms of the Household Cavalry. They were spread out for almost thirty miles, with Jerry & Co. in the lead, creeping along the B604 (check) to relieve the besieged manor of Althorp. The radio message had described a good-sized army of combined Reformed Monarchists, Conservative Republicans, Stuarts, Tudors, Carolines, Guillomites, New Harovians and Original Royalists, all united in their apostasy, their perverse willingness to diss the Madonna Herself. Camping around the walls like old queens.

"You hard girls. It's a conspiracy, isn't it?" Shaky Mo passed Trixie's dusted reefer back to her. "I call you the Cuntry. You are the country, aren't you? You're running it, really. The old girl network. Your mum's their role model. Our madonna's their goddess. A monstrous constituency. A vast regiment!"

"Keep mum." Jerry giggled into his bag. "Keep it dark. Under your hat. Close to your face."

Baroness Brunner began to cackle again. It was high-pitched. Some kind of alarm. Her hideous old eyes glared vacantly into his. "It's all in the cards, lad. All in the tea-leaves. Cards and tea-leaves made up my entire cabinet for a while. That way I could control the future."

"Wonky." Jerry twitched again. "It's going all wonky."

"I warned the wonkers." The old baroness sighed. Her work was over. She had no more energy. "Where am I? Can I say wonkers? I told them it would go wonky. You can't say I was wrong." Independent of her words, her teeth began to clack slowly and rhythmically. She drew a scented silk cushion to her face. In vivid threads, the cushion bore the standing image of the Blessed Diana, with a magnificent halo radiating from around her blonde curls, her arms stretched as if to hug the world in love, flanked by choirs of celebratory angels. There was some sort of Latin inscription, evidently embroidered by an illiterate hand.

Jerry watched her breaking up. She was in worse shape than he was. She had spent far too much energy trying to get her predictions to come true. It made a shadow of you in no time. It had been the death of Mussolini and Hitler. That's what made most presidents and prime ministers old before their time. Memory was the first thing to go. Which was embarrassing when you couldn't remember which secrets to keep.

Jerry sighed. There wasn't a lot of doubt. Things were starting to wind down again.

He shivered and drew up the collar of his mossy black car coat.

TWELVE

Two Billion Broken Hearts

> We think Diana was killed through drunken driving . . . We think. I think. But we do not know. I do not know. Every newspaper and news organization, with the exception of the more excitable elements of the Arab media, has decided it was an easily explained crash. Lurid theories about her death abound on the Internet but that is the domain of students in anoraks—desperate like the fundamentalist Muslims, to pin something on the Satans of the Western security services and their imperialist masters. Yet people who read serious newspapers and watch serious television programmes still have their doubts. Perhaps in this uncertain world they need to find a perpetrator, they cannot accept that the most popular woman of her time was wiped out with her playboy lover in an ordinary car crash after a night at the Ritz.
>
> —Chris Blackhurst, *The Observer,* October 19, 1997

"Are you sure it's not a lookalike or a wannabe?" Sucking a purloined lolly, Trixie stared critically up at the slowly circling corpse. "And he could be pretending to be dead."

The swollen head, the eyes popping, the ears flaring, stared back at her as if in outrage at her scepticism. Oddly, the silver paper crown his executioners had placed on his head gave the Old Contender a touch of dignity.

"We're going to have to burn him." Major Nye came up with his clipboard. He was counting corpses. "Before his followers get hold of him. He's worth an army in that state." He paused to cast a contemplative and sympathetic eye over his former monarch. "Poor old boy. Poor old boy."

The rest of the besiegers were either dead, dying or sharing a common gibbet. By and large the century hadn't started well for the monarchists. It looked like the Dianistas were soon going to be in full control of the accounts.

"Good riddance, the foul, two-timing bastard." Mo had sat down comfortably in the grass with his back against the tree. He was cleaning his piece with a Q-tip. "First he betrays his wife, then his mother, then his lover. He makes Richard the Third seem like Saint Joan."

"He struck me as quite a decent, well-meaning sort of chap." Major Nye glanced mildly at his board.

"I don't think we want to hear any more of that sort of talk, do we, Major?" Trixie had the moral high ground well sorted.

"He gave her a lovely funeral," said Bishop Beesley. "That huge wreath on the hearse with 'MARM' picked out in her favorite flowers. It made the Krays seem cheap. A proper people's send-off."

"The man was a monster." Trixie firmly held her spin. "The Prince of Evil. The Demon King. That's all you need to remember."

"But what of the Web?" Una came walking through with a scalp-pole she had liberated from the Shire Protection Association. "Can you control that, too?"

"Like a spider." Trixie's words were set in saliva. She tasted her own bile as if it were wine.

In a moment they would achieve the culmination of all she had ever dreamed.

"They're getting a raft ready to go to the island," said Una. "I knew you'd want to be there at the moment they dug her up."

Trixie quivered. "You realize this will give us power over the whole fucking world, don't you?"

"It goes round and round." Una put her scalps into Jerry's willing right hand. "Hold on to those for a bit. And come with me."

They stumbled over the ruins of the manor, over the remains of tents and makeshift defenses. Crows were coming down in waves. Parts of the battlefield were thick with heaving black feathers. It had been impossible in the end to save either the attackers or the defenders. But the island, by general consent, had not been badly shelled.

They arrived at the lakeside. A raft of logs and oil-cans was ready for them.

"Good lord." Bishop Beesley gestured with a distasteful Crunchy. "That water's filthy. Thank heavens we don't have to swim across. There's all kinds of horrors down there. What do people do? Sacrifice animals?"

"It's our duty to take her out of all this." Mo picked up a long pole and frowned.

"Clearly the family no longer has the resources." Stepping onto the swaying boards, Trixie Brunner assumed that familiar air of pious concern. "So we must shoulder the burden now. Until we can get her into safe hands."

"You're still sending her to Coventry."

"That's all changed." Bishop Beesley chuckled at his own misunderstanding. "I thought it was the Godiva headquarters. She almost went to Brussels. But we've had a lovely offer from Liverpool."

"Which we're not going to take." Trixie's sniff seemed to make him shrink. "Ten times her boxed weight in generic licorice allsorts? That's pathetic! You're thinking too parochially, bishop. Don't you realize we have a world market here?"

"She's right." Una began to pole them out over the water. "America. Russia. China. Wherever there's money. And the Saudis would buy her for other reasons. It's a seller's market."

"Russell Stover. Hershey's." Convinced, the bishop had begun to make a list. "Pierrot Gormand. My Honeys Tastes a Lot of Lickeys." Thoughtfully he popped the last of his Uncle Ben's Mint Balls into his mouth. "Sarah Lee. Knotts Berry Farm. Smuckers. America. Land of Sugar. Land of Honey. Land of Sweetness. Land of Money." His sigh was vast and anticipated contentment.

"Syrup?"

THIRTEEN

We'll Win World Cup For Diana

> . . . The Royal Family often seem to behave in ways which could actually be called unpatriotic, and their denial of Diana, the world's sweetheart, was the biggest betrayal of all. But then, what can you expect from a bunch of Greeks and Germans . . .
>
> Her brave, bright, brash life will forever cast a giant shadow over the sickly bunch of bullies who call themselves our ruling house. We'll always remember her, coming home for the last time to us, free at last—the People's Princess, not the Windsors'.
>
> . . . We'll never forget her. And neither will they.
>
> —Julie Burchill, *News of the World*, September 7, 1997

"We might have guessed the yellow press would be here first." Trixie had the air of one who was glad she had anticipated the right make-up for an unexpected situation.

She glared furiously down into the empty grave.

"Who are you calling yellow?" Frank Cornelius brushed dark earth from his cords. "Anyway, I wasn't here first, obviously." His features had a blighted look, as if he had suffered severely from greenfly.

"But you know who was, don't you?" Una Persson poked impatiently at him with her long-barrelled Navy Colt. She had chosen it because the brass and cherrywood went best with her coat but it was a bugger to load. "That earth's still fresh. And the coffin looks recently opened."

Bishop Beesley was shattered. He sat on the edge of the empty grave licking the wrapping of his last Rollo.

"This is sacrilege." Mo paced about and gestured. "I mean it's inconceivable."

As usual at times like these, Jerry had risen to the occasion.

"I think we're going to have to torture you for a bit," he told his brother. "To get the information we need."

"That won't be necessary, Jer'." Frank's smile was unsure.

"Yes it will," said Jerry.

"It was all legit." Frank spoke rapidly. "The upkeep of the site was tremendously draining, as you can imagine. After the old earl went down outside South Africa House at the battle of Trafalgar Square, there was a bit of a hiatus. The surviving family has responsibilities to its living members, after all. They brought a copter down while you were shelling the house. She'll be in Switzerland in an hour or two. Procter and Gamble have acquired the cloning rights. This is democracy in action. Think of it—soon, anyone who can afford one gets one! Charities will snap them up. Live! Oh, Jerry, this is what we've dreamed of! Of course, she doesn't actually belong to the people any more. She's a corporate property. It's Princess Diana™ from now on. A dually-controlled subsidiary, People's Princess (Kiev) PLC, own all the copyrights and stuff. But there'll be more than enough of her to go round. Charity gets a percentage of those rights, too. PP are a company with compassion. Their chairman's a notorious wet."

"I wish you'd tell us all this after we've tortured you," said Jerry.

Frank sank to his knees.

"Sorry," he said.

"*You're* fucking sorry." Mo unhitched his big shooter, unsnapping the safeties, going to Narrow Ribbon Fire and pulling the trigger in one fluid, chattering movement which cut Frank's head from its body. It bounced into the grave and rested in the desecrated mud looking up at them with mildly disappointed eyes. A groan came out of the torso as it slumped onto the stone. Blood soaked the granite.

"Loose cannon." Mo seemed to be apologizing.

Jerry was getting pissed off. He rounded on Trixiebell. "I told you this was strictly cash. I should have got it from you up front. And now this little bastard's robbed me of my one consolation."

But Trixie had been thinking.

"Wait here. Come with me, Mo."

She began to tramp through the mud towards their raft. She boarded it and Mo poled his way to the shore.

While Una Persson did something with the grave, Jerry squatted and watched the Hon. Trixie.

She and Mo walked up the shore to where they had parked their Ford Flamefang.

Una came to stand beside Jerry and she too studied Trixie and Mo, watched as they dragged old Baroness B. from the cab. Trixie's mother made peculiar stabbing motions at the air, but otherwise did not resist. Her teeth were half out of her mouth and her wig was askew but the worst was the noise which came from her mouth, that grating whine which people would do anything to stop. In her heyday, men and women of honor had agreed to appalling compromises just so that they might not hear her utter that sound again.

Even after Trixie had stuffed her mother's moth-eaten wig into the rattling mouth, the old girl kept it up all the way back to the island.

Jerry was beginning to realize that his recovery was temporary. He reached for his purple bag and looked on while Trixie and the rest bundled the noisy old woman into the coffin and tacked the lid back on. There were some unpleasant scratching noises for a bit and then they knew peace at last.

"It's a pity we didn't keep one of those gun carriages." Mo was polishing the top.

"They won't know the difference in Coventry." Trixie pushed Jerry towards their car. "Check the raft. Have a root around. We'll need all the bungee cords we can get for this one. Once we get to the car, she'll have to go on the roof."

"I'm not sure of the wisdom of deceiving the Church." Bishop Beesley fingered himself in unusual places. "Where does devotion end and sacrilege begin?"

"Don't be ridiculous." Trixie started to haul the coffin back through the mud towards the waiting raft. At the waterside Jerry and Una took it over from her.

She paused, catching her breath. "Nobody can go further than the great British public. Besides, mum's an authentic relic in her own right. Surely she's well worth a lorryfull of Smarties? It'll be the muscle we need to get us out of trouble. And if she's still alive when they open the box, they've got an authentic miracle. Who loses? A deal's a deal, vicar. Any port in a storm. Isn't modern life all about responding appropriately to swiftly changing situations? And isn't the Church all about modern life?"

"Besides," Mo gestured in the direction of the real world, "we haven't got much choice. We're going to have to buy petrol."

"Well," said the bishop, "we'd better not tell the men."

"We'll divvy up after Coventry, say."

This began a fresh round of intense bargaining.

"There is another alternative . . . " Nobody was listening to Mo. He shrugged and stepped down towards the raft.

"But I understood I would receive part of my share in confectionery." Bishop Beesley was close to panic.

At a signal from Una, Jerry helped Mo aboard, then loosed the mooring rope. He and Mo began to pole rhythmically through the detritus towards the bank.

It was some minutes before Trixie and Bishop noticed what was happening and by then Mo and Una were loading the coffin onto the roof while Jerry got the Ford's engine going.

"Now Church and State will have time to establish a deeper and more meaningful relationship," Una opened her *Diana of the Crossways* and began comparing it to her charts. "Someone has to preside over the last rites of that unsatisfactory century."

After his brief flurry of energy, Jerry was winding down again. "It suited me."

Major Nye's face appeared at the window-slit. He was puffing a little. "Hope you don't mean to leave me behind, old boy."

"Can't afford to, major." Una's spirits were lifting. "We need you to drive. Climb aboard."

As Major Nye's legs swung in, Jerry shifted to let the old man get into the seat. The others settled where they could. The cab had not been cleaned and the smell of vomit was atrocious. From overhead on the roof there came a faint, rhythmic thumping which was drowned as Major Nye put the car into gear and Mo took his place in the gunnery saddle.

Their followers limping behind, they set off towards Coventry, singing patriotic songs and celebrating the anticipated resolution.

"All in all," Jerry sank back onto his sacks and rolled himself a punishing reefer, "it's been a tasty episode. But it won't go down too well in the provinces. I'm beginning to believe this has been a poor career move. Market forces abhor the unique."

What would I know? I say. What would I know? I am dead and a friend of the dead.

We get no respect these days.

The Camus Referendum

WAHAB

Farther Down The Line

> All of a sudden, then, I found myself brought up short with some though not a great deal of time available to survey a life whose eccentricities I had accepted like so may facts of nature. Once again I recognized that Conrad had been there before me . . . I was born in Jerusalem and had spent most of my formative years there and, after 1948, when my entire family became refugees, in Egypt.
>
> —Edward Said, *London Review of Books*, May 7, 1998

Jerry took the July train out of Casablanca, heading East. There was a cold wind blowing. It threatened to pursue them to Cairo.

"It's like you've been telling them for years." He was leafing through *Al Misra*, thinking it could do with a few pictures. "They're academics and politicians mostly, debating whether or not flight is possible or if it is whether they should allow it, and everywhere above them the sky is full of ships." He frowned. "Is that a quote? If we're living on the edge of the abyss, Mrs. B., I think we should make the best we can of it. Love conquers all. A bit of vision and we'd all be more comfortable."

"I have had visions since I was a child." With prissy, habitual movements Miss Brunner arranged her *hadura*. She was calling herself General Hazmin but her old, green fundamentalist eyes still winked above her yashmak. Her accompanist, Jerry's current lover, snored lightly in the corner chair while the gray, flat roofs of Casablanca began to flash past faster and faster. "Originally of the Prophet, but later of ordinary people from history, or people I did not recognize, at least. I always felt very close to God."

"Me, too." Jerry settled himself into his deep chair as the train torqued up to sound minus ten. "With me, of course, it was Jesus. Then the middle ages, mostly. Then the nineteenth century. Now we're somewhere between the end of one millennium and the beginning of another. The blank page between the Old Testament and the New. I had no idea what it was all about. These days I just see things in shop windows. They always turn out to be something ordinary when I examine them. Maybe it was the dope in the sixties? They sell you any old muck now." He patted his heavy suitcase.

"This is the age of the lowest common denominator. I blame America."

"Don't we all?" She stared vacantly at the blurred landscape. "A ram without a brain, a ewe without a heart."

He blushed. "Impossible!"

She looked into the whispering corridor. "Flight is so unfashionable, these days."

DOS

American Tune

> His life was dedicated to the United Kingdom, and he always spoke for all the people of this fair land. Enoch warned us about Europe, about excessive immigration, and he reminded us of our heritage and history. If only we had all listened . . .
>
> —Stuart Millson,
> *This England*, Summer 1998

"A mature democracy is surely a democracy which orders its affairs by public debate and reasoned agreement. An immature democracy is one where affairs are settled by conflict, by adverserial court cases, authoritarian laws resisted by civil liberties groups. Didn't America lead the way in this appalling devolution? Why would any democracy want to repeat that mistake?" Prinz Lobkowitz looked at his dusty drawers and coughed as if embarrassed.

"Immature or corrupted, the body counts are the same. They were almost up to the 100,000 target last year. It's a big market, Major. A lot of citizens. A lot of good gun sales. All I need is for you to give me the slip." Jerry took dust from his eyes with a fingertip, glaring at the disturbing fan above. "And if you could spare a little something for the journey . . ."

"Of course." Lobkowitz found his documents. "Ugh!"

"That was probably me." Shaky Mo Collier spoke from the shadows where he had been posing with his new ordnance. Lazily he flipped and zipped. "You had marmite or something in there. I thought it was resin or ope but I couldn't get the lid off without using my knife. Sorry. You'd know if I was *trying* to make a mess."

"Thanks." With insane deliberation Lobkowitz began to whistle "Dixie."

DREI

Valentine

I dreamed I was in England
And heard the cuckoo call,
And watched an English summer
From spring to latest fall,
And understod it all.

—Enoch Powell, *The Collected Poems of Enoch Powell*

"The land of cotton." Major Nye took Una her gin sling. She was hypnotized by the waters of the Nile white against the steel gray rocks. "The river runs a merrier course nearer to her source than her destination. What?" He sat down in the other chair as she turned, uncrossing her legs. She wore Bluefish, longing for authenticity in pastel luxury. And elegant beyond understanding, he thought. She was unassailably beautiful these days. They sat at their old table on the terrace of the elegantly-guarded Cataract Hilton. Fundamentalists had made tourism a luxury again. It was wonderful. Indeed the fundamentalists were very popular in America now because they had successfully prepared for Western business and attendant human rights legislation by reducing their national economies to zero and attracting the benign authority of the democratic corporations.

Una and the Major were surveying neighboring Elephant Island for an EthicCorp™ which had already done miracles in Egypt. And everyone admitted *DisneyTime*™ had turned Alexandria into the thrusting modern metropolis it was today. They had even removed the original city to the Sinai between *Coca Cola*™ University and *Sinbad's Arabian Fantasy*™, in a successful effort to improve trade, tourism and education in the region. Who could complain? In *LibraryWorld*™ the scrolls could almost be real.

"Of course." Una concentrated on a pleat. She shook her skirt again. "We are making a rod for our own backs, major. Or, at least, putting all this tranquility in jeopardy."

"It's share and share alike nowadays, Mrs. P.," Major Nye

tipped his cap towards the river. "We all have to take a little less. Like the War, what?"

"What war?"

"Last one. Big one. What?" He frowned. "Are you joking, Mrs. P. Or are you in trouble?"

She reassured him. "Just a joke, Major. In poor taste."

"I know exactly what you mean." He offered her a bowl of cherroids. "These are dreadful."

ARBA

Heartland

> "If two quarrel, the Briton rejoices," has long been a proverb. In the course of centuries but few had seriously endeavored to catch the measure of Mephistopheles, and none had succeeded. The wilder the turmoil in Europe, the more might England rejoice, for countries that had got their heads battered were afterwards easily the most docile."
>
> —*Hindenburg's March On London*, Germany, 1913, Eng., Trs, 1916

"Okay, Mr. C., so you never caught *The Desert Rats*. Then rely on me like an old-fashioned officer and I will get us through, okay? There isn't a World War Two movie I haven't seen at least twice and I've always been very fond of a wasteland." Mo's voice was muffled by his respirator, a black and belligerent snout. "Here we go!"

The half-track's caterpillars whistled impotently over the sand. Another shell made a neat, noisy crater only a few yards away. They wiped at their goggles with dirty gloves.

"Libyan." Sniffing, Shaky Mo paused in his busy handling of the gears and gunning of the engine. "You can always tell."

"But we're so far from the border." Bishop Beesley's camouflaged miter oozed from the conning tower. "And a long way from the Basra Road."

"Never very far, Bishop." Shaky Mo did something angry to the machinery and it lurched upwards, back onto the blitzed concrete of the road. "Not these days. Not ever."

PYAT

Across the Borderline

> Then in the year 1870 something quite unheard of happened. About that time there all at once appeared in Europe in the foreground a youth in the fullness of his strength—young Germany! He was a sprig of the good, stupid old-German Michael, who had fared especially badly owing to his horizon bounded by the church tower, and his secluded mode of living. Michael had to sit very far behind in the European State class, and during the last five hundred years he was always several decades behind the others. Young Michael, however, the fair-haired, blue-eyed fellow, was of a different mold! To the schoolmistress on the other side of the Channel he looked a very slippery fish!
>
> —*Hindenburg's March on London.*

They've been chopping up children, mostly, as far as I can tell." General Hazmin had removed her yashmak and now wore a massive gas mask, designed to resist the most fashionable mixtures. It gave her the appearance of a Hindu goddess. She moved ponderously through the village. Every so often, when Jerry slowed down, she gave the rope a tug. He had begun to enjoy the sensation. His giggling grew louder as she dragged him, for a moment, through the gobs of bloody flesh. "Oh, Christ!" He shook. "So cold. Oh, fuck." General Hazmin was discovering the frustrations of trying to punish a creature which had either experienced everything or was grateful to experience anything. "You are no longer human, Captain Cornelius."

He shrugged. "I never was. Was I?"

"We are all born human."

"Somewhere back on the clone line, sure. It's the type, though, that's important, isn't it. Cromagnon, I mean, or Neanderthaal. We should never have got mixed up. It's not their faults." He had a mood swing. He had begun to weep over the remains of a little girl whose throat had been slit and whose mother's hands had been cut off before she, too, had been killed. "Their brains can't make the connections most of us make. They look human. But they're not quite. Thirty percent of the population, at least? Genetics are so important these days, aren't they?"

Una Persson had taken the rope from General Hazmin's gloved hands. She swung her lovely hair as she looked back at him. "So which are you, Jerry, love?"

"Bingo bango bongo, I should never have left the Congo." Jerry sometimes wished he hadn't abused his homo superior status so frequently and so self-indulgently. "I used to be the world's first all-purpose human being. I was really happy in the jungle. Just like Derry and Toms. A new model of the multiverse. But it all turned back to shit. Africa should have negotiated new borders for herself. That's where the trouble began. I should know. I started it."

"Yes, right. You and bloody Sisyphus. " Una exchanged some enjoyable glances with General Hazmin. "What shall we do with him this time?"

SIX

She's Not For You

> "Successive generations of our politicians have failed, or in some cases actively betrayed, their country's interests. Now only the ordinary people can hope to reverse the tide of bureaucracy and centralized control which is already engulfing every participating nation in Europe. Are there enough people who care or dare to do something about it? Or is *Land of Hope and Glory* finally to be replaced by *Deutchshland Uber Alles*?"
>
> —Letter, *This England*, Summer 1998

"I'd like to stop off in Algiers as soon as possible." Una had slung Jerry over her best pack camel. He rubbed his face on the animal's hide. He moaned with tiny pleasures. "I had a wire from my agent. We're doing a revival of *The Desert Song* in Marrakesh next month. I promised them I'd get you to sing."

"Blue heaven and you," croaked Jerry as he bounced. "One alone. We are the Red Shadow's men. One for all and all for one. Or is all one, anyway? One or the Other? Never more than two?

I can't believe in a simple duality. The evidence is all against it. Once a clone . . . Clone away, young multiverse. Clone away. Oops. Oh! Oh! Yes! Watch it, Stalin. The cells are out of control."

"Damn!" By accident she had struck him full across the buttocks with her camel whip. She took some rags and a bowl from the saddle-bags and tried to save the fizzing, strangely-colored sperm running down the animal's flanks.

This amused him even more.

SEBT

What Was It You Wanted?

> Sir: I have recently returned from a business trip to the Arabian gulf and was immediately struck by the presence there of a British export which is rarely found anywhere else in the world. Why is it that when we travel several thousand miles to somewhere as alien to us as Bahrain or Dubai we can still buy a pint of good English bitter, yet those closer to us (geographically and poltically) never stock anything but lager and pilsener? One could tread the pavements of French towns for hours and never find even a smell of anything like traditional English Ale."
>
> —Letter, *This England.*

"Imperialism breeds nationalism and nationalism needs guns. America supplies both, just like ICI and Dupont make bullets and bandages. It's the trick the rubber trade learned early on. Condoms or rubber knickers. There's always a market."

Una signed the form and handed over the remains. From his tank Jerry opened and closed his mouth. Tubes ran from all his other orifices. "What?"

"You'll be fine," she said.

The whole tribe surrounded him now. They seemed proud of their bargain. Discreetly, they pointed out the peculiarities of his anatomy. He was enjoying an unfamiliar respect.

"It is beautiful," said one of the young women. Like the other Berbers, she wore no veil. Her aquiline features were striking.

Her green eyes were exceptional. “Some kind of cuttlefish?”

Una shook her head.

“Not nearly so interesting. Or intelligent. It’s the light. See?”

OCHO

Getting Over You

> “I had allowed the disparity between my acquired identity and the culture into which I was born, and from which I had been removed, to become too great. In other words, there was an existential as well as a felt political need to bring one self into harmony with the other . . . By the mid-seventies I was in the rich but unenviable position of speaking for two diametrically opposed constituencies, one Western, the other Arab.”
>
> —Edward Said, *Between Worlds.*

“You were monumental in Memphis.” Shaky Mo was trying to cheer his exhausted chum. “What a tom, Jerry. What a comeback!”

“Too many.” Jerry smiled sweetly into his restored reflection. “Too much.”

Mo wasn’t really listening. With a thumbnail, he scraped at a bit of hardened blood on his barrel. “It was a shame about Graceland. Could have been a crack. But nobody’s got any money, these days. It had to go to a private buyer. Nothing like the smell of an old Vienna.”

“Land of Song.” Jerry slipped a comb through his locks. “Land of Smiles. Where there’s a drug there’s a way. Millions will pay through the nose to visit that historic toilet.”

Mo put his gun down and carefully got out his maps. “Now all we have to do is find a drum.”

“Boom, boom,” said Jerry.

“I meant a gaff.” Mo folded the filthy linen. “Sometimes I wonder about you.”

ENIA

The Most Unoriginal Sin

Q: Your paper talks about the balkanization of American society and the imminent train wreck we're facing. Any suggestions on what readers can do to help turn this around?
A: I urge your readers to become very aggressive in fighting for the enforcement of the nation's civil rights laws . . . The civil rights laws passed in the 1960s are, for the most part, not enforced or are weakly enforced. A white man like me can pretty well discriminate against Americans of color every day of the week—in housing, employment, public accommodations, schools—with no fear of being punished under the civil rights laws. For example, it's estimated there are four to eight million cases of racial discrimination in housing each year, and yet very few whites are ever punished, even mildly, for this massive discrimination . . .

—Joe Feagin, *Southern Poverty Law Center Report*, June 1998.

We don't have to worry about the Europeans. All the British and the French are waiting for is American leadership.

—Bob Dole to Congress, 1995.

The American general had all the flaky wariness of his kind. He wasn't used to being in this position. Nobody spoke his language. He made complicated, aggressive movements with his cigar to show he was on top of things. His inexperienced lips trembled with frustration. His boy's eyes shifted uncontrollably, sensing the necessity of self-reliance but having no appropriate training, only the rhetoric. The Chlue were as mystified by him as the Sioux by Custer. But, like the Sioux, they had no problems with the idea of genocide. They had some sense of what his rituals meant and were wary of them. Perhaps they recognized the traditional American warm-up to a necessary action. When sentimental speeches failed, there was only the rocket.

The black tents were pitched all along the shallow valley. Sweat and animal dung, cooking fires, tajini, kous-kous. A noise of goats and ululating women. Horses. Metal. A subtle, pervading odor of cordite, a faint, blue haze of rifle-smoke. In the distance were the banners of the Rif and the Braber. All the Berber clans were assembling. Only Cornelius could have brought them here. He was one of themselves. Their cause was his. They asked little more than freedom to roam.

The general settled his plump bottom onto the director's chair which he had brought with him. Everyone else sat on carpets.

"Tell these bastards that they're Berber-Americans now. They can vote. We've given them several choices."

In Arabic, which all the Berber tribes could understand, Jerry said:

"You have no choice. If you do not sell him your villages, he will have you all killed by fundamentalists."

This made sense. Sheikh Tarak, their spokesman, gave it some thought.

"Tell them about human rights." The general was impatient. "War crimes."

"He will then kill the fundamentalists. So all but him and his corporation will perish."

"You will not perish, dear friend." Tarak's old eyes remained amused. "We'll sell him the villages. After all, it's only fifty years or so since our noble grandfathers wiped out the bastards who used to own them."

"They'll sell." Jerry turned to the general. "But they want a royalty."

"Royalty. Fucking royalty? Don't they know we've abolished all that in America." He began to roll up his plans. "This is going to be an eco-complex, not a fucking casino."

"They say there's no royalty on egoes." Jerry responded to Tarak's inquiring eye.

"Good!" The handsome old sheikh understood perfectly. "Let them build their hotels. Then we will come back upon a great *harka*. And lay waste to everything. Thus it begins again."

"He's prepared to negotiate a lease," Jerry told the general.

TISA

Don't Give Up

> Our passion for a city is often a secret one. Ancient, walled cities like Paris or Prague, or even Florence, are introspective, closed, their horizons limited. But Algiers, in common with a few other ports, is as open to the sky as an eager mouth, an unprotected wound. Algiers gives you an enthusiasm for the commonplace: how blue sea ends every street, the peculiar density of the light, the beauty of the people. And, inevitably, amidst all this unprotected generosity, you scent a seductive, secret ambience. You can be homesick in Paris for breathing space and the whisper of wings. In Algiers, at least, you can sample any desire and be certain of your pleasures, your self, and so know at last what everything you own is worth.
>
> —Albert Camus, *Algerian Summer*

In Marrakesh Jerry sat back at his cafe table and watched the German tourists boarding the evacuation buses taking them to their planes and trains. The Djema al Fnaa, the great Square of the Dead, had lost none of its verve. In fact, since the departure of the Germans a rather gay, lively quality had returned to the city. The storytellers were already drawing large crowds as they described the Rif's decision to drive the infidels from their territory. "There is a tendency to play to the lowest common denominator, even here." Prince Lobkowitz leaned to freshen Una Persson's cup. "Sugar?"

Mo Collier was bored brainless. He had set his vibragun on its lowest notch and was giving his back a massage. "You got to admit, Prince L., that they do a nice coffee. The krauts. I've never found this Turkish stuff much cop, even when you call it Greek stuff. Or Moroccan stuff. But your German, now, given half a chance, knows his Columbia from his Java and can brew a bean with the best. If only the rest of Fritz's food was edible, they could have become a nation of restauranteurs and we'd all like them now. They always meant well. But they shouldn've brushed up on the old cuisine and not tried for the macho image. It doesn't suit them. It makes them even more ridiculous than most. They should have gone on laughing at the Prussians. Talk about the lowest CD of all, eh?"

"Bismarck was a great leveller," Prince Lobkowtiz agreed. "And so was Hitler, for that matter. An odd record, really, for so benign a race. They just want to bring the best they have to everyone else."

The tourists were squeezing themselves through the double-wide doors as hard as they could. There were no street boys on hand to push them in. Their proferred francs and marks lay on the ground where they had been thrown back by the crowd. The Rif had made examples of surrounding villas owned by German infidels. The Marekshis were in a jolly mood. The Germans had no power now. Their marks were a bad memory. Some of the Berbers had brought food and video-cameras and were filming the sweating Teutons, in their damp, grubby whites, as they silently embarked.

Una eyed the swollen bottoms with some interest. "Do you think they're growing into Americans?" she asked. "Or are Americans descended from them?"

"Hard to tell. What an aggressive gene, eh? The Germans used to think of themselves as undeveloped Englishmen. They had that in common with the Americans. Now, of course, they need no models. They are all king-size. They have their wealth instead."

"Some day." Mo was in a visionary mood. "People will hunt them. Not much sport, though."

"German?" Major Nye parted his lips in a silent laugh. His pale blue eyes were almost lively. "I thought they were all Scotch. You know—MacDonalds, Campbells, Murdochs. Those chaps own everything. The most aggressive people on earth. Devolution was the best idea the English ever had. Now, with nobody else to blame, the Scotch and the Irish can go back to fighting each other. We can just hope they won't start marching on London again. They drink too much. And then they decide to claim our throne. Those sectarian battles never cease. They're a tradition." The old soldier savored the delicate mint. "Because a few purse-mouthed Yankee scrooges refused to pay for the army that had protected their backsides, borrowed a couple of old English political principles, such as no taxation without representation, to offer a moral reason for welshing on their bills, their descendants now continue to give high-sounding reasons for not coughing up their fair share and see the 'Celts' (actually mostly Danes) as fellow sufferers under the British heel. How long did this suffering last? The peculiar thing is that it's the most aggressive Americans—low Protestants, Scottish Rites Lodge, Orange Lodge—who swallowed the myth. The very people who would have been fighting the Catholics just as their Scotch-Irish cousins do now. Have you noticed, by the by, that all the soldiers in the regiments which massacred the Indians had Irish names? Their Indians, I mean. Not Kipling Indians. Though come to think of it . . ."

As the muezzin began his electronic call from the Booksellers' Mosque, Una Persson bowed her head over her black cup. "That's progress for you."

"And Heinz," said Mo. "And Sarah Lee."

"What?" Jerry was distracted. He murmured the responses.

"General Foods." Mo seemed to offer this as an explanation.

They allowed him a moment's time for himself.

"Nestlés," he added.

"Mo?" said Jerry.

"I thought we were doing one of those guessing games. The seven most powerful food corps. Like the names of the seven dwarves. What's that?" Mo's ear ticked.

"Six," said Jerry. "Unless Private Murdoch doesn't count."

"It's like adding a Greedy. Seems there should be one. But there isn't. OK, no junk media. How about Pepsi?"

"Drinks mostly. And burger chains."

"That's food, too, though. Same with Coke."

"We should stick to—you know—general foods. Basics."

"Are we counting services?"

"No."

"Then you cut out MacDonalds."

"Okay. Three."

"Right," said Mo, narrowing his eyes. "Let's think of the rest."

The last prayer called, the square was filling with its evening population. A wash of deep scarlet and glittering gold raced out of the shadows of the surrounding market stalls—the acrobats had arrived. The fire-eaters and snake-charmers and conjurors called their audiences to them. Fortune tellers were busy with their cards and bones. A squeal of flutes. A mumbling of drums. Dark shapes moved boldly around the parameter and the Pakistani fakir, originally an engineer kicked out of Saudi, lowered himself onto hot coals.

There was a smell of roasting mutton, of chestnuts, of jasmine and warm wax.

Una sighed at the texture of it. Her relaxed fingers traced eccentric geometries over the china. She folded down the collar of her black car coat and unbuttoned. Her chest foamed, white flecked with red. It was her linen, no longer constrained. She hadn't had time to change. She had come straight from the theatre with Jerry. She reached to caress his cooling hand. She had no fear that she was setting a precedent. If it didn't exist now, it wouldn't exist.

She stroked his rapidly growing nails. Entropy and the Absurd. You had to love it.

Jerry raised his head. He smiled. He purred. A jaguar. "My brain's changed."

Major Nye beamed upon the crowd. He had not looked so dapper since the last time he was here, with Churchill, in '44. The prayer having ended, he returned his cap to his head.

"What a blessing religion can be."

Thanks to Willie Nelson and Across the Borderline

Cheering for the Rockets

ONE

Noon

"There is this same anti-semitism in America. I hear the swirl and mutter of it around me in restaurants, at clubs, on the beach, in Washington, in New York, and here at home. No basis exists for the statements that accompany it. 'The Jews,' people say, own the radio, the movies, the theaters, the publishing companies, the newspapers, the clothing business, and the banks. They are just one big family, banded together against the rest of humanity, and they are getting control of the media of articulation so that they can control us. They have depraved every art form. They are doing it simply to break down our

moral character and make us easy to enslave. Either we will have to destroy them, or they will ruin us."
—Philip Wylie, *Generation of Vipers*, New York, 1942.

"Let a Jew into your home and for a month you will have bad luck."
—Moroccan proverb

"Let an American into your home and soon he will own your family."
—Lebanese proverb

"We call them 'sand niggers.'"
—Coca Cola senior executive in private conversation

"A nation without shame is an immoral nation."
—Lobkowitz, *Beyond the Dream*, Prague, 1937.

"They appear to have broken another treaty." Jerry Cornelius frowned and removed something like a web from his smart black coat. Slipping his Thinkman™ into his breast pocket he fingered his heat. His nostrils burned. There was a wired, cokey sort of feel to the atmosphere. Probably only gas.

"Pardon?" Trixiebell Brunner, dressed to kill with a tasteful UN armband, was casting about in the dust for something familiar. "So fill me in on this one. Who started it?"

"They did, naturally." The UN representative was anxious to get the interview over. They had staked him into the ash by way of encouragement and the desert sun was now shining full on his face. His tunic flashes said he was General Thorvald Fors. The Pentagon had changed his name to something Scandinavian as soon as he got the UN appointment. It sounded more trustworthy. He had already explained to them how he was really Vince Paolozzi, an Italian from Brooklyn and cursed with a mother who preferred his cousin to him. His familiar family reminiscences, his litanies of favorite foods, the status of his family's ethnicicity, his connections with the ultra-famous, his mafiosities, the whole pizza opera, had finally got on their nerves and for a while they had given him a shot of novocaine in the vocal chords. But now they were exhausting the miscellaneous Sudanese pharmaceuticals they'd grabbed at random on their way through

Omdurman. The labels were pretty much of a mystery. Jerry's Arabic didn't run to over-the-counter drugs.

"I see you decided to settle out of court." Jerry stared at the general, trying to recognize him. There was a memory. A yearning. Gone. "Are you on our side?"

"What we say in public isn't always what we mean in private?" The general's display of caps seemed to be an appeal.

"A legalistic rather than a lawful country, wouldn't you say? That's the problem with constitutional law. Never has its feet on the ground."

Lobkowitz came to look down at the general. He was behaving so uncharacteristically that for a second Jerry was convinced the old diplomat would piss on Fors. The handsome soldier bureaucrat now resembled a kind of horizontal messiah.

The prince fingered his fly. "Nowadays, America's a white recently pubescent baptist festooned with an arsenal of sophisticated personal weaponry. Armed and ignorant. Don't cross him. Especially if you're a girl. Captain Cornelius, we're dealing with Geronimo here, not Ben Franklin. Geronimo understood genocide as political policy. He knew what was happening to him. Somehow inevitably that savage land triumphed over whatever was civilized in its inhabitants. They are its children at last." Prince Lobkowitz turned in the rubble to look out at the desert, where the Egyptian Sahara had been. His stocky fatigue-clad body was set in an attitude of hopeless challenge. His long gray hair rose and fell in the wind. His full mouth was rigid with despair. He was still mourning for his sons and his wife, left in Boston. For the dream of a lifetime. For peace. "Our mistake."

Jerry sniffed again at the populated air. "Is that cordite?" He touched his lips with his tongue. "Or chewing gum." He had pulled on a vast white gelabea, like a nightshirt, and a white cap. His skin had lost some of its flake. He wondered if he shouldn't have brought more power. He'd only come along for the debris.

"All that informal violence. Out of control. Reality always made yanks jumpy." Shaky Mo licked his M18's mechanisms, feeling for tiny faults. "They're good at avoiding it, of forgetting it. If it can't be romanticized or sentimentalized it's denied. Fighting virtual wars with real guns. That's why they export so much escapism. It's their main cash crop. That's why they've disneyfied the world. And why they're so welcome. Who wants to buy reality? Fantasy junkies get very aggressive when their junk is threatened. You all know that sententious American whine." He tasted again. He was hoping to identify the grade of his oil. He had become totally obsessed with maintenance.

"If I were Toney Blurr I would stick a big missile right up Boston's silly Irish bottom. Where the republican terrorists' paymasters live. Remind them who we are. Bang, bang. And it would make the protestants feel so much better. People in the region would understand. They admire that kind of decisive action. CNN-ready, as we say. Such a precise, well-calculated single, efficient strike would cut off the terrorist's bases and supplies and lose them credibility with their host nation. Bang. Bang. Bang."

Everyone ignored the baroness. Behind her yashmack her mad old eyes glared with the zealotry of a recent convert. Since her last encounter with Ronald Reagan she had become strangely introspective, constantly trying to rub the thick unpleasant stains from the sleeve of her business suit. Not that she had been herself since three o'clock or whenever it was. There was a lot to be said for the millennial crash. It had questioned the relevance and usefulness of linear time.

"Universal Alzheimer's," said Jerry. "Where?"

"Eh?" Lady B's wizened fingers roamed frantically over her ice-blue perm. "Would you say it was getting on for four?"

"Water . . . " General Fors moved pointlessly in his bonds, the stakes shifting in the ash, but holding. His uniform was in need of repair. His cheeky red white and blue UN flashes were offensive to eyes grown used to an overcast world. Even his blood seemed vulgar. His skin was too glossy. They hadn't been able to get his helmet off easily so Mo had spray-painted it matt black. General Fors was also mainly black. His face gleamed and cracked where the paint had already set. "Momma..."

"You're coming up with an unrealistic want list, pard." Jerry was the only one to feel sorry for him. "Anything more local and we'll happily oblige."

"Home . . . "

"You are home. You just don't recognize it." Mo's guffaw was embarrassing. "Home of the grave. Land of the fee. You discount everything you have that's valuable. You sell it for less than the traders paid for Manhattan. Now all that's left are guns and herds of overweight buffalo wallowing across a subcontinent of syrup. They don't hear the distant firing anymore. Or see the clouds of flies."

"Fries?" said General Fors.

Prinz Lobkowitz had now relieved himself. His hopeless eyes regarded the general. "You had a vital, successful trading nation reasonably aware of its cultural shortcomings. Which everyone liked. We liked your film stars. We liked your music. Your sentimental cartoon world. And then you had to take the next step and become an imperial power. Burden of empire. Malign by definition. Hated by all. Including yourselves. You're not a country any more, you're an extended episode of the X-Files."

"Missiles!" The general tried a challenge. His head rolled with the fear of it.

"All used up now, General. Remember? HQ filled them with poisoned sugar and wacoed them into your own system. The bitterness within. Double krauted. Flies? You think this is bad. You should see California." Babbling crazy, Mo appeared to take some personal pride in the decline.

"You told him this *was* California." Any hint of metaphor made Trixiebell uneasy and simile got her profoundly aggressive. "Is that fair?" She cleared her throat. She patted her chest.

"Lies . . . " said General Fors. His big brown eyes appealed blankly to heaven. The sun had long since disabled them.

"I call it retrospeculation." A goat bleated. Professor Hira came waving out of the nearest black tent. With their vehicles, the Berber camp was the only shelter in a thousand miles. The plucky little Brahmin had an arrangement with the sheikh. He was still wearing his winter djellabah. He had his uniform cap on at a jaunty angle. Behind him, above the dark folds of heavy felt, the tribe's cycling satellite dish forever interpreted the clouds. "Anyway. What does geography mean now?"

"Lies . . . "

"Too right. You dissed the whole fucking world, man. Then you ojayed it. But not forever. You were neither brave, free nor respectful. Once we couldn't use your engines what could you offer us except death?" Shaky Mo stepped in the general's lap, crossing to the useless desert cruiser and climbing slowly up the camouflage webbing to his usual perch on the forward gun tower. "Not that I approved of everyone leaving the UN."

"We are the UN," explained General Fors. "At least let me keep my Ferraris."

"Your mistake was to get up the Mahdi's nose, mate. A poor grasp of religion, you people. And what's worse, you have bad memories." Pulling down the general's shades, Mo set himself on snooze. Gently, his equipment fizzed and muttered, almost a lullaby. He swung slowly in his rigging. From his phones came the soothing pounding of Kingsize Taylor and the Dominoes.

To be fair, General Fors had got up all their noses. Leaving old Lady Brunner wandering about in the dried-up oasis, the rest of them moved into the desert leviathan's shade. They felt uneasy if they wandered too far from the huge land-ship Her Kirbyesque aesthetics were both comforting and stunning. But her function left something to be desired. *The General Gordon* had been breaking down ever since they'd fled Khartoum. The vehicle had been the best they could find. At a mile to the gallon it wasn't expensive to run. The world was full of free gas. From somewhere inside the ship their engineer, Colonel Pyat, could be heard banging and cursing at the groaning hydraulics and whispering cooling systems. Sometimes it was hard to tell the various sounds apart. The machine had its own language.

Jerry wondered at the sudden sensation in his groin. Was he pregnant?

He paused and looked up at the pulsing sky. At least they'd had the sense not to fly.

TWO

Non

Last winter, in the first precious weeks of war, our Senate used three of them to argue the moral turpitude of one member. That is as sad a sight as this democracy has seen this century.

—Philip Wylie, *Generation of Vipers*

We kept reporting to our officers that there were large number of Germans all around us, together with heavy transport and artillery, but the brass told us we were imagining things. There couldn't be Germans there. Intelligence hadn't reported any.

—survivor, The Battle of the Bulge

For some weeks after their arrival in Bosnia the Americans spent millions of dollars in a highly-publicized bridge building exercise. The whole time they were building it local people kept telling them there was an easy fording place about half a mile downriver. Intelligence had not reported it.

—survivor, Bosnia

You have to tell the White House and the Pentagon what they want to hear or they won't listen to you. That's how we got blamed for the Bay of Pigs after we'd warned against it.

—ex-CIA officer.

We Don't Dial 911
Commercial Texan home signboard painted on silhouette of a sixgun.

"Everything's perfectly simple." General Fors had rid himself of his various stigmata and had repainted his helmet a pleasing apple green. His attempts at Arabic lettering were a little primitive, but showed willing, even if his crescent looked like a sickle. "It's just you people who complicate everything. We were so comfortable."

They had made him security officer and put him near the revolving door. The hotel was deserted. Through the distant easterly windows guttered a wasteland of wrecked cars and abandoned flyovers, a browned world.

"Too many you know darkies." Jillian Burnes, the famous transexual novelist, was the only resident now. She was reluctant to leave. She had been here for six months, she said, and made a little nest for herself. She had come on a British Council trip and lost touch for a while. Her massive feet up on the Ark of the Covenant, she was peeling an orange. "This operation was aimed at thinning them out a bit."

"So far it seems to have firmed them up a bit." Jerry was helping the general buckle his various harnesses together. He dusted off his uniformed back. "All this red plush is a natural sand trap."

In the elegant lobby, its mirrors almost wholly intact, they had piled their booty in rough categories—domestic, religious, entertainment, military, electronic, arts—and were resting at the bar enjoying its uninvaded largesse. Even the sky was quiet now. The customers had all fled on the last plane. And the last plane had gone down in the rush. They could have been in New York or Washington. Had there still been a New York or Washington.

Giving the general a final brush, Jerry wondered why so much of Jerusalem was left.

The other British Council refugee was dwarfish Felix Martin, son of the famous farting novelist, Rex. A popular tennis columnist in his own right and virtual war face for the breakfast hit *Washington Toast,* Felix dabbed delicately at his dockers and looked tragically up at Trixiebell.

"Baby?" said Trix.

"Have you been over here before? Is that blood do you think?

THREE

None

> But, until man is willing to pay the cost of peace he will pay the price of war, and, since they must be precisely equal, I ask you to consider for how many more ages you think man will be striking balances with battles? . . . But recollect that, to have peace, congresses will be compelled to appropriate for others as generously as they do now for our armies, and the taxpayers will have to pay as willingly, and as many

heroes will have to dedicate their lives to the maintenance of tranquility as are now risking them to restore it.

—Philip Wylie, *Generation of Vipers.*

Man is still so far from considering himself as the author of war that he would hardly tolerate a vast paid, public propaganda designed to point out the infinite measure of his private dastardliness and he would still rather fight it out in blood than limit the profitable and vain activities of peace in order to study his personal conscience.

—Philip Wylie, ibid.

Once you get it (your market economy) in place, you'll take off like a rocket.

—Bill Clinton to the Russian Duma, September 1, 1998

"They must have felt wonderful, bringing the benefits of German culture to a world united under their benign flag." The three had strolled out to what was probably the Reichstag or possibly a cinema. The set, so spectacular in its day, had received one of the first strikes specifically aimed at Disney. Jerry picked up a fluffy dumbo.

"These aren't Germans." Trixiebell tucked everything back in. "These are Americans." She remassaged her hair.

"Did I say Americans? They loved the Nazis, too. I remember when I worked for Hearst in '38. Or was it CBS? Good old Putzi. A Harvard man, you know. Or Ford? Or Goebbels? Or '49? Uncle Walt admired the art-work and slogans, but he thought he could make the system function better over here. And they were, indeed, far more successful. Still, the patterns don't change."

"You have to take the jobs where you find them." Trixiebell, in sharp black and white, pouted her little mouth. In her day she had firmly enjoyed the ears, tongues and privates of cardinals and presidents. She was a prettier, modern and more aggressive version of her old mum, who had been bought by a passing trader.

"It's what the fourth estate is all about.

It's what the public says.

It's what we say.

I mean, this is what we say, right?" Felix was having some trouble getting his sentence going. He didn't like the look of Mo's elaborate ordnance. "Are those real guns?" His melancholy nose twitched nervously above prominent teeth, a glowering dormouse. Tough cotton shirt, serviceable chinos, jumper, jacket, all bearing the St. Michael brand. Marks guaranteed middle-class security. Lands End. Eddie Bauer. Oxfam gave him the shudders. He was strict about it. His life was nothing if not exclusive.

He withdrew into his clothing as if into a shelter. It was all he had left of his base.

"Oh bum. Oh piss. Oh shit.

Oh bum. Oh piss. Oh shit.

Oh bum."

"Hallelulla," said Jerry. He was beginning to feel his old self. "Or is that Hallelujah?"

"Bum again?" Trixiebell scented at the wind. "Was that Felix. Or you?"

"Childish bee. Where's the effin loo, lovey?" Jillian Burnes hefted her magnificent gypsy skirts and stepped lushly into the shaft of light coming through the roof. "Must be the Clapham Astoria." For years she had survived successfully on such delusions. "I used to be the manager here." She swung her borrowed mane. She fluttered her massive lashes. She smacked her surgical scarlet lips. "This is what comes of moving south of the river. What actually happened to the money?"

"Computers et it." Mo was admiring. He had found some more glue. "The Original Insect et it. Millennium insect. Ultimate bug. Munch munch. Bug et everything. Chomp. Chomp. Chomp. Et the time. Et the dosh. Et the info. Et the control. Et the entire lousy dream. The house of floss. It all went so quickly. Gobbled up our world and all its civilization and what do we have to show for it?"

"Some very picturesque ruins," she pointed out. "Heritage sites. Buy now while they're cheap. Especially here at *the center of our common civilization!* Imagine the *possibilities. Yes.* Yummy."

"Yum, yum, yum," said Jerry.

"Yummy. That's so right," said Trixie.

"Fuck all," said Mo. "I mean fuck off."

"How?" Jillian swung like a ship at anchor. Then she remembered who she was. She sighed, as if making steam, and continued her stately progress across the floor. Mo traipsed in her wake.

"Lies," said the general.

Jerry whacked at the old soldier's head with a sympathetic slapstick. "Those aren't lice. They're locusts."

FOUR

No

> To maintain our low degree of vigilance we had to adopt the airy notion either that nobody was preparing for war or else (since almost everybody was) that the coming war could not touch us. We necessarily chose the latter self-deception.
>
> —Philip Wylie, *Generation of Vipers*

> . . .The news out of Jonesboro, Ark., last week was a monstrous anomaly: a boundary had been crossed that should not have been. It was a violation terrible enough to warrant waking the President of the US at midnight on his visit to Africa, robbing him of sleep till daylight.
>
> —*Time*, April 6, 1998

> It is our goal to teach every school child in Texas to read.
>
> —*George W. Bush election commercial*

"Faid-bin-Antar" touched his cup to the samovar and his servant turned the silver tap. Amber tea fell into the bowl. Listening with delight to the sounds it made, the old sheikh seemed to read meaning into it. His delicate, aquiline face was full of controlled emotion. Behind the RayBans his eyes held a thousand agonies.

Brushing rapidly at his heavy sleeve, he stared through the tall ornamental window to his virtual garden where Felix Martin's head, its bushy brows shading uncertain eyes, continued to present his show. His body had been buried for twelve days. His ratings were enormous. The virtual fountain continued to pump. The antique electronics flickered and warped, mellow eccentricities. Sepia light washed over Jerry's body, giving it strange angles, unusual beauty. Jerry was flattered. He was surprised the generator had lasted this long.

"We who work so hard for peace are insulted by every act of aggression. When that aggression is committed by individuals, whatever cause they claim, we are outraged. But when that aggression is committed in the name of a lawful people, then we have cause to tremble and fear the apocalypse."

The sheikh sighed and looked carefully into Jerry's painted features. He turned his head, contemplating the dust.

"For fifty years I have struggled to bring understanding and equity to North and South. I have brought fanatics to the discussion table and turned them into diplomats. I have overseen peace agreements. I have written thousands of letters, articles, books. I have dissuaded many men from turning to the gun. And all that has been destroyed in a few outrageous moments. Making diplomats into fanatics. To satisfy some pervert's personal frustration with the United States and to make an impotent president and his overprivileged, under-informed constituency feel good for an already forgotten second. The very law they claim to represent is the law they flout at every opportunity." Sheikh Faid was still waiting for news of his daughters.

Jerry took a handful of pungent seeds and held them to his nose before putting them in his mouth. "They're trying."

But the sheikh was throwing a hand towards his glowing, empty screens. His voice rose to a familiar pitch.

"As if any action the Americans ever attempted didn't fail! They never listen to their own people. Those officials are all swagger and false claims. True bureaucrats. When will it dawn on them that they have lost all these phoney wars. When will they be gracious enough to admit failure? How can they believe that the methods which created disaster at home will somehow work abroad? They spread their social diseases with careless aggression. It's a measure of their removal from reality. There was a time, sadly, when the US people understood what a farce their representatives made of things. They used their power to improve the world." He beamed, reminiscent. For a heartbeat his eyes lost their pain.

"I used to enjoy those Whitehall farces when I was a student.

Do they still run them? Brian Rix's trousers fell as regularly as the sun set. Simpler satisfactions, I suppose."

"Failure," Jerry said. "They don't know the meaning of the word. Imperialism's no more rational than racism. That's why they fly so well together."

"Well, of course, you know all about imperialism. You'll enjoy this." With both hands the sheikh passed Jerry the intricate cup. "The English love Assam, eh? Now, what about these Americans?"

Jerry shrugged.

He reached beyond the carpet to run his gloved hand through the ash. It was fine as talc. You could powder a baby with it. "We're defined by our appetites and how we control them. They've made greed a virtue. What on earth possesses them?" He tasted and returned the glittering cup.

Folding his slender old fingers around the bowl's delicate ornament, Sheikh Faid savored his tea. He considered it. He scented at it.

Jerry wondered about watching a video.

After a while, Sheikh Faid began to giggle softly to himself. Behind him the endless gray desert rose and fell like an ocean. The wind cut it into complex arabesques, a constantly changing geometry. Sometimes it revealed the bones of the old mosque and the tourist center, but covered them again rapidly, as if disturbed by memories of a more comfortable past.

Soon Sheikh Faid was heaving with laughter. "There is no mystery to how those Teutons survive or why we fear them. It is a natural imperative. They migrate. They proliferate. Like any successful disease. It's taken them so little time. First they conquered Scandinavia, then Northern Europe and then the world. And they wonder why we fear them. That language! It reminds me of Zulu. It buzzes with aggressive intelligence. It cannot fail to conquer. What a weapon! Blood will out, it seems. Ah, me. It costs so much blood. The conquest of space."

As if remembering a question, he reached to touch Jerry's yielding knee. Signalling for more tea, he pointed to the blooming horizon.

"It is their manifest destiny."

Philip Wylie (1902–1971) wrote Gladiator *(1930), the direct inspiration for the Superman comic strip. The co-author of* When Worlds Collide *and* After Worlds Collide *(1933 and 1934), he wrote a number of imaginative and visionary stories including* The Disappearance *(1951). His non-fiction, such as Generation of Vipers, is relevant today. His essay on "Science Fiction and Sanity in an Age of Crisis" was published in 1953. His work was in the Wellsian rather than in the US pulp tradition and remains very lively. He scripted* The Island of Lost Souls (Dr. Moreau) *(1932) and* The Invisible Man *(1933). Other books included* Finnley Wren, Corpses at Indian Stones *and* Night Unto Night. *Much of his work was a continuing polemic concerned with his own nation, for which he invented the term momism to explain how sentimentality and over-simplification would be the ruin of American democracy.*

Firing the Cathedral

Heavy Fighting in Jerusalem
"Jerusalem, Saturday
The heaviest fighting for over three weeks broke out in Jerusalem tonight when Jews using mortars, opened fire on the Arab area of Katamon.

Two big explosions shook the city as the attackers blew up Arab houses, which they claimed were snipers' nests and operational headquarters.

Firing then broke out in other quarters of the city. Army bren carriers moved up to vantage points and fired into the fighting areas, gradually bringing the situation under control and quietening the city."

—*News of the World*, March 14, 1948

Nothing Heard from Air Liner Six Minutes After Leaving Calcutta Comet Missing

"A Comet jet air-liner with 43 people—including 10 women, a child, and a baby—on board was missing last night on its flight from Singapore to London.

The Comet, owned by BOAC, left Dum Dum Air-port, Calcutta, just before 11 a.m. for its three-hour flight to New Delhi. Six minutes later the Comet made its routine report 'Climbing on track.' Then there was silence."

—*Sunday Dispatch*, May 3, 1953

Stormbringer

"Upon the 10th inst., we began the storm; and after some hot dispute we entered, the enemy disputing it very stiffly with us. Our men that stormed the breaches were forced to recoil; they made a second attempt and became masters both of their retrenchments and the Church. Divers of the Enemy retreated into the Mill-Mount; a place very strong and difficult of access. The Governor, Sir Arthur Ashton, and divers considerable officers being there, our men getting up to them, were ordered by me to put them all to the sword: and indeed, being in the heat of action, I forbade them to spare any that were in arms in the town: and, I think, that night they put to the sword about 2000 men; about 100 of them possessing St Peter's Church-steeple whereupon I ordered it to be fired, when one of them was heard to say in the midst of the flames: 'God damn me, God confound me; I burn, I burn.'

The next day, the other two Towers were summoned. When they submitted, their officers were knocked on the head; and every tenth man of the soldiers killed; and the rest shipped for the Barbadoes. I am persuaded that this is a righteous judgement of God upon these barbarous wretches, who have imbrued their hands in so much innocent blood; and that it will tend to prevent the effusion of blood for the future, which are satisfactory grounds to such actions, which otherwise cannot but work remorse and regret."

—Oliver Cromwell on the Lenthall Massacre, September 17, 1649

"This Axis of Evil."

—David Frum (Speechwriter for G.W.Bush)

ONE

Buffalo Soldiers

"Jerusalem: This is where it all began.
This is where it will all end."

—CNN, January 16, 2002

"It is true that whenever difficulties arose with awkward Governments of backward oil areas, they were always worsened when the Great Powers intervened. Of course, as soon as the first World War had demonstrated that oil was the most important of all war materials, the Great Powers never stopped interfering. In *The Oil Trusts and Anglo-American Relations*, a book which I wrote in 1923, I revealed some of the undignified squabbling between the victorious Allies which had been raging over the oil of the Middle East . . . The unseemly commotion was sufficient to put the Governments of the backward oil countries wise to the politics of international oil."

—Nicholas Davenport,
Oily Spectacles New Statesman and Nation, October 6, 1951

"The business of America is business."

—Calvin Coolidge, January 17, 1925

"Aha, young patriot! And what do you desire the Gandalf to bring you for July 4th?"

In his faded gray cassock, puffing on a churchwarden and wearing a patriotic pointed hat instead of his miter, Bishop Beesley was doing his seasonal job at the WTC Memorial Mall. He had a small living in St. James's, John Street, so it wasn't far to walk. He did Uncle Santa or Sam Claus from September 11th to December 25th, took a break until Easter, then started the Gandalf job again around the middle of May. "A moveable feast?" Shaky Mo Collier twitched up the bishop's cassock with his MK51, sniffing critically at the sweet smoke. "Know what I mean, Denis? Is that your own beard?"

"Bugger off at once, you cheeky young sprig," boomed the Gandhi, "or you'll feel my sandal on your sitmedown. Mark my words, young hobnob, I am old and wise. I know better than anyone. While I appear to make ill-considered decisions on the spur of the moment, I am, just like our president and all his sages, actually behaving according to a carefully pre-arranged plan. *White men in gray this world shall rule, Till justice come to Kent State School.*" He cast a benign eye down the line of kids and handlers waiting to have their wishes granted. They were all security tagged and lightly tranked. The mall was a haven. It was a paradise. "I wonder if you would be interested in the leg of Saint George, a genuine relic, with full provenance. A fake went on Ebay for over a million dollars last week. Pickled, but considering the age . . . ?"

"Dragon's Claw?" Mo hated buying dope from the clergy. He couldn't help it. He came from a time before consumerology. As an anachronism, he now had a mysterious and unexpected power. He liked the taste of it. The economics defeated him but the idea of the blood feud provided a deep sense of security. Reagan and Thatcher should have been made king and queen of the world. You knew where you were with them. A tooth for a tooth. But the liberals had done their usual meddling and now war was endless, which was some consolation.

The Gandalf felt about inside his robe. He seemed to be listening for an emergency warning. He dropped his voice. "Cash only. Mill a lid." He caught a movement through the pseudo-glass and cast a nervous eye out at the ragged New York skyline. "Azrael?"

From a stylish, queerly-stained flak jacket Mo pulled a big wad. His meaning frown settled on the National Guardsmen looking after the crowd. They were soft-faced college footballers, drafted for the season and glad of the extra money. They checked their watches. "Coffee break." Zonked on Afghani black they had been chilling through most of the century. The heavy tar had got to their blood and their arteries were hardening so fast they moved towards the *Syrup Dog* concession like tin men who had lost their oil can. Mo sighed deeply. He was free of any immediate anxieties. A Golden Age like this normally lasted at least a year.

Wasn't it time Jerry turned up? It didn't seem fair otherwise. He'd been on ice for too long.

The Gandalf slipped into his plastic cave for a moment. He

came out fast, holding the remains of a Mars bar. Aware of his watching customers, he fussily adjusted his points. But he was all over the place. His nose lifting with disgust, he slipped the lid into Mo's blackened hand. "Some little oik's wanking over the hobbit costumes. Where's a policeman when you need him?" The Nats were still enjoying their Caramel Corn Dogs, watching the adventures of Sweet Doggy on the overhead screen. Seizing his chance, Mo dove inside to see what pleasure he could get from the situation.

Bishop Beesley smoothed his gray smock and used the diversion to recover himself. He cleared his throat. "Ho, ho, ho, ho…"

Slowly he began to beam. He had some brief sense of authority. He turned back to his customers. From the tent, they heard a dull thump and a squeak, some muffled grunting.

The Gandalf discretely settled on his stool. The moment was now Mo's.

The whole mall was silent for ten minutes, awaiting the inevitable gunshot.

TWO

Tell Me There's a Heaven

"I want to bite the hand that feeds me.
I want to bite that hand so badly."

—Elvis Costello, "Radio, Radio"

"A new George W. Bush last Tuesday addressed a transformed country, wholly unlike the one he campaigned in, and as not quite the man who campaigned . . . He leads a country in which the political terrain has been utterly altered, with old constraints leveled, and new possibilities revealed. It is too early to tell what these may lead to. But not to describe what they are."

—Noemie Emery, *The Weekly Standard*, February 11, 2002

"He has no soul."

—George W. Bush, Fox TV, December 18, 2001

Jerry Cornelius had popped into Gaucho's for a swift tequila sunset. He moved through the chattering crowd, a little underdressed for the evening, reached the bar and looked for service. He had shredded his retro threads in Houston and now wore a bum-freezer suit in style since 1960. It made him look a bit of a mod, a movie crook, an east ender. The sunglasses were the final touch. There was nothing like the comforts of convention. Sunglasses were a classic. He never listened to anyone's advice. He had weak eyes, these days.

They couldn't fault the whistle, though. "There's always authority in a nice plain suit," his brother assured him. "A short haircut, a touch of gold and plenty of cuff. It speaks volumes."

Jerry still wasn't too sure about the head shave. He couldn't help being reminded of electric chairs and Jews. He was on his way to Princelet Street now. In spite of his disgust with the heritage industry, Taffy still sometimes used the synagogue as a rendezvous. He had some last message tapes to hand over, he said. They needed an honest broker. He had examined all he was interested in. The Home Office pathologist had developed a special research study of the final words of the dying. He knew there was a truth eluding him. Ever since Jerry had known him Sir Taffy Sinclair had been up to something. Jerry still didn't know what it was. Sinclair had helped him out of the eighties and stayed with him through the nineties, so Jerry owed him. That had been a deadly dull twenty years with almost nothing to show for it but the *Belgrano* and the Basra Road. Sinclair had been more than decent. He had delivered Jerry to some nice holiday spots in the Middle East. There had been no shortage of skirmishes, but very little to get your teeth into. So when Sinclair sent a message, the old assassin was going to come through. But the trail back wasn't always easy, these days. Every second brought a thousand choices. Surely it wasn't only the fault of information technology?

When the old troupe effectively split up, Jerry had looked forward to spending some time in the Cairo pyramid he'd bought from the Egyptians when property values sank so suddenly in 2001. He had spent a fortune on restorations. He always got delusions of grandeur on holiday. It hadn't been long before he had returned to London. The coming collapse of New York made him realize he only felt thoroughly easy in a big city. But he had kept a low profile. You knew when your age was over. You just had to wait and hope that you'd get another chance. It was a turning world, at least for now.

"And when all's said and done," he told Mitzi, behind the bar, "London's the place to be."

She enjoyed this. "Not many places left," she said. "Not big ones. Just bits. And little ones."

They were old friends. Mitzi flirted at him. She was only a bishop's daughter but she knew how to juice up a Jesuit. "You can't beat a police bike. You can't match the classic Royal Albert." Her gorgeous mascara fell like blue junk onto the damp bar and bonded with the rest of her ashy droppings. An unlikely grin broke through her lip-rouge. It defied her powdered cheeks, it cracked her neck and blacked her eyes. It brought back something Jerry hadn't seen since the early seventies. "Your dad doing all right?" he asked.

"Well, he's working regularly. He's got a job in the States. They spent a fortune on reproducing The Two Towers. Then someone took out the Empire State. So tourism's up again. They want him for his accent. They love us over there. They think we're on their side." She turned to dust at her picture of Margaret Thatcher in its red, white and blue frame. "But things aren't the same, are they? I was going to move to Hastings. Or Worthing? What do you think?"

"My mum preferred Worthing," said Jerry. "She liked the minstrels at the Delaware Pavilion. Or was that Bexhill?" It was all South London-on-Sea now, which made everything simpler. Indian restaurants and racist raffles. It was a matter of time before the yardies took over Hove.

Almost his old self, he lit a triumphant Sherman's. He was back on home territory. This was the real thing. The big finish. He was enjoying it no end. "I'm getting myself a little place in the Lakes after this. I've had enough of international tourism. It's my last Smoke Opera." At her look of discomfort he added: "Well, naturally I'll be home to die. To become one with the concrete from which I was conceived. From concrete we come and to concrete we return. The only place you're allowed to grow old and die without a lot of fuss being made about it is a proper city. And, when all's said and done, there is no more proper city than London."

She was used to his self-pity. "Well, at least you haven't changed much. You back in the seminary?" She tasted her own lips with her tongue, staring a little critically at his shaven scalp. "It doesn't make you any younger, you know. Have you seen those sculptures of Bedlam loonies at the V&A, is it? You look like an 18th century murderer."

Jerry accepted the crititicism. "That's where it started for me," he said. "One crap, half-baked revolution after another, then seventeen seventy-six and every sodding thing went pear-shaped. Revolutions are about people either trying to keep things the same or restore a golden age. The Americans were successful in holding back the march of time for over two hundred years. They're a bigger version of late 18th century Britain— hangings, harsh prisons and disgustingly rich autocrats above the law."

"They can't help it." Mitzi relaxed into a reminiscent smile. "They're a very unvolatile people. They're mostly krauts, aren't they?"

"Well, they all blew their bloody revolutions. Trust Cromwell to fuck everything up. All this stuff could have been thrashed out over a table in ten minutes. But they got too scared. People really hate liberty. First sniff they get of it and they dive back into their familiar captivity. They fight to the death to keep those chains."

Mitzi snorted. Various essences clouded the air around her head. "Tom Paine, eh? And *Common Sense*. If you ask me the Canadians are the ones who had the common sense."

Jerry looked up at the clock. "Is that the right time?"

THREE

Oliver's Army

"The Christians had gathered for Sunday services and the disciples expressed an interest in seeing the services, and the Master agreed. As they entered the building, the priest and the congregation recognized them and went over to greet them. There was so much joy that everyone began to experience an uplifting spiritual state. Several Sufi singers in the Master's group asked permission to chant verses from the Qur'an and the priests granted it.

The joy of receiving our Master, combined with the singers' praise of the Lord, brought an ecstatic state to those present. Many were in rapture. When the signing was finished and Abu Sai'd prepared to leave, one of his disciples exclaimed enthusiastically, 'If the Master wills and mentions it, many Christians here will abandon their garments of Christianity and put on the robe of Islam.'

The master retorted, 'We did not put their garment on them in the first place that we should presume to take it off.' "

—Ibn Munawwar: *Asrar at-Tawhid*, ed. Shafi-Kadkani, 1, 210.

"They get a white bucket for emergency squirts, while they are instructed to hold two fingers up for the alternative. At that time, a guard shackles them and takes them to the port-o-loo. While the military has spared no expense in construction costs (in three weeks , they built a completely operational field hospital staffed by 160 medical personnel—two more than there are prisoners), they've saved a fortune in toilet paper. It's the detainees' cultural preference not to use any. 'We don't shake hands,' says one camp guard."

—'*Guantamo's Unhappy Campers, The only abuse the detainees are experiencing is self-inflicted*,' by Matt Labash,
The Weekly Standard, February 11, 2002.

"All American soldiers are left-handed," said Jerry. "I read it in a magazine."

"I can't look at CNN without thinking of my poor, silly son." With a broad smile, Abu Said stretched his rule from shoulder blades to thigh. "You've put on a little length since we last had business. But you could do with fattening up. I'll take you home with me tonight. We are, God willing, having a good dinner."

"What was that you were saying about sheep?" Jerry reached for his jacket.

"I was talking about sheepdogs. I've known some funny sheep-dogs. I admire your collies, of course. Who couldn't? I always made a point of catching the trials on the telly." He had come home to Jelalabad when things started to get tricky in Tipton.

"Ever known one that killed sheep?" Jerry lifted his arms. Abu Said read off numbers to his palmtop.

"Never. There's a lot of wolf to a good sheepdog, as anyone will tell you, but there's something in them, just like there is in a lot of humans, that just won't let them do it. What sort of wolf is that, Monsignor Cornelius?"

"A fairly ineffective wolf."

"But a very effective sheepdog."

"You must get a bad cross, every so often. They can't all be naturally good."

"Oh, perhaps." Abu Said retracted his measure. "Are you familiar with Camus? I have been re-reading *Le Myth de Sisyphe.* Constant striving. Constant disappointment. Constant joy. Always a consolation in times like these."

Jerry was uncomfortable with this posture of acquiescence. "When did the world's leaders learn the trick of talking aggres-sively and putting civilians in the front line? It saves a fortune in military spending." He slid his right index finger down the silk swathe his companion offered him. "As smooth as oil. You'd hardly know what it was."

"No, but it's worms as usual." The tailor indicated big bolts of cloth racked along the three walls of the shop not facing the street. "The rest is oil. Man-made, as they say. Think of that one—that gauzy pale green up there for instance—starting some-where in the desert, underground." His amused brown eyes looked hard into Jerry's face. "You were speaking of the Rif. Abd' el Krim, I think his name was. Didn't he die of tuberculosis in Paris? They usually do. Are you still called the Raven in the Magreb?"

"You're thinking of Texas. A different, more complicated age." said Jerry. "They could have called me the Red Shadow and put on the same show."

"Men of toil and danger, would you serve a stranger, and bow down to Burgundy? Fight, fight, fight for liberty," sang Abu Said inexpertly. He couldn't help adding classical Egyptian flourishes. "Why are you so interested in that shitty little country?" He shook his head and took out a pack of Camels, offering them to Jerry. "Smoke?"

"It keeps us forging ahead." Jerry fished a battered cigarette from the pack and very gently placed it to his lips, as if he tasted the paper. He felt the ghost of memory. "It keeps us happy."

" 'Ah,' said Christ, brushing at his tears with bloody hands, 'would you re-crucify me?' " Abu Sad drew a breath for a further quote then became alert. He sniffed the air. "Can you smell it too? That's a wolf. I thought the Jews had killed them all." He got up hastily, knocking over his dummy, opened the little door in the back and ran through the house, taking down a long switch from the rack and going outside to check his sheep pens.

Jerry followed him. On the dark horizon were the outlines of Bethlehem. The sleeping sheep began to rise, blinking in the glare of Abu Said's sweeping flashlight.

Jerry sniffed the wind.

"Is something burning?"

FOUR

Pig Alley Blues

> "You've grown up in a world that says you don't belong to it. So you make one you *can* belong to. But it takes a bit of nerve to go to Selfridge's dressed as Boadicea."
>
> —Boy George, BBC Radio 4, January 16, 2002

> "Captain Marvel Battles THE AXIS OF EVIL!"
>
> —*Captain Marvel Adventures*, January 1945

> "Islam means peace."
>
> —George W. Bush, September 2001

"Eat pork, mother-coverers!"

Trixie Brunner was getting it on at the VR arcade. There were dozens of great news games. She had her name down for *Daisycutter Panic* and *Towelhead Run*. Meanwhile she was playing *Iman Hunt* with one hand and *American Terrorist* with the other. It improved her sense of balance. "*Frum, frum, frum* . . ."

Trixie's prim foxy face was bright with carmine and torquoise. She wore a little red dress and five inch black spikes. With her pale skin and platinum rinse she looked like a Nazi poster. Her mother, waking from one of her long reveries, was convinced Trixie sported a false bottom. "It doesn't suit you," she said. It was a pathetic stab at regaining power and Trixie, feeling sentimental, didn't respond. Her mother soon drifted off again. The junk Trixie was giving her kept her comfortable.

The baroness had been almost all gangrene before they operated. Now she was mostly mouth. Trixie was using her own old stroller to take her mum for her weekly spin to the arcade. She had given up the bingo. Her mother kept insisting the numbers on her card were all winners. She would shout "Bingo!" in the middle of a game. Her fellow players had turned against her.

"She's a bit of an archosaur, I'm so sorry." Trixie apologized to Mo Collier who scratched his stubble and grunted agreeably. The idea of a prosthetic arse was turning him on.

With uneasy grace he offered Trixie's dam one of the Mars Bars he'd taken off the vicar. "Would she like to mumble something?"

"Better not," said Trixie. "It goes all over her."

"Anyway," Mo carried on where he'd left off. "You know, I was thinking if you fancied a you know, bit of fun."

"I'm having a bit of fun." Trixie pointed out. "If it's you, I'd rather bang than bonk. But I don't mind doing a VR double-up. Want a round of *Screw You?*"

Mo's pride threatened his lust, but eventually he agreed. "How much is it?"

Trixie shouted into her drooling mum's ear. "Hear that, mum? He's learning."

It was too much for Mo. He swung his MK800-50 off his shoulder and threw a small, showy, irritable needle burst into the machine's slot. The tiny heart-searchers clattered about for a while. Finding nothing organic, they settled down to wait. They had an active lifespan of twenty hours.

This gesture interested Trixie. "What are you doing for Christmas?" she asked absently, leaning back to straighten the seem of her stocking, her bottom bending awkwardly. "Or are you invited down?"

Mo's juices began to rise.

FIVE

On the Beach

> "Frodo: 'I wish none of this had happened.'
> Gandalf: 'So do all who live to see such times, but that is not for them to decide. All we have to decide is what to do with the time that is given us.' "
>
> —New Line Cinema Ad, December 2001.

> "For all the talk about he country moving on from Sept. 11, one group isn't quite ready, and that's the nation's marketers."
>
> —*The Wall Street Journal*, February 5, 2002

> "This smug, self-righteous, ignorant and aggressive people, whose myths are supported by self-deception and self-serving lies, have been breaking treaties since their history began. They have habitually invaded and settled territories guaranteed to others and, ultimately, driven those inhabitants to violence as a last resort. This violence, then condemned as savage and unprovoked, they punished with vicious, genocidal and horrific intensity. In the languages of those they invade they are called The Treaty Breakers, but they call themselves the Chosen People, whose manifest destiny is to occupy the lands promised to them by God. They have used their scriptures to justify all the crimes they have committed against their own Biblical commandments."
>
> —Lobkowitz, *The Monotheists*: *A Trail of Tears* 1952

Bishop Beesley had reverted to his richer robes and miter. "Boston?" His golden crook was blotchy with chocolate. He licked at his fingers with what was almost sensuality. “There’s much to be said to falling back into the old routines. The cardinal virtues. And, of course, the cardinal sins. Still, I shall miss dear old Hobbes.” Beesley reluctantly offered a bon-bon. He was relieved when Jerry refused. He began to gush.

“Dear colleague!” He indicated a chair.

Jerry walked towards the bookshelves.

Beesley had been glad to get this job after that awful Russian affair. He turned to his hi-fi shelf. He took up the arm of his record player and lowered it onto the record. “Jazz, okay? Italian-American? I’m secretly a bit of a rebel, as you’ve no doubt guessed. You’ve probably never seen my soft shoe shuffle. This is *Abyssinian Stomp*. Do you know it?”

“I heard it in Rome once.” Jerry sighed as the cleric began his awkward jive. “It never did much over here.”

The light through the stained glass windows gave the Gothic room the detailed richness of an early Pre-Raphaelite. The light reflecting from copper, brass, silver and gold. The old books, the iconography, the boxes with the logos of Mars and Smuckers blended well with other muted colors. The rest of the shelves were stacked with Utilitarian pamphlets. In some surprise, Jerry fished out an early copy of *The Newgate Calendar*. “Did you read this?”

“My illiterate daughter/thought/it had something/to do with/nougat.” The bishop was still shaking his stuff. A dance to set the earth vibrating on her axis; but for the moment the aftershocks were confined to the untrustworthy towers of Oxford. Jerry turned to the window. Outside, a steeple gasped and fell languidly to the rubble. Beesley was celebrating his return to the Anglican church. He called it a reconciliation and received what was left of the parish in return. All his entrepreneurial attempts to found a new proselytizing sect had come to nothing with the legalisation of Class A drugs.

Still, there wasn’t much more mileage in the Oxford Movement. To Bishop Beesley, Muscular Christianity seemed something of a contradiction in terms. His maiden sermon had been called “Keep It Sweet” and had gone down a treat in the ruins of Christ Church. You wouldn’t get too many customers, these days, with a pile of gloom.

The spring of the gramophone had begun to run down. Beesley boogied faster and faster, as if to compensate for the record's melodic groan.

"You're not worried about a heart attack?" Jerry picked up the arm and replaced it on the rest.

"Oh, we're not likely to have another for a while. I think they've made enough of an example of Oxford, don't you?" The bishop subsided, reaching for a Snickers.

"You can still get batteries, you know." Jerry turned the handle of the instrument. "You don't have to use springs and clockwork. You'll rediscover steam next. This is real life, not some kind of exotic urban fantasy."

The bishop sat down suddenly, panting and crimson. "Are you trying to wind me up? I've been ordered to do this by the quack. He suggested Soul, but Dixieland's the furthest I'll go. Weren't you here on business?"

"I'm back with the Jesuits," said Jerry. "I was sent to suggest an alliance."

Bishop Beesley calmed his jowls with a grubby pink hand. Suddenly his ambition had returned. He was only one conversion away from being the next Pope.

"This is from where?" He straightened his miter and picked up his crook. "Vatican?"

"Via Westminster."

"Westminster? I thought the survivors were snorting the dust! Blowing in the wind, Monsignor." He uttered a small, reflective fart. He was determined not to seem a walk over. "Who are you really with?"

Jerry showed his fake badge. Bishop Beesley admired it. "So who are you really with, then?"

"The Society." Jerry laughed. "The old Co-op."

Beesley was clearly convinced, but he had to be absolutely sure. He reached for an instrument.

"What's your number?"

"Four nine four oh six." Jerry displayed the brass tag on his watch-chain. It was well-used. Bent and battered. It looked like a Roman coin.

The atmosphere became suddenly cheerful.

Beesley thoughtfully peeled a Yorkie. “So how’s old Poppa?”

SIX

What’s Your Movie?

“Soldiers of the King
A series of 36
25: Skinner’s Horse, 1st Duke of York’s Own Cavalry (India)
This fine cavalry regiment dates its history back to 1803–14; it is an amalgamation of Skinner’s Horse and 3rd Skinner’s Horse. The present designation was given in 1927. ‘Captain Skinner’s Corps of Irregular Horse’ was raised from a body of horse who came over to the British after the battle of Delhi; at one time they were called ‘1st Bengal Irregular Cavalry’. The 3rds were originally styled ‘Second Corps of Lt.-Colonel Skinner’s Irregular Horse’. Composition is Hindustani Musalmans and Musalman Rajputs (Ranghars), Rajputs (U.P. and Eastern Punjab) and Jats.”

—Godfrey Phillips Cigarette Card, c. 1935

“When I get into a lift full of business men when I’m wearing full make-up, you can tell by the way they behave whether much has changed or not.”

—Boy George, BBC Radio 4, January 16, 2002

Maximus Minor
“As America’s victory in Afghanistan unfolds, what keeps coming up for me are the opening scenes of the movie ‘Gladiator’. The barbarians, dressed in skins, have thrown the decapitated head of the Roman peace negotiator at the Romans’ feet, and are jumping up and down in maniacal, murderous frenzy. The Roman General, Maximus, calmly reaffirms with his commanders their most cherished values—‘strength and honor’—and then quietly orders: ‘At my signal, unleash hell.’ In the war on Moslem terrorism being waged today, George. W. Bush has become America’s Maximus.”

—Jack Wheeler, *Soldier of Fortune*, March 2002

“The clowns have taken over the circus.” Major Nye was driving Una Persson down to the coast where she had six weeks in *Oh, What A Lovely War* live on Brighton pier where it had all originally happened.

"Have you heard the news today? I suppose it was inevitable. I wasn't so worried when they were simply running politics. But the circus! I used to love the circus. We had a big one come through every year when I was a lad."

The old administrator was showing his age. His pale blue eyes were bright in his weather faded face. His handsome skull was almost fleshless. His thin gray hair was smartly combed but his moustache lacked its old bristle. In a dark suit a couple of sizes too large for him, he looked as he had when a young man, coming back from the Burma Road and being handed his civvies.

On the black wheel, his pale, lightly veined hands stuck out of his gloves like picked bones. "Billy Smart, I think. Or Lord George Sanger was it? They were great rivals at one time. Then there started to be these visiting acts from Russia and France and so on. Very chic, I suppose. Not my taste. Elephants and clowns is what I call a circus. Lion tamers. Equestriennes. White ponies. Sharp shooters. My uncle met Buffalo Bill, you know, at Earl's Court. I would love to have seen Buffalo Bill. And what about Annie Oakley! Was she Jewish, do you think?"

Gearing expertly, he swerved to avoid the potholes created by a cluster bomb blast across the M-25. "Bloody American gunnery. Makes you wonder about the actual prowess of the outlaws and the riflemen and all that. I suppose that was true once, but you know how dangerous it is to rest on your own military or political laurels. I think they got used to easy shots. Instead of putting men in the field, they spent their money on gadgets. They all learn in arcades, you know. Virtual experience. Virtual authority. You can't blame them for wanting to simplify everything."

"It's grids," said Una. "They can't get enough of them. Once they've got it in a grid and named it, they think it's theirs."

"They were already very insecure before this started. Their lack of education was beginning to dawn on them." A straight stretch coming up, he sought his smokes in the top pocket of his boiler suit, flipped the top open with his thumb and fished a thin roll-up into his lips. "Forty years ago, when I was first dealing with the C.I.A. it was full of smart, humorous young men who knew a thing or two. They had decent degrees. A few languages. Good manners. Sporting attitude. They were like Foreign Office johnnies. The best of them tended to go native, of course, but always remembered their duty in the end. Like Lawrence and Samson. Nowadays, it's a bunch of smart-alec apparatchiks installed by the Busch gestapo.

Business isn't much good at running business, let alone nations. Soldiers are no good at politics. It's business, not politics, builds empires. They can't help themselves. What was it Marx said about stupidity?"

Una was growing a little irritated with this litany. "We're all USUKs now, Major Nye."

The old soldier was unrelenting. "Look what happened when we let them get in on the last German war. First they backed Hitler and Mussolini with great enthusiasm and cash. Then it soon became obvious their bets were barking barmy and losing seriously. So they sent us all those poor, badly trained boys for cannon fodder, and used Wall Street money to install their own awful glory-seeking generals who, as now, threw away lives faster than Kitchener and made enough blunders to extend the fighting in Europe by a year."

Major Nye cleared his throat.

Una tried to arouse herself long enough to interrupt him. Too late.

"They then make films claiming our victories. Thieves as well as incompetents. But I suppose that's what happens when you draw your labor force from Middle European peasants. You get the crusades all over again. Thank God for Oppenheimer, various Hungarians and the A-bomb or we'd still be fighting the Japs."

This woke her enough to stir and speak.

"What's up with you, major?" She pushed her dark hair back from her eyes. She needed a hairdresser. She was amused. "I thought you admired Woodrow Wilson. You always rather liked the yanks."

"I still do. I just don't think they're any good at wars or politics. They have no proper experience. They didn't have to work for a Magna Carta or a Bill of Rights, you see. They got them imposed by Jefferson and Co. Entirely different approach. Easy victories. Most of them just started out wanting a reasonable tax break, a bit of respect. Badly handled. Easy victories usually mean a long war. Johnny Turk discovered that after he took Constantinople."

He braked a bit sharply to avoid a crater.

"Do what?" Una was paying attention to the road.

"It's their Achilles heel, really. Easy victories over under-equipped enemies made us complaisant, too."

He did his best to see the truth. Too many of his beliefs had been successfully challenged and he was a conscientious bureaucrat at home and abroad.

"They always get back at you somehow and you always get stretched too thin. We did the same. The problem is they have never known true shame."

"Shame," said Una. "Shame."

She began to brighten.

"Ah, look—the road's still there. We should be in Hove by lunch-time."

Privately she thought the Americans had saved her life. Without the GI audiences tonight she'd have been playing to one old lady and a deaf dog.

SEVEN

Shorty Says

RAF's Missiles on Alert in Far East

"Britain's Bloodhound missiles in Singapore are ready to fire in defence of the city, now threatened by Indonesia's trouble-mongering President Sukarno.

An RAF announcement in Singapore said yesterday: 'The missile systems have been activated and are fully operational.'

The 25-foot long Bloodhounds are 'purely defensive anti-aircraft weapons' said an RAF spokesman.

They home on to their targets by radar.

> Activating involves tests of the guidance and firing systems to ensure that the rockets are ready for launching.
>
> Rocket firing Hunters yesterday attacked jungle hideouts in South-Central Malaya, flushing out five more of the Indonesian paratroops dropped there eleven days ago."
>
> —*Sunday Mirror*, September 13, 1964

> "I made peace with all the people in the world, resolving never to wage war on anyone, and I waged war against my self and have never since made peace with it."
>
> —Kharanqani in 'Attar: *Tadhkirat*

Jerry met Mo coming out of the rather flashy and over-cleaned Arndale *Kebabarama.* It was doing well since the trams had stopped coming in to central Manchester. Mo widened his mouth and took a large bite of his lamb-burger. The rich curry sauce ran down through his stubble like a flood in the desert. "Wotcher, Mr. C. If you want another of these, don't bother. They just ran out of meat."

Jerry looked up and down the street outside the deserted complex. It was a big brutalist anachronism. These days, people were building down, rather than up. All the show was on the inside. "You were supposed to be looking after Taffy."

"Bugger!" With unconscious ease, Mo transferred his guilt into a belligerent glare. "He said he wanted fish and chips. There's supposed to be a chippy in Deansgate. What a bastard that geezer is. Going on about jam tarts." He peered nostalgically about him, at the huge tower block, the spanking clean shops. In his memory he drew in the dust of his ancestry. "It was all ruins round here once."

An eastern breeze carried the faint chords of George Harrison's ukulele as he did his famous Formby imitations. *Tee hee missus . . .*

"Oh, come on." Jerry's instincts were buzzing. He holstered his heat and ran with long, economical strides towards Deansgate. "The old Savoy farts. He'll be sniffing out the ghosts of departed jailbirds. He's only interested in something once it's compost for his own necromantic art. I know exactly where to start." This was too boring to be a trap.

Mo opened up a manhole cover. He couldn't help himself. He shouldered his clumsy MK907-243 and began to descend. "I'll meet you in the basement."

His caution served him well.

Taking the corner by the looted car show-room, Jerry ran headlong into a squadron of "Cossacks." These mounted Bengalis sported long lances from which fluttered the various pennants of their clans. They had found an old Jew in the street. As the Jew ran towards him, clutching at a straw, Jerry hesitated.

The heavily bearded and turbanned lancers reined in their miscellanous mounts, waiting to see what Jerry would do.

He turned to the terrified septuagenerian. "I suppose it's too late to talk?"

From up the street he heard a burst of celebratory gunfire. The Bengalis turned their horses and galloped towards the source. It was their instinct. If there was a gun, they would charge it.

Jerry relaxed. Mo would deal with them.

He peered into the twitching face of the man they had been going to murder. "Didn't you used to be a bloke called Auchinek."

Auchinek was grateful for any recognition. "I was a promoter," he said. "One of the best. I had no enemies. At least to speak of. Then all this had to happen. Is there still time to get to Jerusalem?"

"Not now," said Jerry.

"What about London? The West End?"

Jerry didn't know what to tell him.

They strolled slowly after the disappearing Bengalis. "It's a musical," said Auchinek. He was cheering up in his own hangdog way. "It will run forever, believe me. I was hoping to get the backing in Israel. Do you have any idea of the current political climate. I've been in a cellar for a week."

"Well," said Jerry, "someone's got to tell you, so I'm going to. There's been a reality shift. The world turned upside down. Things are still settling at the moment."

"A perfect time for a new musical." Auchinek beamed. He was pleased with himself. There had been a period when he had only been able to do this on Prozac. "Remind me to buy you a drink. This will be a natural for Broadway."

"That's what I'm trying to say," said Jerry.

EIGHT

Black, Brown and White

> "If I'd arrived in Esfahan first, I kept thinking, instead of Tehran, I would have had a whole different first impression of the Islamic Republic. Iran, as personified by its *chador*-cloaked women, would have seemed much more impenetrable to me…The chador the Esfahani women taught me, was not just a swathe of black fabric but rather a formidable garment to be reckoned with."
>
> —Christiane Bird, *Neither East Nor West*, 2001.

> "It's not surprising that a Republican governor should take a dim view of children's health insurance. It was Perry's predecessor, George W. Bush, who unsuccessfully fought expansion of the CHIP program in the 1999 Legislature, even as he was campaigning for president with a promise to 'leave no child behind'."
>
> —Michael King, *Austin Chronicle*, February 15, 2002

> "EVERY WEDNESDAY! **ASIAN NIGHT!** TOPLESS FEMALE SUMO WRESTLING! ASIAN BEER, SUSHI AND SAKE SPECIALS!"
>
> —Advertisement, Penthouse Austin, *Austin Chronicle* February 15, 2002

> "TOTALLY EXPOSED. **OIL WRESTLING**. WEDNESDAY FEBRUARY 20TH"
>
> —Advertisement, the Show Palace, *Austin Chronicle* February 15, 2002

"What sort of time do you call this, then?" Taffy was distant with irritability. In his loose, green suit he issued from the shadows of the Princelet Street synagogue and closed the doors behind him, a lofty Norman abbot.

"Bloody hell," said Jerry. "Do you know how many Ainsworth diversions it took to get from Manchester—"

The Home Office pathologist hated tech talk. He brushed past his visitor and, lighting the way with an early bicycle lamp, climbed the wormy stairs to the weaving loft. Below, the creaks and groans of the wood echoed the cries of long dead patients, of dismantled looms. The shrieks and wails of sawn bones.

"Lord, the pain." Taffy had recovered himself. With an habitual air of resolution, he opened his bag, took out his gloves and slipped them on. "Once a pathologist . . . "

He was all that was left of the Home Office. He would be retiring soon, to St. Leonards-on-Sea where he had a lease on a small sweet and tobacconist's. His wife didn't like his idea of having a second hand book section, or even some sort of lending library, where the videos would normally go. She had scotched his grave, sub-Morrisian scheme to re-install newspaper deliveries and possibly a milk round. "Sometimes," he had told Jerry, "she loathes my nostalgia and I must admit it's not the nicest side of my nature."

He scratched suddenly at his cheek. He was ferociously clean-shaven. A Roman patrician, an Iroquois sachem. A Benedictine reformer. A puritan, like Milton, with a devilish soul, an unprincipled curiosity. His stern spectacles glared in the dawn light, biting through the dust of the transom. "This is where they operated," he said. "No anaesthetic of course. Just speed and a spot of luck." He cocked his ear to the light. "Was that a voice?"

"Gus Elen," said Jerry, "or probably George Formby." His tears fell like rain.

A clear, sweet soprano, too Gertie Lawrence for the real music hall, began to sing with brisk self-mockery:

I feels a cove should fink afore 'e talks abaht th' woar,
There's blokes as talks as dunno wot they mean,
But yer tumble as yer 'umble knows a bit abaht th' Boar,
When we calls me nibs 'The Bore o 'Bef'nal Green'.

It was Una, of course, waiting for them in the eaves, dressed as a West End masher, a collapsing topper under her elegant arm, hand in pocket, the other hand sporting a cigarette holder, a smouldering Gitane. "Nobody remembers the good old days."

She winked. "There's more money in murders and villains. *Sweeney Todd* always did better than *Nell of Old Drury*. In the provinces at least. When I refer to good old Jack, I'm talking Buchanan."

A little below Jerry's height, she slipped elegantly towards him, embracing him. "Oh, I just don't know what it is about you? You lovely little wanker." She remembered her manners, stepping back. "Sorry Colonel Sinclair." She went to pick up her sword stick. She left Jerry still trying to work out what this had to do with *Greenmantle.* "Business as usual I'm afraid."

Sinclair despised that kind of formality. He judged people by it. "No need," he said. "Honestly." He was firm. A strong-minded the bishop, driven by the truth.

"Shalom," said Jerry. "Shalom. Shalom."

Una smiled. "What I tell you three times will be true." She popped her hat open, to disguise her despair.

"Pain." Sinclair sucked at his suicide tooth and then remembered his manners. "Pain will do it."

Through the house's groaning frame, her uneasy boards, came a sudden prayer, a distant chorus. "Haunted," said Una. "Haunted as hell."

"Pain." Sinclair was firm.

Hastily Jerry sought his reflection in the dusty windows and was relieved when he found it. "It's amazing none of them are broken," he said. "What would they have had originally do you think?"

Sinclair looked at his watch. "I think I've done pretty much all I can do here. I'd better be off."

"Taxi?" Una produced her cell phone.

Sinclair shook his head. "I drove myself in."

Jerry was growing uneasy. "I think we should all probably get out of here. Don't you?"

In some disgust, he looked down at his hands and feet and recoiled from the blood. "Oh, shit. Here of all places."

Una sighed. "I suppose we can't ask you for a lift in this state?"

The pathologist shrugged. "Don't worry I have some old polythene in the boot."

NINE

When Will I Get to Be Called a Man?

> "*BEGINS TO-DAY. No. 1 of a great bunch of stories about the No. 1 man of the North-West Frontier of India.—THE WOLF OF KABUL*
> The Afghans, the Pathans, the Kurds, the Afridis, and all the bandits from Baluchistan, on the coast of the Arabian Sea, to far Kashmir and the borders of forbidden Tibet, live in dread of The Wolf of Kabul, the man who can make them or break them."
>
> —*The Wizard Weekly*, September, 1930.

> "A society which punishes those who do not agree that it is perfect, can never, of course, progress. It will, however, grow increasingly aggressive even as it inevitably corrodes from within."
>
> —Lobkowitz: *Time and Meaning*, 1938

> "Keep from me, God, all forms of certainty."
>
> —Moslem prayer

Prince Lobkowitz was doing his best to pull his weight. But his palsy was growing worse. He held his arms to his sides, trying to stop the shaking. There was something wrong with this brain, he insisted. He was subtly out of synch. He had no previous experience of the condition.

"If time is a field, Monsignor Cornelius, and space but a dimension of time, the few dimensions we are able to conceptualize are surely a comment upon our paucity of invention, rather than our boasted prometheanism?"

Jerry Cornelius was beginning to regret falling back on religion. He'd always known there was a flaw in this escape plan. But Prince Lobkowitz was his only wholly trustworthy ally. Mrs. Persson was probably on the square, but you could never be sure of her overall game plan. Lady Luck was sometimes his only hope. The cards built houses wherever they fell.

His long-term memory was improving. He remembered the medrasim in Cairo and Marrakesh, the years of meditation in the retreats of Oom and Cadiz. All in order to take a few extra steps in the never-ending Dance of Time. It was so easy for

Mrs. Persson. He didn't have the mental discipline. He had paid a high price, not being able to follow her when her skills had surpassed his own. He was still paying it. "*I sometimes feel I lived my life like a candle up your qui—*"

"Ladies present," warned Lobkowitz, who hated vulgarity.

Jerry paused to lock the door of the church. Prince Lobkowitz had come to take him down to the village, where there was still a reasonably good tea-shop which could tell the difference between a tea-cake and a muffin. "Ladies?"

Too late, he sniffed the air.

"Oh, thank God, Monsignor, there you are!" The self-pitying shriek of her threatened species.

It was Trixie Brunner from the manor. She was distraught. "I, as you know, have not one racist bone in my whole body. Yet why I have to pay taxes at eight billion pounds in the pound just to keep a bunch of greasy little oiks from God knows where when my whole family has lived and farmed and had businesses in these parts for years. Well, where *are* they from, Monsignor? And don't tell me all my chickens committed suicide."

Jerry was recalling his schooldays. "I'm so sorry, Miss Brunner? Was it the Jews?"

"Oh, no." She was genuinely disgusted. "These aren't intellectuals at all. I'm talking about asylum seekers." She frowned. Something had just occurred to her. "Who on earth would wish to live in an asylum?"

Steadying his shakes, Lobkowitz stood to attention and when he was introduced he clicked his heels and kissed her trembling hand. She was immediately reassured.

The old diplomat had lost none of his graceful trickery. "We in Europe long for your English freedoms," he said. "That is why it is so important for you to join us in this alliance of nations. You have so much to teach us."

"Well the first thing I'd do is abolish Brussels. Not exactly the farmer's friend, are they." She had found the remains of a constituency in the Country Sidereal Alliance. She was doing what she could to fit in. Her awkwardly slung buttocks proclaimed her a horsewoman, but all her life she'd had an aversion to getting close to any living thing even a few inches larger than herself. The faux-derrier swung like panniers on a camel, reminding Jerry that when he had last seen her she had been reluctantly returning from a trans-Saharan expedition, commanded in the name of her mother, attempting to discover a Middle Eastern route to the past. She had not wanted to tell him what she had found. When she eventually let her mother know, it had nearly knocked her off her throne.

"We have our own pipeline now, you know." She spoke brightly, attempting to impress Prince Lobkowitz. "You can adopt a length. But we're funding a whole line through Afghanistan. It's the patriotic thing to do." She tugged off her head scarf.

Jerry stopped by the prince's new Lexus pick-up. It was the only working vehicle in the car-park.

Lobkowitz drew on his driving coat. "Can we drop you anywhere?"

TEN

Joe Turner Blues

> "As part of Operation Plumbbob tests conducted in 1957, the Atomic energy Commission hung nuclear weapons as large as 74 kilotons beneath blimps. The nuclear balloon era came to a close in 1963 after a pair of freak accidents destroyed the AEC's two airships on two consecutive days."
>
> —*Popular Mechanics*, March 2002

> "There is a remote human reflex known, to those who witness it most often, as the 'flashpoint'. This is when a calm person moves suddenly into hysteria. A 999 operator learns that it can be triggered by as little as the words, 'Hello, ambulance service.' Even the coolest emergency caller has trouble coping with the question 'Are they still breathing?' "
>
> —Emma Brockes, *Guardian*, February 6, 2002

> "George Bush's budget is not for the faint-hearted. His $2.13 trillion spending plans for 2003 include a 14% increase in the defence budget, the biggest rise since Ronald Reagan, as well as doubling of spending on homeland security. It is bold. By keeping overall government

spending outside defence and homeland security to a 2% rise next year (compared with a recent annual average of more than 7%) Mr. Bush is proposing a dramatic shift in America's spending priorities.

And it is brazen. Far from trimming his tax cuts to help pay for more guns, Mr. Bush reinforces, nay increases, his proposed tax cuts by almost $600 billion over the next decade…

The result is a dramatic turnaround in America's fiscal outlook. Far from using the Social Security surplus to pay down debt or restructure America's pension system,—a goal both parties claimed to be overriding only nine months ago—Mr. Bush's budget uses the surplus to pay for defence spending and, particularly, tax cuts."

—*The Economist*, February 9, 2002

Wrong-Way Lindbergh turned his mild, expectant blue eyes drunkenly on Jerry. He patted vaguely at his own bottom, looking for a back pocket, a pint. "I was expecting Captain Ewell. He was bringing me something."

"Fancy a drink, general?" Jerry slipped a slender flask from inside his black car coat. "I hope you don't mind. It's Armagnac and it might be on the turn. It's Napoleon." He wore his long hair Jacobin style and, with his full lapels, had the look of a romantic Deputy in the days before the Terror.

Mrs. Persson reflected that it was good to see him in youthful good spirits again. He had been taking his work too seriously.

"So old 'Four Eyes' Ewell isn't here yet?" The general stoked his almost hairless head.

"Well, it's my fault, I think. I'm pretty bad at the rituals."

Continuing to pedal his exercise bike, General Lindbergh studied the full length mirror. He was still not satisfied with the rake of his cap which had originally been worn by Sterling Hayden in *Doctor Strangelove.* Lindbergh had always coveted it. The guys at the last base he commanded had, at his suggestion, clubbed together to buy it for him. There wasn't much he could have said to them without choking, so he had saluted them instead. They had returned his salute with their own.

"Any kind of politics." He concentrated on the mirror. "I'm no friend of politics. We could have finished this job in ten seconds. But all we got was interference. We could have taken out the whole lot of them."

"On one card, I bet," Trixie Brunner. "I love Americans. I love your generosity. Why can't we all be Americans? I'm so jealous of your wonderful optimism."

He nodded agreeably, his eyes still on the mirror. He tipped the cap a little further to the right. "Guess who?"

The door behind them opened revealing a tall black man in a fatigue jacket from which the insignia had been ripped. He was clearly in poor spirits. "Sir?"

"How's the war going, captain?"

"Sir, until we realize we are over-confident, under-informed and over there, we are not going to move forward. Sooner or later we must conclude the obvious. We sound good but we are crap at real life. Every boast we have made, we have been unable to deliver on. I suggest we waste no further time. I further suggest we do not compound our mistakes. We have been living a fantasy. Sir."

"Well-spoken, Corporal Ewell. You can tell them I'll be down for my photo-opportunity in a couple, okay?"

"Sir." The black man closed the door slowly.

Wrong-Way shared a confidence with Trixie. "He lost it. He's a screamer. You know what I mean, don't you, sweetheart? Poor bastard. He was doing so well until he started wetting his panties. A tribute to his race. But that's war for you." He paused in his pumping and looked around for his cigar.

Jerry felt the phone vibrating in his back pocket. He fished it out while Mrs. Persson got Wrong-Way by the goolies and hauled him off the bike. "Pentagon Emergency Room," he said.

"Where is this?" he asked the grimacing general. "Approximately?"

"You're asking me?" Wrong-Way was beginning to relax into familiar discomforts as Mrs. Persson gave him another squeeze. He winked at her. "I've always been attractive to strong women. It's the uniform, isn't it? What do you think of the cap?"

Jerry went to find a window.

He met Trixie sorting through the ruined office. "What a mess. You'd think someone had let off a bomb in here." She was depressed. "I'd expected something a little more, well, expensive."

"This is the twelfth Penta-cabin they've built. They were supposed to fool the enemy, but they made them too big. It was a matter of prestige, apparently. You can't really have a *tiny* pentagon. It would send out the wrong signals."

Wrong-Way was sweating and giggling. "Is this a bust?"

"Or is it a bust," Trixie agreed. She had found a player and was hooking it up to the computer. "Here we go-go." The Pet Shop Boys were soon strutting their stuff over the microwaves.

She was living out the life her mother had missed.

"I say, Jerry." She began to bop. "Did you ever see Freddy Mercury at the Flamingo?"

"Only as I was leaving." Jerry closed his eyes and took a grip. It was time to order a pizza. He reached for his phone again.

It was missing.

Trixie waved it as she left, anxious to catch up with Corporal Ewell, who was walking slowly, with shoulders slumped, down the porta-passage. "Sorry. Force of habit." With an apologetic shrug, she popped it in her purse.

Jerry went to see if there was still a fridge. The way things were going, he'd be perfectly happy with a Coke and a pretzel.

ELEVEN

Digging My Potatoes

> "Over 23,00 American steel workers have lost their jobs because of unfair foreign trade practices. The US Department of Commerce calls it 'the thirty-year history of repeated unfair trade actions…' Foreign countries dump their subsidized steel in US markets. It destroys American jobs and devastates communities. Since 1998 alone, 29 steel companies have gone bankrupt and over 23,000 workers have lost their jobs. The International Trade Commission ruled that surging imports have seriously injured the US steel industry.
>
> It's time to level the playing field for American steel workers. Under Section 201 of the Trade Act of 1974, the President can institute a strong remedy that gives workers in America's steel companies a fair chance to compete. Urge the President to implement strong 201 trade relief."
>
> —Advertisement, Minimill 201 Coalition,
> *Representing America's 21st Century Steel Companies*

> "The effects are also touching Wall Street. In the past few weeks, investors have shifted their attention to other companies, making a frenzied search for any dodgy accounting that might reveal the next Enron . . . This week shares in Elan, an Irish-based drug maker, were pummelled by worries over its accounting policies . . . All this might create the impression that corporate financial reports, the quality of company profits and the standard of auditing in America have suddenly and simultaneously deteriorated. Yet that would be wide of the mark: the deterioration has actually been apparent for many years."
>
> —*The Economist*, February 9, 2002

"It was probably a bit short-sighted making the States autonomous, although that was the thinking of the day." Professor Hira embraced his favorite occidental. "You have to admit the idea has merits. But as the states divided, the corporations united. Oh, Jerry, you are looking so fit and chipper. You were so beautiful when you were young." It was very warm. There was a smell of new-mown grass. Somewhere, over on the other side of the cholera ditch, a game was still going on.

Jerry leaned his bat against a yim-yum tree and stooped to remove his pads. He knew that his whites were tightening over his bottom, distracting the physicist. He also knew how good his thighs and buttocks looked again. He wanted something out of Hira and he knew he had to use every possible device.

Hira was blooming, too. The little Brahmin radiated good health. "Weren't we right to start with, all those years ago? But can this be the beginning of the end? So soon? Something will follow us, surely?"

"Well, it's Hobbes eat Hobbes round here at the moment," said Jerry. "Worse than usual. The problem with the imperial leviathan, as you know, is feeding him. If we are going to make anything to last, we'd better get busy."

"I have always had control of the juggernaut. I needed your engine." Professor Hira beamed. He passed a plump, delicate hand over Jerry's left cheek, arm and hip. "Your energy is high. I hope you are wiser than the first time we met."

Jerry grinned.

The Hindu was surprised. "Have you been filing your teeth?

Have you had trouble with your meat?"

"No," said Jerry. "I've been living in France."

Professor Hira followed Jerry gingerly into the big double hammock. It took him a moment to stop swinging. "I always said that's where you'd end up."

"We resist the inner voice," said Jerry. "It is our destiny."

"*Nous verrons...*"

Professor Hira took some long, deep breaths. He sat up carefully, removed his crumpled linen jacket and threw it towards the table where they had taken their drinks. "Isn't it astonishing how possession of the atomic bomb immediately robs one of moral authority?"

For a time there was silence. In the distance there still could be heard the clip of leather on willow, the cheering, the clapping. After some years, Kashmir was once again playing Bengal. It had taken a while to build back the teams. But there was unlikely to be much violence, now. Sometimes people took a game altogether too seriously.

Jerry swung out of the hammock and went to find his cigarettes. The dirty glasses had been removed. The collapsible card table was new. A fresh bottle was in the ice-bucket. Two glasses on a side table.

Hira approached on weakened legs, tucking in his shirt. He squinted against the sun. Jerry offered him a Sullivan's.

"Do you need moral authority, once you have the bomb?" Jerry sat down opposite him at the dark green baize. He took a fresh pack of cards from the side box, broke the seals and spread the deck before him, shuffled, spread, shuffled again. He put the deck in the middle of the baize. Hira picked it back up and began to shuffle left to right.

He admitted to feeling a little uneasy if his various gods were not treated with proper respect. Even though he was a rational man. "There is a certain authority demanded by even the smallest household god," he said. "I'm not sure that's our best model. But pantheism must always be preferable, surely, to monotheism? You lived in a world which promised choice but denied it at the the most fundamental levels! A complete perversion of the ideals, the enthusiasm which it harnessed. Thank the great Lord Ganesh that it's over. Look at the awful trouble you get into by cutting your road straight, no matter what the nature of the landscape. It's a mind-set which, to say the least, leads swiftly to a *cul-de-sac*."

"Oh, it's just communications and demographics." Jerry was determined not to get into anything too heavy. "News travels faster, ages come and go faster, one generation swiftly succeeds another. *Ovem lupo committere.*" It was odd how his Latin was coming back.

He fingered the elegant cut of his vestments. He was getting used to this reversal in his fortunes. He had been the underdog for too long.

Jerry was to be the first Catholic governor of Kashmir. He looked across the lawn at his wonderful palace, white filigree like carved ivory in the evening sunlight. The Society had been persuaded to pay for the building. Locals were only impressed by lavish lifestyles. They respected you for it. Most of all, as he had explained to the Pope, they admired a religion which could afford such extensive building work. India had been fine under the nabobs. It was the bureaucrats who spoiled everything.

This job was really a sort of retirement. He had been removed from the active list. The locals looked after the paper work and saw any would-be converts. There were fewer and fewer these days, as the Muslim population dwindled. There had been only two conversions to Hinduism. It would have been graceless to point this out to Hira. Christianity had a way of turning its aggressions into effective instruments. It must have something. He had never been able to stand outside his culture as much as he would have liked.

Without speaking, they sat staring at their hands. Temporarily, they appeared to have forgotten the game they were playing. "What a shame our religions have so little in common." Professor Hira frowned. "Was it always so?"

"You once argued that physics and Hinduism moved in the same direction to the same end."

"Oh, that was a very long time ago. I was so optimistic about everything. A very twisted tiny twig on the great multiversal tree.

We have come a long way, Monsignor Cornelius. We have learned something fundamental about the nature of time. Such a very, very long way. Now we are closer to discovering what time actually is, we are almost free of the concrete. Don't you feel your load lightening, your feet walking on air?"

Jerry wasn't sure.

Reaching across the table, Professor Hira smoothed Jerry's hair. "It is a terrific responsibility, old boy. Am I supposed to represent courage, temperance, justice and practical wisdom? And, if so, how? It's a bit of a stumbler, that one.

Greeks, now, was it? Jerry was beginning to wonder what he had ever seen in his little buddy.

TWELVE

Lively Up Yourself

> "Perhaps the most common observation at the annual meeting last week in New York of the World Economic Forum, that feast of self-congratulation by the business and political elite, was that most businessmen are gloomier about America's economic prospects than most economists are . . . corporate American fears a rather weak recovery."
>
> —*Economist,* February 9, 2001

> **"Soldiers of the King**
>
> A series of 36
>
> **36: Sudan Defence Forces**
>
> The Sudan Defence Forces consist of a Cavalry Corps, Camel Corps, Eastern Arab Corps, Sudanese Machine Gun battery, Western Corps, as well as engineer troops and various departmental corps; a typical member of the Camel Corps is shown. With the exception of one regular battalion the units are made up of irregulars who enlist for three years. The force is jointly officered by British and native officers, and consists of approximately half Arabs and half Sudanese and Equatorial Africans; the language used is Arabic. A private is known as a 'Nafar', a lieutentant 'Mulazim Awal' and the commandant of the force 'Kaid El 'Amm.' "
>
> —Godfrey Phillips Cigarette Card, c. 1935

Freedom Is Being There

"The freedom to go where you want to go, when you want to go, is a precious liberty. And with government and industry taking important steps to ensure your comfort and safety, the nation's skyways are once again ready to help you make the most of that freedom."

—Advertisement, Boeing, *Forever New Frontiers*

The Scottish Special Forces were pulling out of Nova New Washington when Jerry and Taffy turned up. It had been a dodgy journey from Hollywood. Their ancient Westland Whirlwind had barely made the journey. It needed oil. It had been under wraps in the Long Beach Spruce Goose Aviation Museum until they found it.

Captain Hamish "Flash" Gordon came up over the rubble on sturdy legs, his sporran swinging. He saluted Taffy Sinclair. He adjusted his cap on his orange hair. He was sternly freckled. "Not much for you, sir. We've found most of the mines. Those bastards must have been digging for years. Guy bloody Fawkes, sir, if you don't mind. All over again. But it's not safe."

"Oh, it's all right, Captain." Sinclair took off his leather gloves. Underneath he wore another pair, made from medical rubber. "I just want a souvenir, really. Anybody hurt?"

"Not a scratch, sir. A bit of collateral damage, but I don't think we'll get many complaints." Overhead a squadron of black F117s flew in irregular formation towards the north. "That's our lads finishing off the job. Those Dutchies will find it was a mistake to take out Glasgow."

Sinclair shrugged. "Call them Dutchies if you like, Captain, but they are Americans. Our allies. This is a bit of an embarrassment."

"If they're not Dutchies, sir, why do they all have German names?"

"They're more comfortable with them. I think they sound more warlike. They've always admired the old Germans. It's the new ones they have trouble with."

"Well, they'll settle down again as soon as we get a railway built." Captain Gordon was an engineer by nature. "There's nothing like a good bit of track and a couple of sturdy locomotives to pull a people together. Didn't these Dutchies invade Canada once, too?"

"They're not famous for learning anything." Fastidiously Sinclair leaned down and picked up a small, bloody door handle. "What's this off, do you think?"

The men had prisoners. Hooded and handcuffed, they were being bundled towards a helicopter. Jerry recognised the muffled voice of General Lindbergh. The tone of his threats was not confident. Wasn't Una supposed to be looking after him? He wondered if one of the others was Corporal Ewell. He would find out soon. He might never have been sure it was Wrong Way but for the cap he clasped in his chained hands.

Easy come, easy go.

Jerry looked around for his sergeant. He was enjoying all this authority. He felt he'd earned it. The simple euphoria of optionless violence.

He kicked at some limbs sticking out of the concrete. "I thought you said you'd cleared up."

Taffy Sinclair was grateful. He kneeled on the broken slabs to get his samples. "These will be invaluable to future generations."

He was taking a keen interest in maggots. "It's amazing how the blowfly finds corpses so quickly. Any decay, really." He was having to pretend to collect DNA samples. Until the Scots established order, he had worked unofficially for the FBI. Of course, the world was running out of manpower. The new cadet corps might help. Meanwhile the local gasmen were striking, claiming that their civil rights were threatened by the Federal people having sexier uniforms. They also wanted their breathing equipment redesigned along more fashionable lines.

"Monsignor Cornelius. I'm told I have you to thank for my release." General Ewell, his uniform brilliant with the symbols of his redemption and Trixie tripping happily in tow, clambered manfully over the ruins to shake Jerry's hands. "You are a saint, sir."

Jerry nodded absently. He was, in fact, several saints. Meanwhile he had to get this awful smell of white smoke out of his nose.

"We're talking tidal waves here," General Ewell was saying to Trixie. "Massive waves which could hit the coast of Texas and sweep all the way inland to Dallas."

"I know," she said. "I'm so pleased they gave you your uniform back, aren't you? Do they zip or button?"

Spontaneously this veteran of the psychic wars put his arm around her. "Hold on there, young lady. I'm a married guy." He laughed easily, full of the comfort of her flattery. "At least I think I still am!" His eyes had the steady, unflinching gaze of a man who had been through hell, humiliation and high water and had come out the other side stronger, wiser and even more determined to fight the forces of evil. Trixie sighed with wonder at her good fortune.

THIRTEEN

No Love at All

> **Where 'GSVT' spells 'Gorilla'**
> "Rwanda is now a Guaranteed Secure Vacation Territory.
> Fly on Air France High Security Jet Liners to your glorious holiday amongst the gorillas of Rwanda's famous hill country. Visit this beautiful region's historic sights and shop in the newest mall concepts, including the Jungle River, Deep Congo and Heart of Darkness, all situated within convenient high security compounds."
> —Advertisement, *The Port Sabatini Advertiser*, July 2002

> "Our Kinda History—Egypt and the Holy Land!
> Open for Business."
> —Ibid

> "Do the Dunes
> Arabian Style
> Lands of Two Thousand and Two Delights
> Do the Dunes Saudi Style
> A big Saudi hug awaits you in Arabia's friendliest state."
> —Ibid

Africa was developing nicely. Services, security and surveillance—the famous Triple S option of the World Tourist

Organization—had never been higher. The smart money was in Nature Reserves, Safaris and Marine Expeditions. Barundi, the seventieth state to join the union, was flying the stars and stripes over the Federal Capital of Washingwood, a city of light, a city of ethereal towers and splendid armament, the center of a glorious sisterhood of emergent nations and entertainment capital of the free world.

Jerry was glad to be back from Europe. He just couldn't take the cold, these days. Still, sooner or later he would have to go and get his sister out of her drawer. Their Ice Age had come so suddenly, it had caught them napping. It was more like a slow avalanche, taking roads, railways, tunnels and burying them under tons of rapidly hardening snow. Global warming was just the second law of thermodynamics doing exactly what he had hoped it would in his optimistic, entropic youth. Energy dissipating rapidly. Everything speeding up. Get the whole farce over with and enjoy it as much as possible. The universe moving faster and faster into the great sphincter, the black hole which might or might not be its own. Rapid heat: rapid cool. Even Rwanda was cooler than this, but they hadn't installed their AC yet.

"Lord, lord," said President Ewell. He was putting on weight. His faux-gravitas had given way to a film of vulgar self-confidence. "This is just the right place to hang out and plan our strategy. It's perfect. Thank you, Colonel."

Colonel Frank Cornelius cracked an adoring smile which worked in unison with his perfect salute, which seemed to click his heels together. Jerry was proud of his brother. He should have been dead. Nobody had ever made a come back from so many different overdoses. Frank had been diligent. He had studied German clockwork toys for years. He had wanted only the source. The model. The inspiration.

"Now, your holiness, how about a run-down on these European girlies. They still getting' a touch of the vapours?" President Ewell clenched his massive, well-kept teeth around a vast cigar. By his slightly surprised expression it appeared he had found, in his mind's eye at least, true love.

Jerry wondered how he had ever worried about his feminine

side. He flicked at his boot with his dog-whip. He was here as Papa Beesley's personal bodyguard. These were to be very high level talks. They had to be, of course, since so much of the rest of the world was uncertainly flooded. You could never tell where the next wave or downpour was coming from. That was what made life such a pleasure. You could run a book on whether it would be Iowa or Indonesia which would go under next. He couldn't help grinning, remembering those ludicrous conversations Mitzi and Trixie once had at every dinner party about how the sea-levels wouldn't rise higher than Bognor or Atlantic City. But, as he'd tried to point out, the sun also rises.

He gave his leg a celebratory tap. Africa was climactically more stable and that meant a lot these days. Especially to the surviving Africans. Political stabilitization had taken a few months, but all that was behind them now. Africa, Trixie had announced to the fashionable world, was the new United States. It had all the old features and was scarcely developed. A brand ready for re-investment. The continental US was too unstable, too old-fashioned, too saturated. In the end the Constitution and the Bill of Rights had become embarrassing. When the time came, the Land of Liberty could re-launch herself as the Fjord of a Thousand Islands. It wouldn't take long. Even now the water was hiding a lot of very unattractive ruins. They would improve when the barnacles and coral had begun their work. People's romantic imaginations would do the rest. But this still wasn't the right time to be buying fjords, not until they settled down a bit. Canada, as usual, had the moral high ground, as well as the high physical ground, and had missed much of the southern ice rush.

They crossed the helipad and entered the gorgeous security lobby of the G.W. Bush Memorial Pentagonican, the elevator bearing them rapidly down below ground level, to the deep, safe bunkers where calm-faced young creatures busied themselves with security assignments. Jerry rather liked it. He was reminded of the Vatican. He didn't mind one of the boys relieving him of his heat, but he insisted he keep his shades. While one young man kneeled to pat his leg, Jerry rather ostentatiously blessed him, then unzipped. "Better check inside," he said.

There was a strong smell of popcorn. General-President Ewell slipped his arm around the intoxicated Trixie. "Ah. They have the Chief's favorite snack ready and waiting. Who loves popcorn?" His brown eyes brightened and focussed on the door marked DEN. He strode forward.

Jerry felt a hand teasing his penis. He had forgotten to rezip. He smiled amiably and winked at Trixie. He didn't mind her coaxing up a little extra support. Mrs. General Ewell had not taken quietly to the annulment of her marriage, the bastardization of her children, and the loss of her Lexus Strongbow. There were some podunk little broadcasters who were giving her publicity in urban Rangoon, but that was about all it was worth. Nonetheless, Trixie had to do what a girl had to do and Monsignor Cornelius could only applaud her prudence. This did, unfortunately, bring him back to thoughts of his sister. She was still in her drawer in the cellars of the Convent of the Poor Clares, Ladbroke Grove, 1971. He couldn't find his notes about the exact dates. But it had been traumatic and he had to get back there somehow. He had a bunch of dogs to feed.

President Ewell snapped his fingers and at this signal a ring of hand-picked young marines surrounded him. He gave them all a manly punch, a manly hug. Some of them blushed to the roots of their crew-cuts. A hug from President Ewell meant more than meat and drink to these unflinching patriots. This was where the war against the Death Star Terrorists and all other rogue nations would begin and there was no doubt who would be attracting the tourists next season. For the DST, there would be no "next season."

His triumph, his luck in surviving, gave his hips the swing of a high-class pimp. "I love it here," he told Jerry. "I love it. It's my roots, you know. It gets to my soul. You don't know what it did to me when that bastard took out Jerusalem. That's stupid. Get rid of the problem by getting rid of the disputed territory? It'll take years to reproduce. It was one of the most valuable heritage sites in the world."

Trixie spoke significantly to Jerry, her eyes urgently enigmatic. "Well, we all thought it looked okay in the rehearsals and nobody bothers to listen to those projections any more."

"Run by a bunch of little novice nunnies, Monsignor, if you'll forgive the reference." President Ewell flung himself into his big easy chair and reached for his remote. "But in those days we didn't know any better. New Jerusalem seemed just the idea to stop Britain bumping along the bottom. We owed that to our allies, at least, what was left of them. Oh, Jesus, was that a waste of time and money!" He laughed and lit his cigar. It was a massive blunt. The glorious smell of Pakistani Mountain began to ease through the corridors of power. Almost every passive smoker was pleased the President was home.

"Fucking bagpipe fuckers." While his guests settled themselves about the room, the president snapped on his control. Road runners and cartoon mice raced back and forth in awesome clarity. "My mother named me after the Lord of Loch Awe, you know. We had ties with the Scots. And that's what they did to us." A tiny screen appeared in the main picture. Smoke and rubble, but there was no way of knowing exactly where.

"It confounded the futurologists, anyway," said Trixie. "Just shows you what their warnings were worth. Scottish independence all the way! I blame that awful Blurr."

Scotland was the latest rogue state. Parachuting in and firing a few shots, the Black Watch had raised the cross of St. Andrew over the Great Temple. Their Sikh and Pashtoon allies had secured the Great Mosque and they thought it politic to let the Covenanters bring the Church under Christian control.

Britain conquered, it was a Race to Nova Nova Washington, which the Scots, with their battle blimps, won easily, wiping out most of the opposition. The President had opened the prisons and armed the inmates in a desperate rearguard action, but the prisoners had fallen on one another, settling old scores, and again the Scots needed to do little but watch. Given enough time, Americans would always wipe one another out. The miserable climate cheered the Scots up. Flash Gordon was never more ebullient. He exposed a sturdy groin for the camera.

"But we're already working out how to get back what's left of our native real estate." Trixie nodded confidently.

For some reason President Ewell remembered Jerry as an ally

at one of the old pentagons when he was, as he had put it himself, going through his baptism of shit which had turned him into the man of steel they saw before them. He liked to keep Jerry around, he said, even though he would be forced to shoot his brother. Sometimes he needed a little spiritual consolation. The dandy priest was no threat and he made an ideal bodyguard, a perfect mouthpiece. He was a great all-rounder.

Jerry murmured something ecclesiastical and went to pour himself a glass of wine.

"Back in the saddle are we, Jerry?"

It was Una. She was as friendly as ever. Still a little disconcerting. But they were lovers again, at least when it suited her, and the sex was almost as good as home-made.

"Where's Catherine?" Una wanted to know. It was clear, too, that she was enjoying herself. You could tell from her clothes. She was wearing her long, tailored coat, her high boots, her black, silk scarf, her black bearskin hat. Given the heat of the den, with its massive home entertainment center, she seemed over-dressed. And yet when she spoke, her breath steamed.

"They took all my weapons at the door. Even my little Swiss Army knife. I use that for my nails." She stopped to cough. More white vapour came out of her mouth. It was like ectoplasm. This disconcerted him. He moved to embrace her.

"Oh, darling," she said. "It's been hideous without you."

FOURTEEN

Ghost Riders in the Sky

> "In the early, emotionally charged days after 11 September, I am told, Bush gave the go-ahead to the CIA and the US military to use torture against captives; this I suspect, could return to haunt him.
>
> Not with the American public, who in their current mood would heartily support Bush and endorse not only torture, but slow death by strangulation and molten iron if they could. But such visible unravelling and official wrongdoing, if exposed, would certainly give the rest of the world a 'bad case of the vapors.' And the US will have found

that, in its enthusiasm, it has burnt bridges to overseas which, it will turn out—perhaps before too long—Americans need desperately."

—Andrew Stephen, *New Statesman*, February 25, 2002

They had tracked down the GB Oil Gang, or what was left of it. Ewsuck had been forced in the end to give them up. There were one or two small time oil lords still at large, but most of the organization's high-ranking members were all accounted for. It was now just a formality to declare their former homeland a terrorist state and send in the daisy cutters.

Someone had clearly warned the Barbecue Kid. The Kid had created a diversion and escaped. There wasn't much left of Houston or Dallas. Every so often he issued a video.

President-General Ewell was still reassuring his economists. "This is like the Hundred Years War. Out of that came a stronger Germany. It paved the way for Bismarck. And whereas it took them generations, we can do it in a week. That's the wonder of modern IT technology. Don't worry. I'm looking out for any frauleins wearing dynamite vests."

He glanced at them for their approval. They nodded. He returned his attention to the TV.

His captured predecessor was munching pretzels and watching reruns of college football games. He still didn't know he was under arrest. He gasped and pointed and waved his fists in the air.

They sat in his tower, looking out over the campus of the University of Texas, at Austin. The city was virtually untouched. Her parks and lakes were tranquil in the afternoon sun. She had been collaterally cleansed with a new kind of audio weapon. When they had arrived, only the Kid's soft-eyed fighters patrolled the streets. These had been quietly taken out by some Gurkhas who had jokingly cut their heads off and then stuck them back again the wrong way round. From hiding they had watched as other fighters had discovered their comrades. Much of the time it looked as if they themselves had inadvertently knocked their colleagues' heads off. Usually the Gurkhas gave themselves away by giggling.

Now they were mopping up. It was mostly blood. It would

take the usual three days, but there wasn't much left of any value. From where he sat with his advisors, General-President Ewell pointed up suddenly. He could see the full moon through his window. "Isn't that perfect. Wouldn't you call that perfect?"

His prisoner took another chocolate brownie from the piled plate beside him. "Make yourselves at home, my friends. Presumably you want to talk about peace terms. Well you won't wriggle out of the consequences of your action quite so easily. You've run up a big bill there." He turned squinting, vacant eyes on them. "It's going to have to be paid."

They ignored him. He returned his attention to the television.

"I was never sure of those chaps whose eyes were too close together. Say what you like, Roy Rogers was untrustworthy." Una handed Jerry a barbecued french bean. "Could I ask you for some spiritual advice?"

"Always open for business for you, dear Mrs. Persson." His beautiful white and gold vestments rose and fell as he sat down on the edge of a floral sofa. "But I hope we're not plotting. You know how I prefer to put the pieces together later."

"What would that gain us? A perpetual Byzantium?"

"Which was a hectic place for most of the time. A Greek Empire should have been our goal, not some awful second hand Rome."

"Did you know the Caliphates despised Rome?" She cracked a carrot. "They weren't interested in anything about them. You could call it rivalrous, but I honestly believe they saw Romans as barbarians, just as the Egyptians saw the Saudis."

"Well, they were right about the Saudis. The last bunch of Egyptians I saw were stripped to the waist and working on the roads. But it is very difficult to revitalize a nation without the resources of the outlaw economies. When will we be getting the oil through, do you think?" She felt about in a salad for some bacon.

"We don't need oil any more." Jerry took her greasy hand. "It's all wind-power, these days."

The Prisoner-President had heard that. His frown deepened. He raised his voice. "There are some things I don't want to hear on my watch, gentlemen." He rose up, magnificent in his special Indian set. "Let's remember our language. There is a lady present." With a geeky gesture, he stooped to kiss her hand, but she withdrew it fastidiously. She had a feeling he was after her Rolex. "Why are you all obsessed with watches."

"Watches are responsibility," he told her. "And time is money."

"I hate to break into your last big wank," she said, "but did you know you're under arrest?"

"I never put my own family interests ahead of this great nation's." He had become a rich, dark plum color. "Because my family interests are the fucking country. You know what—there's guys out there want me to be king. King George sounds a lot better than King Ko-leen. That ain't a monarch, it's a country song. How does that sound? Ko-leen? Studies have shown this. Many studies. They have shown it. That's what you socialistic assholes fail to determinate." Without his autoprompt, he was losing his inhibitions.

"I don't have to apologize to anyone in the world."

"There's nothing to apologize for," said Jerry, cocking his shooter. "Turn him over, Mrs. P. We might as well finish the job right here. It's what his inner man would have wanted."

She took a step back. She had never approved of Jerry's taste in torture. Or revenge. Or, in this case, what could be sex.

Averting her eyes, she handed him the tube of KY.

FIFTEEN

Who Is That Man?

> "It is on George Tenet's watch, after all, that the CIA was unable to penetrate al-Quaeda in order to determine its capabilities, and more important, the terrorists organization's intentions, prior to September 11.
>
> It is on George Tenet's watch that the CIA allowed the bombing of the Chinese embassy in Belgrade because it didn't have the right maps.
>
> It is under George Tenet's watch that the Khobar Towers and U.S.S. Cole bombing investigations have been botched.
>
> And it is under George Tenet's watch that the Counterterrorism Center was in the words of J. a former CTC official, 'eviscertated.' "
>
> —John Weisman, *Soldier of Fortune*, March 2002

"Fourth came what is universally seen here as the 'victory' of the war in Afghanistan by an invincible military, despite its failure to apprehend Osama Bin Laden, or virtually any of the rest of the top al-Qaeda leadership, or even the pathetic Mullah Omar.

This has led to what the late Senator J. William Fulbright called the 'arrogance of power' here. Even Colin Powell has rudely and condescendingly turned on America's European critics."

—Andrew Stephen, *New Statesman*, February 25, 2002

"Soldiers of the King
A series of 36
31: Jodhpur Lancers
Jodhpur, or Marwar, is the largest Indian State in the Rajputana Agency, and the State Forces include a regiment of lancers, an infantry battalion, and a transport corps. These troops are maintained by the Maharaja—who has a salute of seventeen guns—and placed at the service of the Empire in case of great emergency. The Jodhpur Lancers upheld all their ancient glory and tradition when they fought side by side with other units of Indian cavalry in France and Palestine during the Great War of 1914–1918. Jodhpur was taken under British protection in 1818."

—Godfrey Phillips Cigarette Card, c. 1935

Hitler Plans to Reinforce Franco
"Germans in Spain Claim Five Divisions May Join Rebels
Warning from Army Chiefs ignored."

—*News Chronicle*, December 21, 1936

Almost diffidently, Taffy came into the cell. "How are they looking after you?" His white coat made him look like a Smithfield trader. The old pig pens under the market had been adapted to a jail. Mo, of course, was an obvious suspect and had been caught red-handed in the basement of Bertran Rota's, desperately trying to find a first edition of *Across the Pampas* by G.A. Henty. Someone had told him he was mentioned in it.

Mo was reconciled now. He knew the locals were hoping for a hanging. Through the little barred window, not far away, came the sound of merriment as they played curling and quoits on the Thames ice above Blackfriars. Taffy had, in fact, just returned from a curling match in which the Home Office played the

Foreign Office. He had never met the Foreign Office before who had remarked on his excellent Welsh.

"Very well," said Mo. "Oh, very well, indeed. I mean, this is luxury. Though they won't let me have my gun. Other than that—perfect. Very good. And they haven't touched me. Universal human rights and all that. Impeccable. But boring. My only serious complaint. I've tried everything to wind them up, but they're Mormons, you know, or Seventh Day Adventists, and it's not altogether sporting. The drugs are excellent. I've no complaints, Guv'nor. That's why I'm not complaining." His arms and hands were covered with small, bloody cracks. As if they had split suddenly and then healed.

Taffy was looking at the marks. "I've never seen stigmata like them. What happened?"

"It's a long story," said Mo. "It started in Carthage. The date was well BC, but I couldn't tell you exactly how long ago. Not me, you understand. Someone I know. You can pass this stuff on. It can stay dormant in the blood for centuries. He didn't know it. I never bothered. Then, about a year ago, I saw the prison doctor."

Taffy smiled to himself. "I am the prison doctor. The only one they need."

"Don't worry, doc." Mo rolled up his sleeves. "I won't tell them, if you don't." He offered loyalty as a matter of course. He loved being loyal. He loved a good cause. "How's that fine lady of yours." He rolled down his sleeves. "What about some Iron Maiden?" He snapped a CD into its player.

"Not now," said Taffy. "I've come to take blood. And spot of DNA, if that's okay. We're eliminating today."

Mo wasn't sure if they were joking. "Not in my cell you don't. What's happened? Lost your enema machine again? My guess is the yanks have got it."

"But you don't know about Brick Lane." Taffy began to prepared the syringe. "Not about what happened at Number Eighteen?"

"When was this?" Mo hopefully eyed the syringe. "Few months ago, or longer? Number Eighteen? Is that the top end or the bottom end? We did a lot of houses that day. Straight through the walls, Israeli-style. Those guys are hard, right?"

Taffy pressed the "record" button of his old-fashioned tape player. "And when did you discover they were hard?"

"Not long after it started. I was watching the news and eating an apple. I always used to eat an apple in those days. Of course they weren't organic. Do you think that could have done it, doc? Turned me stupid, like that?"

"I don't know. They still want to get you for murder, if they can."

Mo began to laugh spontaneously. "I haven't killed anyone in weeks. That's not murder, that's enemy crossfire. You know you can't afford a bunch of prisoners when you're going in. There's only one thing you can do for them. I wasn't in the SAS for my health, doc. Although, I have to admit, I picked up some healthy habits. Never lost them. They were like brothers to me, those guys. I could have wept when they busted up the unit. I loved those guys. We had a bond." He brushed away a manly tear.

"How did they do it?"

"Oh, some sort of fragmentation device. They had no idea what they were using. I was pissed off. I could have done a lot more with it. But that's sodding American gunnery for you. Worst in the world, after the Turks. And the Turks have an excuse. Most of their guns are about five hundred years old. Great while they lasted, I have to admit."

"So how were you captured?"

"Captured?" Mo began to laugh. "I wasn't captured. I walked all the way here from Watford and signed myself in. I know the Yeomen of the Guard, see. Then I went to find my book." He brandished the handsome three-decker. "And they came and picked me up when they were ready. Not much left around Piccadilly, eh? It wasn't a bad walk. Nothing left of Leicester Square, of course. Funny fires. Very fatty. Buggers your nose up."

"What?" said Taffy, who had been fiddling with his tape-recorder. "All the way through?"

SIXTEEN

Get Yourself Another Fool

As Terrorism Grows, the More Vital Battle Blimps become
" 'A lot of NASA Helios technology has found its way into what we are doing,' Charles K. Lavan Jr. tells *Popular Mechanics*. He is the principal engineer for advanced programs at Lockheed Martin Naval Electronics and Surveillance Systems in Akron. The company has designed a high-altitude airship that can carry telephone- and internet-switching equipment. Lavan heads a team that comes up with a design that uses nacelle-mounted, brushless DC motors to keep a blimp 'on station'. Hydrogen and oxygen are stored in hollow tail-structure tubes—and there will be plenty to store."

—Jim Wilson, *Popular Mechanics,* March 2002

'We're Back In A Nightmare Of Aggression'
" 'We are in a menacing world, but we're British, we'll pull it off,' declared Mr. Herbert Morrison at Birmingham last night. Mr. Morrison said that before we had really had time to grasp the balance of payments crisis the bad news from Prague came as another blow in the rear. 'In fact on top of all our economic troubles we find ourselves back in the same sort of nightmare of aggression we thought we had banished by disposing of Hitler.' "

—*News of the World*, March 14, 1948

"The action taken by Washington on August 20, 1998, continues to deprive the people of Sudan of needed medicine.

Germany's Ambassador to Sudan writes that 'It is difficult to assess how many people in this poor African country died as a consequence of the destruction of the Al-Shida factory, but several tens of thousands seems a reasonable guess.' "

—Noam Chomsky, *9-11*, Seven Stories Press,
New York, October 2001

"This country is not strong enough to face such a war without the wholehearted and immediate support of the United States. There was never the slightest chance that the United States, which by established tradition expects its capitalists to take care of themselves, would pluck Anglo-Iranian's chestnuts out of the fire for Mr. Attlee or Mr. Churchill or any other combination of British Interests. The Americans might indeed have been dragged in eventually, but only if

Abadan had become the Sarajevo of 1951. The morality is equally simple. If the world is to have a chance of making progress towards freedom and peace, it can only be by recognizing that commercial enterprises in backward countries must no longer be backed by guns. The rule of law means the end of sterling imperialism; and Britain accepted that doctrine as binding in subscribing to the Charter of the United Nations."

—*New Statesman and Nation*, October 6, 1951

"Are you sure this is the appropriate time to be escaping?" Una held the co-pilot's controls as Jerry stripped off his heavy djellabah. The C-Class Imperial Flying Boat flew with her usual steady grace. Kept in good order, she would last until the end of time. Jerry drew a deep, relaxing breath, enjoying the familiar finishes of his instrument panels, the purist aesthetic of his deco passenger quarters.

"You don't know what this means to me," he said. "I was just beginning to slip away again. I couldn't have lasted. Didn't you see me thinning out?"

"My guess is, you're looking for your mum."

"God knows, Mrs. P. I'm in this for the fun."

"Well, I'll believe you when I see the run."

"Annie Get Your Effing Gun?"

A little pettishly, Jerry took the controls. The aircraft dipped and recovered. Judging by the smoke, they were still somewhere over Kashmir. Jerry turned right towards the sea.

"Steady on!" cried Major Nye from the starboard toilet. "Having a bit of trouble in here, as it is."

Side by side in the comfortable seats, Taffy Sinclair and Mo Collier were going through an old cigarette card collection they had found in a locker. "Look at this one!" Mo showed it to his new friend. "Fifty Famous Chickens."

"See," said Jerry, setting the automatic pilot and accepting a Russian Tea from Mitzi Beesley, who had found the bar and was loving the retro implements. She had mixed far too many cocktails already and was running out of glasses.

Jerry sipped his tea. "How did we go from living like this, to living like that?"

"It has to do with how we trade." Una got up and smoothed down her skirt. "But you know me. Economics was always my Achilles heel." She went to look at the drinks, gently vibrating on the bar. "What's that pink one, Mitzi?"

"It's meant to be a Shirley Temple, but I forgot not to add the gin. It's a bit sweet."

Una placed her fingers firmly round the glass. Sipping, she grimaced and looked down through a window. "Oh, that's so beautiful. The torquoise water. Where is that?"

"Well, it was Bengal." Major Nye came out of the toilet. His hair was freshly brushed and he had spruced his moustache. "Very little of her left now, poor bastards. I was stationed there once, as a young man. Not a rich country. But the tigers were magnificent."

He went to look for his Singapore Sling.

"What happens next?" asked Mitzi happily. "Do the tigers all evolve into fish?" Her sense of evolutionary time was derived entirely from half-hour Nature documentaries. "I expect the people will do some beautiful fish farms. You know how they can make anything gorgeous from a few fronds and a rock. And they're *so* spiritual."

When Mitzi had wiggled into the loo, Mrs. Persson pulled the shutters and closed her eyes, trying to see a way forward. All she could make out was a tangle of highways, twisted into unnavigable shapes by some astonishingly malevolent force. Was she at last about to confront Satan?

She was kicking herself for letting Jerry talk her into this. She had fallen for his charm all over again. Well, it was too late for regrets. Besides, she was by and large having a very good time. Just as some people were designed for untroubled rural peace or constant love affairs, others were designed for crisis. They needed almost constant adrenaline surges or they could not feel properly alive. She was beginning to remember who she was. She was recollecting the subtle flavors of different livers.

"Tasty," she said.

Jerry put on his headphones. From his skull came the faint tones of Mose Allison's "Everybody's Cryin' Mercy." The plane flew gracefully over the water, disturbing herons and other water birds. He reached his hand towards the bank of toggles and began to flick them on and off in rapid, coded sequences. Then he turned up his headphones until he could hear only the music.

As soon as she was back, Major Nye rejoined Mitzi at the little bar. "Same again, my dear, if you please." He glanced at his watch. "We should be there soon, with a spot of luck."

SEVENTEEN

Last Train to San Fernando

> "Former vice-president Al Gore said tonight there should be a 'final reckoning' with Iraqi President Saddam Hussein's regime in the war on terrorism . . . "
>
> —*Washington Post*, February 12, 2002

> " 'This is going to be a war of attrition,' Mr. Davis said of the Republicans' strategy against Democrats nationwide in a meeting with one of his recruits, 'and we have more tanks, more helicopters, more troops than they do.' "
>
> —Rep. Thos. M. Davis III,
> Chairman of the Republican Congressional Campaign Committee,
> *New York Times*, March 3, 2001

> "Unlike in Afghanistan, there is no obliging opposition to do the dirty work. There is little hope that the elite Republican guard . . . will turn traitor. That leaves the prospect of a ground war involving up to 200,000 US troops, and deplored by every section of Mr. Bush's crumbling alliance… Mr. Bush's motives are more murky. They are about oil, naturally. (Iran's 'evilness', for instance, rests on its democratic tendency's wish to exploit its energy reserves with other partners) . . . They are about imposing a Pax America from Georgia to the Philipinnes. They are about double standards."
>
> —Mary Riddell, *Observer*, March 3, 2002

As the flying boat circled over the lagoons and waterways of High Calcutta, Professor Hira came from the back of the plane to sit in the navigator's chair, behind Jerry. "Is that the marina?" he asked.

Jerry banked for a landing.

"The whole place looks abandoned," said Una. "Who was it responded to your phone call?"

"I didn't ask," said Jerry, checking his instruments. "But it sounded like an elephant. Would that be Ganesh?"

"Not likely," Hira said. "Not after the big one. But it was a deep voice, eh?"

"It had to be a demi-god, the way the whole phone shook. Didn't they build this place?"

"Well, they had the vision, but their worshippers did the grunt work. I'm really not happy with all this myths and legends stuff. I blame Hollywood. It's just revived the worst regressive aspects of everyone's DNA."

Una put a placatory hand on Professor Hira's sleeve. He had turned his eyes to the floor. He had lost touch with his own metaphysics and he wasn't sure he could get back. Einsteinian logic had meant so much to him. But now everything he had placed his faith in was proving to be as disappointing as everything he thought he had escaped. Oppenheimer had known what was going on. But it was not in his nature to complain.

"It was nobody's fault," he said. "All the punters moved to Nanking."

They were coming down fast.

Jerry lifted his nose and felt the floats touch smooth water, slowly taking purchase as he cut the engine and lifted the ailerons. The plane swung a little on the surface, then he switched on again and began to taxi towards the huge white marble quay.

The quayside was completely deserted. The signs, the stores, the few office buildings, had all received the worst of the recent hurricane. The last Hindu Nationalist government had built these massive marble sea walls and monumental quays, each dedicated to a major deity. But the huge brass statues had been lost to the elements as their pedestals crumbled into the aggressive ocean. Above the water poked the massive head of Ganesh, part of an ear, an eye and a tusk, encrusted with algae and nameless flotsam.

"He doesn't look at all happy," said Jerry. Jerry himself was full of high spirits.

He cut the engine and let the flying boat float towards the steps. The place had a morbid, sinister air.

They bumped gently against the quay.

Professor Hira was first off the plane and running up the steps with a mooring rope. He wound several turns around the broken capstan. Then he waved to them and, beneath wide, gray skies trotted towards the flattened remains of the Customs House. Una Persson stepped down onto the float and with some elegance reached towards an iron ring, putting her foot onto the sea-stairs. Rapidly, followed by Jerry and Major Nye, she began to climb.

A damp wind blew across the deserted quays and Una turned up the collar of her black, military coat. Overhead wave after wave of gray cloud rolled. Jerry pushed his hands deeper into his pockets. "Parky," he said. Was this really the end of Empire?

"Who'd have thought it? Brought low by a few heavy showers?" The Americans had fought a war on too many fronts, yet they had good domestic reasons to know that nobody beats the weather. The English had understood that for centuries. Especially where Ireland was concerned.

Major Nye looked behind him. "All ashore that's going ashore!" He was almost jovial now.

Back in the tiny kinema, Mitzi and Mo Collier were snuggled up watching a Seaton Begg thriller, *The Terror of Tangier.* For Mo a new Seaton Begg movie was a sort of epiphany. In other lives, the stars had been close acquaintances of his.

Gloria Cornish had never been more sexy and sophisticated than when she played the infamous adventuress Mademoiselle Roxanne, G.H. Teed's finest character. Mo had read the book and didn't think it was a very good adaptation but was enjoying this scene. Shackled in his cell, guarded by sinister Arabs, Seaton Begg's assistant Tink hasn't a chance, but, disguised as a dancing girl, Roxanne sneaks in to his rescue.

Gloria Cornish played the dashing Frenchwoman and Sir Seaton Begg was, as usual, played by debonair Max Peters. Mitzi never tired of Mo's boasting of his acquaintance with the stars. It was one of his most attractive features.

EIGHTEEN

Not Dark Yet

"Law Enforcement Products
For
Law Enforcement Professionals
Smith & Wesson
American Made American Owned
* Handguns * Handcuffs * Bicycles *
Smith & Wesson"

—Advertisement, *Guns & Weapons*, April 2002

"The phrase 'business as usual', which we make a show of trotting out whenever we suffer a terrorist attack here, seems to have no resonance on the other side of the Atlantic."

—Simon Heffer, Spectator, February 9, 2002

Ammo as Street-Ready as the Officer Carrying it
"Law Enforcement professionals face a greater variety of tactical situations than ever before. That's why TAP™ ammunition from Hornady is quickly becoming the standard by which all ammo is measured.

Hornady has developed a complete line of rifle, handgun and shotgun ammunition that delivers reliability, incredible accuracy, and hard-hitting terminal performance."

—Advertisement, *Guns & Weapons For Law Enforcement*, April, 2002

Colonel Pyat had never looked younger to Jerry. He wore his fur cap on the side of his head, sported a fancy silk dark green coat with light green frogging, his baggy trousers tucked into soft riding boots. Belts of ammunition were over both shoulders and hanging from his saddle. He had a sabre in his right hand, a pair of Webley .45s on his hips, a Martini carbine in the holster on his saddle. From his belt hung a long black and silver Cossack dagger.

Pyat had risen swiftly in the Canadian hetman's ranks and by the time the Cossacks reached Boston's lagoons he was in command of five squadrons and a number of flying machine-gun carts, drawn by sturdy Arab horses, ridden bareback by the careless boys who took them into battle. The method of temporary causeways developed by the Cossacks' Bengali engineers were ingenious.

The colonel's massive moustache made him look like Josef Stalin, but his dark brown eyes were full of a life Stalin's had never known.

He saluted as he rode up on his stocky steppe pony. He resheathed his sabre, staring over the water-logged landscape. The well-trained pony scarcely moved. "My dear Monsignor Cornelius? You are very welcome. As you know, you have co-religionists here in New Ukraine, though most of us prefer the more ancient resonances of the Orthodox Church. Still, many of our lads are dutiful Catholics and would welcome a little confessing, I'm sure." He had become more tolerant as his military successes increased. "I have friends in both Rome and Venice. You?"

"Well, I did have." Jerry was a little baffled. "Rome, Mecca and Jerusalem were all taken out. It was President Guiliano's big initiative. When they banned the Old Testament? Tough on terrorism. Tough on the causes of terrorism."

"I wonder why everyone was so tolerant towards Poland." Colonel Pyat was not one to give up on old grudges.

"Religion is the gunpowder of the masses," said Archbishop Beesley, heavy in his new Greek vestments and sporting a false black beard several sizes too big for him. It was attached around the mouth by what his acquaintances knew to be chocolate.

"Well, the flintlock at least." Mrs. Persson was a good horsewoman but she was not fond of horses. She sat her mount with disdainful detachment. This appeared to depress the horse.

"The more advanced forms seem to leave them a bit cold."

"Turkey," said the Bishop. "Now there's a problem. How do we peel them out of the alliance?"

"Oh, that won't be any trouble." Mrs. Persson flipped up her mobile. "Their leadership is riddled with fanatical zealots who have sworn on the gun and the Qur'an to spill the blood of Christian babies. I'll just let New New Nova Washington know."

Bishop Beesley uttered a small, appreciative belch. He frowned in some dismay. "I appear to have singed my beard. It's all this foreign food I'm being forced to eat." Gloomily he took a tin of crystallized figs from beneath his cassock. "Still, it's a sacrifice one makes for Mother Church."

"I used to love her chicken." Shaky Mo Collier, almost invisible beneath an arsenal of assault rifles and rocket launchers, led his horse to join the group. He spoke with some reluctance. "Could someone give me a hand. I can't seem to get up into the stirrup."

Jerry cast an eye over the swamp. He had a feeling this was going to be the easiest part of the campaign.

For as far as he could see, on any little hillock or grassy knoll, the combined Cossack horde was beginning to set up its fires and tents. They were living off the land and their nick-name for themselves was "the locusts." Certainly there was very little left behind in Wendy's and Wottaburger after they had been through, but generally speaking they tended to leave Taco Bell and Jack-in-the-Box alone. Jerry Cornelius wondered how long their triumph would last. He had no argument with Major Nye. Flying cavalry was the answer to high-flying bombers, most of which had no bombs left anyway and helicopters were no trouble to sideline. But what happened when they got to the serious wetlands? It wouldn't be long, after all, before this lot was completely under. They didn't need to do a sweep to the sea. The sea was doing a sweep to them.

At this rate it would take centuries to build an infrastructure good enough to supply his particular needs. The movie industry was already reduced to defending an enclave swiftly retreating to Sherman Hills and Fort Davey Crockett. Given Crockett's history, Jerry wasn't entirely sure he'd feel safe in any fort named after him.

He shook his head as he spurred forward to have a word with Major Nye. The signs were all pointing south and he had a feeling it was time they let the Cossack momentum carry itself to the beaches while they peeled off to seek more settled political climates. He didn't care what the others thought, but he was heading down to Texas and wouldn't stop until he had crossed the Rio Grande.

Mrs. Persson reined in beside him. She could probably read his mind. "Don't they still call you the Raven there?"

"It's just the clothes," he said. "*Sartor resartus*, eh? I was just re-reading it."

She was tolerant, but she found his references to the old days too self-pitying for her taste. Any moment now he would reach into his saddle-bag and slip on a stetson.

"I'll come with you as far as Laredo," she said. "I have someone I'd like to see out there. Then I'll head for Mexico City and fly down to Rio. A little Portuguese is what I need after all this excitement."

Major Nye pulled at his moustache. Since seeing Bishop Beesley's beard, he had become self-conscious about his own facial hair and was afraid he had caught some food in it. "I only need to get down to Belize, so I'll turn right as soon as I need to. I'll be perfectly comfortable, there. It's still more or less British."

Jerry steadied his antsy pony. "I always said the South would rise again."

"Funny about the weather." Jerry turned, miserably searching for her. But it had only been his mother's voice he had heard. He suppressed the anger which he had distilled so rapidly from his self-pity.

"Funny about the weather," he said. "It was the same with the Spanish Armada and the Luftwaffe invasion of Britain. Just as you think you're buggered, along comes a bit of wind or rain, and Bob's your uncle. Sometimes you even have to think there's a bit of justice in the universe. Or God really is an Englishman. Those who live by the Big Engine, get run over by the Big Engine."

They all looked at him with a mixture of disgust and bewilderment.

"Not turning preachy on us, are you, old boy?" asked Major Nye. In his father's day their village had seen off four vicars who tried to introduce an unwelcome gravity into their sermons.

"Just something I read in the *Telegraph*." Jerry knew by now how to get out of an English foxhole in a hurry. But he could tell he was still a bit rusty or he wouldn't have fallen in at all.

None of this would have happened if he had read more modernist fiction as a boy.

"Don't mind him." Mrs. Persson was surprised to find herself coming to his defense. She laid a hand on his arm as he lifted his toe for another bash at his leg. "He's shell-shocked. Or has been.

He has his mother's eyes. I'll have an export pale. Six letters and it's not 'wanker.' "

While they were considering this, she took his horse by the bridle and led it away.

"Come on," she said. "There's nowhere else."

Jerry relaxed. From a saddle bag he retrieved his little ukulele. It would take him a while to tune it up.

At last they began to see cactus. This caused Shaky Mo some excitement. He had to shoot a couple to be sure they were real. His horse was covered with pale green pulp. Bishop Beesley, who had lost his hat but was stuck with his false beard, put his plump hands over his ears. "Oh, dear!"

Major Nye rode in beside him. "Too noisy for you, vicar?" He turned to Jerry. "Come on, old boy. Help us out with a sing song!" "A Four Legged Friend."

It would be a week before they found the old Chisholm Trail.

By the time they left Oklahoma, Mrs. Persson had grown a little tired of "South of the Border" and "Happy Trails", especially after Jerry lost his G-string, but even that was better than Major Nye's nostalgic rendering of the Moore and Burgess Minstrels' favorite "I'm My Own Granpa":

And I have no hesitation, when I make this declaration,
Not a nation in creation, can produce another man,
In this trying situation, of relation complication,
I invite investigation, introduce him if you can . . .

A shadow went by swiftly overhead. She looked up. She saw a hint of something already merging with the line of hills on the horizon.

"Azrael," she said.

NINETEEN

Roll On Texas Moon

"For Trans-Ocean Travel . . .
The SR.45 long range flying boat
For Maritime Defence . . .
The SR/A1 fighter flying boat
The 80-120 passenger SR/45 flying boats, now under construction, redesigned to lead the world in safe, comfortable and economic long distance travel.

The SR/A1, the world's first jet propelled fighter flying boat, performs all the functions of a land based fighter, with the added advantages of operating from easily camouflaged bases and runways that cannot be made unserviceable be enemy action.

In all parts of the world Nature provides suitable operating bases for both these types of aircrat.
Saunders-Roe"
—Advertisement, *The London Mystery Magazine*, No. 1, January 1950.

"British-based Price Western Leather may not be a familiar household name in the United States, but in many of the world's hotspots PWL holsters are held in high regard as equipment that can be counted on. Americans can now purchase this high quality gear as PWL-USA has opened its doors down in Georgia. USA sales representative Ron Bunch recently sent me a sampling of PWL gear and I've found it to be outstanding.
Model 120TS
This is the original PWL covert holster and it has been in constant production since 1976."

—Dave Spaulding, *Guns and Weapons For Law Enforcement*, April 2002.

The End of Sterling Imperialism
"The showdown at Abadan has arrived. The British Government, rather than landing troops to sustain our commercial interests by force, has appealed to the Security Council and by implication accepted for the moment Dr. Moussadek's notice to quit. By now the last of the British oil men has left Persia. No Government can expect to escape criticism in such a situation by soberly choosing to obey the law rather than resorting to some flashy gesture of defiance or retaliation . . . an unworthy, and probably ephemeral, emotion."

—*The New Statesman and Nation*, October 6, 1951

Pig Alley Blues

"In the middle of the song two young hipsters scraped their chairs as they left. I could not contain my fury. Big Bill took me aside. 'Why blame those kids? What do they know about a mule? They never had a mule die on them . . . When I visited Europe after WWII, I saw where all the bombs fell and destroyed all the people. What do I know about a bomb? I never had no bomb fall on me. The only bomb I saw was in the movies. Same thing with those kids and the mule.'

'Bill, are you telling me that we must experience horror such as war in order to understand it?' Bill nodded. 'I am afraid that's so, unless we learn something from the past.' "

—Studs Terkel, edited liner quote for *Big Bill Broonzy, Trouble in Mind*, November 1999.

"I'd forgotten about those multiple orgasms." Mrs. Persson rolled towards the blind and opened a chink. Jerry lit two Shermans. The smell of their juices had intoxicated him all over again. He ran his hand up her soft inner thigh. It was good to get away from those muggy New Mexican swamps. Even better to get away from what Texas had become. The rainfall and rising tides had been a catalyst for the vast areas of chemical, nuclear and human waste, one of Texas's main money spinners in the good old days, and something unlikely was being born there. He whistled a few bars of "Maybe It's Because I'm A Londoner", realizing what a fool he had been to move out in the first place. He handed her the Shermans. She inhaled its rich, unadulterated smoke.

From somewhere in the far northern part of Ladbroke Grove came the familiar whine of a Banning cannon. He had been wondering when the New Alliance would revive that one. They had been banned under the Geneva Convention and, of course, It was a typical irony that Geneva, ultimately, had been the first to be shaken out by a Banning.

The Banning's relentless vibrations were so familiar that it relaxed them, like the sound of the sea. Bass and drums. They could hear the buildings falling with regular precision. There was plenty of time. Soon the Banning would stop and whoever was using it would have to do some mopping up while the weapon recharged.

Jerry checked his watches.

"Where to next?"

She went into the bathroom and tried the shower. It was still working. She tested the water for serious pollutants. "I'm thinking," she said. She got in.

Jerry pulled on his fatigues. He was longing for some R&R, a little peace time, so he could get back into something elegant again. He remembered he had forgotten to check his answering service.

The first message. "The war is endless. The most we can hope for is an occasional pause in the conflict."

It was a prerecorded solicitation and sounded familiar. But Jerry couldn't work out what they were selling. There was only one other message and again there was something familiar about it. It could also have been a sales pitch. Another obscure reference in a voice so lugubrious Jerry thought they must be selling suicide packages:

My "Azrael."
Every few hours now,
Mostly in the day,
I'll spot the shade
I name my "Azrael."
"You hint at death," I say,
"Your darkness tenders me
A taste of resolution,
So I'll call you 'Azrael.'
I'll call you 'Azrael'
To translate my terror
Into something else.
So, 'Azrael,' I'd look
You in the eye to
Maybe catch some clue
About my future, 'Azrael,'
Before I die."

"A friend of yours?" Una knew enough not to spend too long in a shower. She was towelling herself robustly. She, too, was curious about who had left the message.

Jerry thought he recognized the voice. It wasn't Taffy Sinclair, was it? Someone older. "I haven't been called the Angel of Death for a quarter of a century, at least. It's a bit flattering. Do you think it's accusatory?"

"Oh, I'm not sure." She reached for the repeat button, then changed her mind. "It might be a warning. Or a threat." Jerry thought she sounded jealous. "I mean if that's meant to be poetry, it's crap."

Jerry had no opinion. The Banning had stopped. "We'd better get it together," he said. "Can't you imagine the kind of pain those things cause? They shake you inside out. You can even live like that for a little while, with your face where your brain should be and your guts unravelling onto the carpet."

"You don't have to tell me." Sighing with her usual distaste at his vulgarity, she started zipping up her battle rubbers. "I was at Mecca *and* Seattle." She pulled the protective helmet down over her head and zipped it at her neck. Now she would hear nothing until her receivers were switched on. She let her breathers rest against her chest while she stepped over the empty cartons to give him an affectionate kiss.

"I never expected an ending as good as this," she said.

He was getting edgy. "What's that?" He cocked his head.

She sniffed and crossed to the french windows at the back of the abandoned apartment. They looked out into a large communal square, with trees and playgrounds. "They're having some fun out there. They're burning the Straw Jack. You can hear it squealing, that's all. Sounds almost human, doesn't it?" Through the dusty gloom of the morning, she watched the local savages dancing around the manikin as it bounced, jerked and cackled in the heat. Their rituals and language had become increasingly primitive and desperate as their certainties collapsed.

Una plugged in her communications. Jerry winked at her as he pulled down his goggles.

They took the basement exit, climbed the area stairs, checked for any movement in Elgin Crescent, then began to run towards the guns.

Life had never been sweeter. Jerry was his old self again.

TWENTY

I Shot the Sheriff

£1,000-a-year Plan for Life Peers
"There May Be 100 New Barons

It is now fairly certain that when official information is available about the progress of talks on the reform of the House of Lords it will be disclosed that an entirely new class of peers will be created. These will be chosen as life peers, and they will number 100, possibly 150. They will be created for the express purpose of bringing into the Second Chamber a cross-section of the community which would not otherwise have the means or background to justify an hereditary peerage. These talks have gone on at the highest level, and it is understood that the King has been kept informed of the progress made.

The question of salary for life peers has been raised, and the figure I have heard mentioned as gaining most support is £1000 a year—the same as that received by a Member of the House of Commons."

—*News of the World*, March 14, 1948

What Next in Korea?
"A massive demonstration by the American people that they are fed up with the Korean war was the true significance of the vote in the Presidential election. This is clear from the enormous rally to Eisenhower himself and the comparative failure of his Republican Party."

—*Daily Mirror*, November 7, 1952

A Feeble Argument
"The Prime Minister gains in political stature week by week. Why? Because he is honest, intelligent and entirely devoid of self-seeking personal ambition. Those are the qualities the British admire. It was therefore disappointing to find Mr. Attlee taking refuge behind a smoke-screen of a somewhat murky character when he answered Mr. Crossman's question as to whether or not we were still engaged in military collaboration with the USA."

—*Leader Magazine*, December 7, 1946

Mo Collier was in poor spirits. It had taken him days to reach London and when he got there most of the South Bank was down. He'd been promised a go in the demolition and had been working out how he could collapse the Queen Elizabeth Hall with four well-placed charges. In his view this was not a level playing field. "Bannings just aren't bloody sporting," he complained. "Otherwise there would have been no point in banning them." Actually named for the California town where it had been invented, the Banning had shaken the buildings to dust. There wasn't even so much left as a miniature London Wheel.

"They told me there was a seventy five year cycle on this sector. I was sure I had at least another five years. It's hard to take, Mr. C, I'll be frank with you. At this rate you're going to find increasing backing for linear time and that'll fuck up your plans, eh?"

"I haven't got any opinion, at the moment."

Mo swung his empty MK2000. "*Ak—ak—ak—frum—frum—frum . . .*"

"Oh, god, can't you keep a bit of respect?" Jillian Burnes, the transsexual novelist, straightened her Dusty Springfield wig with prim dignity. She was regretting accepting his invitation. This was beyond slumming. She cast an unseeing eye over the few remaining ruins. "Of course there's no way to deal with this. Not yet. Not in fiction. I haven't absorbed what it means to me. You know, I haven't taken it in. Maybe, I could have one of my characters walking by and seeing it . . . This is such a difficult art, isn't it?"

"Not when you got the right equipment, Jill, mate." Mo winked and admired her pearls. "Are those real?"

"Naturally," she said. "This costume's pure *Salammbô*, Mr. Collier, not some bit of sub-Lotian oriental tat. I resent that implied criticism."

Jerry had to admit she was beautifully dressed in a whole variety of Liberty's silks and feathers. She might have been a character in an early Melvyn Bragg movie. "Is that a parrot in your bosom, or are you just pleased to see me?"

Automatically, Jillian glanced down. She was self-conscious about these things.

"I just don't think they should have done it." Mitzi Beesley was close to tears. "I loved this place. I grew up with it. I had a subscription to the National Film Theatre when I was a student and everything."

"But you have to admit it was crap," said Jillian. "I mean, it was crap, right? I mean crap architecture, right? Ideas inherited from the bauhausers. Or am I wrong here?" She had seen Mo's other clip and was doing her best to fit in. "Is that live?"

"I'm not going to waste it, if that's what you mean." Mo kicked at the vibrated dust. "That concrete was all imported. Otherwise, I'd have minded more. You want some respect for your ancestors, right? Or am I wrong here?"

"I don't think so," said Jillian. She hated her thing for little men. "What was that song you were singing?"

"It's an old one." He knew what was happening and had begun to strut around her. "Goes back hundreds of years. *I've got gangrene, jolly, jolly gangrene. I've got gangrene to take away my life. I've got gangrene that's black and gangrene that's green but some gangrene's a funny shade of white.* My dad got it off his grand-dad who got it off someone who was in the Crimea and they got it off some Russian geezer who said he got it off his grand-dad, who was French. So there you have it." He spoke carefully, accenting his vowels and consonants, almost one at a time, in a way he thought was posh.

Responding in her own half-cockney, Jillian carefully inspected her bosom while he faced the river. She began to make small adjustments to her silks. "Blimey! Goes back a bit, then."

"Oh, yes." Mo nodded slowly. "It's very antique. I prefer the antique to the modern, any day, by and large." This was his effort at social chit-chat.

He looked across to where the House of Commons clock tower still stood, saved at the eleventh hour by a band of heritage salvagers flying in with massive battle-blimps to throw up an electronic net which made a Banning even more dangerous to the user.

The Americans, driven back by bouncing vibes, had taken to the river. Like Rif clans on a *harka*, they preferred to avoid major conflicts and simply massacre the nearest *mellah* before going home. The Rangers planned to finish the job they should have finished in Oxford the first time around. There were old scores to settle. It had only been an hour or so since the sound of their squealing merrimac engines had died away.

Mo offered his free arm to Jillian Burnes. "If you've seen enough, I'll take you back to the motor."

TWENTY ONE

Sermonette

Haifa
"Haifa Women in Black are now at
Shederot Ben-Gurion and Hagefen
Friday, 1–2 p.m.
Contact: Dalia Sachs
Men are Welcome"
Jerusalem
"Women in Black
Hagar (Paris) Square and junction of King George,
Gaza, Ramban, Keren Hayesod, and Agron.
Friday, 1–2 p.m.
Contact: Judy Blanc"

Nixon's Vision of Peace
"It is in the most unlikely times that Richard Nixon's hopes for peace shine through most strongly. With the Mideast in torment and Vietnam still a bleeding sore, there is more talk than ever in the back corridors of the White House and the State Department about what is seen as the approaching era of negotiation.

Nixon's persistent vision, that he will usher in a generation of world peace, illumines his often dark Washington days and gives him reason for cautioning his men to avoid petty political and bureacratic squabbles. 'Always look beyond these things,' he told one group. 'There's a bigger picture.' "

—*Life Magazine*, September 25, 1970

The Spirit of America
"On Sept. 11, our lives and our nation were changed forever. We are now engaged in a struggle for civilization itself. We did not seek this conflict. But we will win it. And we will win it in a way that is consistent with our values. More than anything else, America values its freedom—the freedom to worship, the freedom to assemble, and the freedom to pursue our dreams. These are the freedoms that make America great and good."

—George W. Bush, *100 Years of Popular Mechanics*, March 2002

"Fuck me with a small priest!" President Ewell was checking his co-ordinates. "We've gained almost a mile. That can't be bad, can it?"

"Well," Jerry read the corrupted screens. "If they're right, you've extended the borders of the USA almost as far inland as Rhode Island."

"It's a beginning," said President Ewell. He was not looking young. His face had taken on a peculiar patchy grayness, like thin coffee. Jerry was beginning to wonder if it was some form of leprosy. There had been a huge increase of sufferers in South New York. During the brief period when one of the warlords had been in control, there had been some attempt to bring in doctors, but the drugs had turned out to be fakes. "Washington didn't do it in a day."

Or, Jerry wondered suddenly, had the Old Man been bleaching his skin. Personally, he couldn't see the point of it now. There were, after all, seventeen black self-proclaimed Presidents of the United States, along with another forty or so Latinos, Euros and Asians, most of whom were controlling various small island regions roughly the size of the Isle of Wight. He looked up as Prince Lobkowitz pushed back the tent flap and came into the Portapent. "Cheerful news, eh?"

"We've pushed them back for at least a mile and are about ready to re-take New Jersey." President Ewell's skin was slowly changing color even as Jerry watched. It was a phenomenon he hadn't witnessed since the early seventies. "At this rate, we'll be in Pittsburgh by Easter and will be sitting down to our turkey dinners in Baltimore by Thanksgiving."

"Isn't that a little optimistic?"

"Not when you have a Banning." Ewell lit a fresh blank.

"You have a Banning?"

"On the way." Ewell looked at Jerry and winked. "If that clever brother of yours comes through, eh, Jerry?"

Prince Lobkowitz pursed his lips. Jerry knew when his old friend was losing his self-control. "The president was telling me how Alfred the Great started with similar set-backs, burning the cakes and everything, but eventually went on to found the British Empire."

"There's a lot to be said for starting from the bottom," Lobkowitz agreed.

Jerry smirked.

A small explosion, quite close.

As soon as President Ewell had found his cane, they walked outside. A shell had landed in a lagoon and splattered even more mud over the quonset huts and canvas-sheltered ruins of the presidential compound.

"Damn." Ewell carefully put out his cigar. "So who the hell is this?"

Jerry pointed out across the lake. At first he had thought it was the steeple of the church sticking above the water-line, but this was moving towards them and growing taller. Then, with a rush and a roar of her jury-rigged nukes, the submarine began to rise, shedding plastic bottles, old milk cartons, broken computer parts and all the usual detritus which normally lay undisturbed upon the surface of the American waters.

President Ewell grinned. He saw the two Bannings bolted to the top of the conning tower. They didn't have to be covered. That wasn't how they worked.

"I think your brother made it, Jerry!"

Jerry said nothing. He waited until the submarine had settled. As the hatch began to hiss open, he sighed. He had already recognized the scent of lavender.

Major Nye clambered unsteadily through the hatch and came to stand on the deck. He held tightly to a rail as he waved his white handkerchief. "Sorry about the shell. This old girl's a bit quirky. We thought we were stopping engines. Lost the manual overboard while I was trying to see how the periscope came up. Nobody hurt I hope?"

Prince Lobkowitz walked down the beach until he stood at the water's edge. "I trust Her Majesty is in good health."

"Well, old boy, between you and me, she was never a great sailor." Behind him, the electronic flagstaff was rising jerkily. There was a reluctant click and the rust-proof Union flag appeared, like a souvenir tea-tray. "Presumably you are the diplomatic representative here? Good afternoon, Monsignor Cornelius.

Good afternoon, President Ewell. You no doubt understand that I am reclaiming this territory in the name of its rightful ruler, our good queen, Gloriana the Second and must ask you to refrain from using any weapons or giving any hindrance to Her Majesty's representatives." He frowned, going over the points to himself. "I think that's everything. Are there just the three of you?"

"Three here—and ten thousand coming up from Georgia armed to the gunnels with Bannings and convies. Seventeen merrimacs should be enough to blow *you* out of the water, Johnny Redcoat."

"I imagine they would, sir."

Jerry never ceased to admire American virtuality. They really did believe if they spoke strongly enough and used enough will power what they wanted to happen would happen. Even now he found himself being persuaded by Ewell's total conviction.

"Meanwhile," said Major Nye almost apologetically, "I wonder if you would mind coming aboard. We have to do a little Banning work on those ruins. No point in building anything until you've established some good foundations."

"It's been a long time since I heard so much common sense." President Ewell made an elaborate bow. He also recognized lethal reality when it was offered. "And my people have always remembered that Great Britain outlawed slavery fifty years before the United States."

Then, keeping his hands dry, he began to wade into the water towards the hull. Jerry was puzzled. The hull was painted khaki, but the disfiguring patches were identical in color to those on the ex-president's skin.

"I think I would feel much more at ease with myself if I were perhaps merely the governor of a small colony. I do have certain British honors, as you know. I would imagine they would count for something."

"Oh, no doubt about it, old boy." Major Nye was decently reassuring. "It's not as if you were ever a rebel or anything."

Though glad that the farce had ended so happily, Jerry could not help keeping an eye on the horizon.

There was always a chance that Frank would outwit them all and keep his word.

President Ewell was swimming strongly now towards the sub. Major Nye threw out a rope to him. He looked up at the others. "Won't you join us, gentlemen. It could get very buzzy here."

Jerry shook his head. "This is the last pair of decent boots I own. And you have to look after the threads, these days, don't you?"

Prince Lobkowitz shrugged and began to tramp back to the other side of the little island. "We can probably get the merrimac far enough away in time."

As Jerry turned to join him, Trixie Brunner appeared in the conning tower.

"Not coming with us, Jerry?"

The old assassin shook his head. He had never been interested in power for its own sake. And nowadays there wasn't anything interesting you could do with it.

Prince Lobkowitz had started the engine by the time Jerry got down to the beach. "If we're lucky, we can make it back across the Atlantic in a couple of days. It'll have to be sandwiches, I'm afraid. The microwave's on the blink." As soon as they were settled in their chairs, Lobkowitz closed the silver-platinum canopy. "These little jobs are expensive, but they were built to last. Are they French?"

"Originally," said Jerry, starting the rotor. "But this one's Chinese, I think. Let's get busy, Prince. The faster she warms, the sooner she cools."

He stretched and yawned. "Good to be back on the old entropy wagon, again. It's where I belong, really."

Prince Lobkowitz hit the "Heidegger" button. "You've always been a romantic, Monsignor."

TWENTY TWO

On the Road Again

It's Time to Fight Back!

"It's the crime that plagues the town—and we are giving you the chance to fight back . . .

Today we launch our DON'T campaign which gives you the readers the opportunity to hit back against the car thieves who cause misery to thousands of us each year. Each week we will carry a series of stories and features highlighting what you can do to make sure you are not a victim. It will also give you the chance to help bring the criminals to justice."

—*Hastings and St Leonard's Observer*, January 25, 2002

"Wherever mullahs are not around, it's there
That paradise can be found. Where mullahs' ire
And crazed rage and delirious fits do not
Exist, there heaven's own land is found to be.
From mullah fury and mullah zeal may
The world all be set free, so none again
Take heed of fatwas and mullah's mad decrees!"

—Dara Shikuh in Hasrat, *Dara Shikuh*, 139

"Dhu'l-Nun was asked: 'What causes a devotee to be worthy of entrance to paradise?'

He said: 'One merits entrance to paradise by five things: unwavering constancy, unflagging effort, meditation in God in solitude and society, anticipating death by preparing provision for the hereafter, and bringing oneself to account before one is brought to judgement.' "

—Attar: *Tadkhkirat*, 156

"Notwithstanding what vicissitudes the world visits upon us," Bishop Beesley dipped his ring-heavy fingers into a bag of Maltesers, "we need never again fear slipping back into ruin. To maintain our economies it is necessary to be rich. Almost everyone alive today is rich. There are so few of us. So our needs are fewer. But we still have satellites and decent dishes. Disposable wealth. Our lifestyle, those of us who survive, is threatened only by the unpredictable. The lunches might not be entirely free, Mrs. Persson, but at least we don't have to pick up the bill."

"Not yet," said Una Persson. "Not until I've had a chance to chill with my friend."

Beesley chuckled. When his face had settled, he said: "Never, one hopes."

The British ice age not entirely over, Catherine Cornelius was still a bit blue. Every so often her teeth chattered tunefully. It sounded to Una like "Mother of a Thousand Dead" but she had never been an uncritical Crass fan. With an aggressive gesture, Cathy poked back her pale hair. "Could you turn the heat up? Or not?" She embraced the mug of tea Una handed her. "Is Jerry still here? Not that it awfully matters."

"Of course it matters." Ecstatically reunited with her baffled friend, Una took off her military coat and put it over Catherine's shoulders. She wore the remains of her old battle suit. She apologized for her appearance.

"I think it looks romantic. Especially the burn marks." Mitzi popped out of the little mini-sphere marked *Office*. It vaguely resembled Santa's Grotto. She had been working for Beesley at the Grasmere Boating Mall ever since she had returned to the Lake District. The climate-controlled William Wordsworth Dome still attracted a fair number of customers, especially during the season. She herself wore a Cinders Claus outfit. A fetching elfette in a tastefully torn ragged cheerleader skirt.

Catherine felt an artery begin to warm in her right leg. The blood flowed with increasing enthusiasm. She took a breath. With some relief, she heard a thin, tuneful whistle. Another vein pulsed rapidly in her left leg. She knew who was whistling McCartney's "Give Ireland Back To The Irish." It made a change from "Oliver's Army," which she had to hear over and over again ever since they had left the ice age. Even the dogs had begun to complain.

Una looked up optimistically at the newcomer, but it was, as Cathy knew, Jerry. He had slipped through on a Universal Access card he had won in a quiz show and was picking his way elegantly across the little wooden bridge to join them. The walls of the dome were tinted against whatever it was created such a glare on the wide delta water. Bishop Beesley was trying to make adjustments with his hand control. He had been certain he had put a filter on the gate. "How did you find us?"

Jerry winked at Cathy. The atmosphere was already improving. "I hope you don't mind. I left the dogs outside. Have you got some sort of electronic fence up?" He unzipped his massive parka. "Hot enough for you?" He turned to give the thumb to a group of airmasked and goggled punters waiting on the other side of the bridge. Hesitantly they began to cross. Mitzi rushed to distribute brochures.

Bishop Beesley was disturbed by this turn of events, but he had a job to do. "I didn't object when you asked if your sister could take a go at our heating unit," he said, unwrapping a Mighty Mars, "but we closed to regular customers at three."

Mitzi pressed forward in a haze of hairspray and cologne. "Congratulations," she chirruped. "Brave souls searching for freedom. May I say first how I applaud your courage in deciding to risk the undoubted terrors of our rather mercurial weather. But now you're here, you'll find it worthwhile, believe me."

"Climate choice is the next big freedom." Mitzi cracked a monster smile. "Any bubble you like. Personal vacation. Security. Seashore. Golf-side. We are in direct contact with the manufacturer and can personally guarantee every level of workmanship, from plumbing to sky-toning. This is what makes our prices so competitive. It's perfectly safe, by the way, to get rid of that breathing and seeing apparatus. In our domes, there is no chance of a leak. That is also personally guaranteed." The bishop coughed on his Mars. Mitzi guided the customers on. "Now why don't we go and enjoy the hydroponic herb garden to get us all in the mood. Everyone's aware, I'm sure, of the great precursors of our domic movement. After the Dome of Discovery there was the Millennium Dome which did so much for London, in the end, and the EnviroDome in Cornwall which, until the collapse, had become such an important part of our countryside heritage." She led them past the row of mud and wattle cottages where they could stay if they decided. "These are what we call jokingly 'the Hovels,' but of course they are thoroughly modernized."

"Azrael," said Una brightly, looking up. "Azrael!"

"No need for the kind of unpatriotic talk young lady." Beesley adjusted his beard. Red, white and blue didn't really suit him.

"Let's remember where we are, shall we? The great privileges we have in our womb-like comfort: This securisphere, this hemisphere, this sceptered sphere set in a spherical sea. No longer need we fear the elements. No longer will the future be uncertain. We have, out of confusion, found Paradise."

The bishop cocked his top-hatted head. He jigged his gaitered leg. "A globe is forever. No longer need you worry about it raining on your parade or waterlogging your fête. Global warming? Global cooling? These aren't important when you're safe inside your heavenly sphere, where the skies are as sunny or gray as you demand. For it is in today's natural climate, dear co-religionists, that the social and economic reflect. And we must be sure ours is a brand which says 'Reflect', which lets us see ourselves full length in the best possible light."

The bishop cast a slightly anxious eye over the wide water. It was clear that he and his daughter were not entirely reconciled.

From nearby she was turning up the volume of her PA. He glared, grinning, towards the demonstration tent.

She was bright, warm, sympathetic. "The personal dome is the ultimate in freedom and personal security. And long, arduous trips are a thing of the past. Snow at Christmas, sunshine for July 4th. For the more gregarious amongst you, we also do a metrodome, large enough to protect most small cities. But frankly, my friends, the day of the city is done. Today is the day of the dome. A noble day. A day by which we remember all victims of terrorism and show our conviction that such a thing shall never happen again. The future of our uncertain hemisphere is the thoroughly predictable hemisphere. By blurr and boosh our world's restored, so on your knees and thank the Lord. Floods and storms might roar and rain, but you'll be snug as a rat up a drain."

"That's terrible," said Catherine.

"It's a hymn," she apologized. "You need to hear the music. An organ gives it more dignity. More resonance."

"Depending on the organ," Jerry said. He was embracing his sister. Slowly, Cathy was coming back to a normal color. "I used to have one of those Hamptons when I was with The Deep Fix, but I never really got the hang of it. Too many consoles for my taste. You know how I like to keep things simple."

"That's the reason they always get so complicated," said Catherine, swinging her arms. One last puff of icy air emerged from her mouth and hung there for a moment like a speech balloon. "You're always trying to reduce everything down to something you can understand. As a kid you were constantly obsessed with pi. Do you remember? Dad used to tell us it would be pi today, possibly pi tomorrow, but pi had no prolonged future. And you proved him wrong, as you've been doing ever since. But does that make you right, Jerry?"

"I'm not interested in being right. I'm interested in what happens. Like with the test tubes."

"A little of this and a little of that. You blew up two of my dolly stoves and broke the windows."

"But I found out what happened." He raised a reminiscent finger to his face, tracing the lines of his re-grown eyebrows. "Most people try to stop things happening. I try to make them happen quicker. Then we can get on to the next thing."

"You're not worried about the human cost?"

"You mean taxes?" said Jerry. "They're a thing of the past. It's mutuality we go for these days. Anarchism in action. Green solutions. Co-operation. Call me a radical. Call me a visionary. But the way I see it, if you get a grip on the future, you might as well bring it along as quickly as possible."

"I prefer," said Bishop Beesley, "to preserve the best and embrace the worst." He frowned. He was sure he had just seen Mo Collier go by outside in a speed boat, heading for Huddersfield. So that was where the little bastard was buying his ammo.

Una put her arm around Cathy, who was shivering again. "You were doing 45 rpm when you should have been doing at least 100. I thought you were just getting old or something had gone wrong with your roots. For a while everything was in stasis there. Talk about dodgy ground. What a snotty score of years that turned out to be. After 1980 I thought the sodding century would never end."

They turned to look out at the blossoming islands, like so many large, transparent eggs.

"Still, it's all right now," said Jerry. "I mean the worst is over, isn't it? Soon it will be safe to head for London." He breathed against the wall, rubbing a clean spot on the curved, transparent shield. A cackle from overhead as a flock of gulls settled high on the surface. They might have been doves. He began to whistle. The world was altogether brighter.

He had never felt fresher.

Musical references to Peter Keane, Willie Nelson, Chris Rhea, Mose Allison, Elvis Costello, Big Bill Broonzy, Lambert, Hendricks and Ross, Bob Marley.

THE WISDOM OF SUFISM *compiled by Leonard Lewisohn is published by Oneworld of Wisdom, Oxford, UK.*

Crap, I told you!